Praise for Diana Finley from readers:

'A thought provoking read'

'Couldn't put this book down'

'I found myself eagerly turning the pages'

'An enthralling tale of love, hatred, secrets and joy'

'I absolutely drank it all in and wished there was more'

'Captivating from beginning to end … the characters were
beautifully drawn'

'Diana Finley is perceptive in her character building and of
domestic and everyday situations'

DIANA FINLEY was born and grew up in Germany, where her father was a British Army officer. After a move to London, at eighteen, Diana spent a year living with nomadic people in the remote Pamir mountains of Afghanistan - an experience about which she wrote several stories and accounts. These helped secure her first job, as copywriter and then as writer of children's information books for Macdonald Educational Publishers.

A move to North East England meant changing direction. Diana took a degree in Speech and Psychology, and worked for many years as a Specialist in Autism, publishing a professional book. In 2011 she completed an MA in Creative Writing with distinction at Newcastle University. *Beyond the Storm* is Diana's First novel, originally published as *The Loneliness of Survival.*

Beyond The Storm

DIANA FINLEY

ONE PLACE. MANY STORIES

HQ
An imprint of HarperCollins*Publishers* Ltd
1 London Bridge Street
London SE1 9GF

This paperback edition 2019

First published as The Loneliness of Survival in 2014
This edition published in Great Britain by HQ in 2019

Copyright © Diana Finley 2019

Diana Finley asserts the moral right to be
identified as the author of this work.
A catalogue record for this book is
available from the British Library.

ISBN: 978-0-00-834834-2

MIX
Paper from
responsible sources
FSC™ C007454

This book is produced from independently certified FSC™ paper
to ensure responsible forest management.

For more information visit: www.harpercollins.co.uk/green

Printed and bound in Great Britain by
CPI Group (UK) Ltd, Croydon, CR0 4YY

To my parents

Chapter 1

2014

She squeezes her eyes tight shut and then opens them wide. As on other mornings, she wonders if perhaps she is dead, and exactly how she would know. The sun has not fully penetrated the maroon silk curtains, but creates a rosy pinkness in the gloom of the bedroom, which could be taken as heaven. A moment later the clatter of the drinks trolley in the corridor convinces Anna that it is not heaven, and that she is still alive. She remembers that today is her hundredth birthday.

The continuous preparations have become more than a little irritating, but she's tried to keep quiet, to accept it in good humour. Tomorrow is the great day, they kept reminding her, making a ridiculous fuss about it. As though one day makes such a difference, even this day. Doreen had done her usual 'popping in' and asking if Anna was excited. She said yes she was, just to please her.

'But don't make too many advance preparations. After all, I might die in the night.'

'Anna! Honestly, shame on you!'

'There's no shame in death. What a waste of effort it would be, and such a disappointment for the other residents.'

1

Doreen didn't like that.

'You're a terrible pessimist, Anna.'

Such a fool. Did she think optimism would ensure eternal life?

'Not at all. I'm not a pessimist – just a realist. We all have to die. In fact, at one day before my hundredth birthday, the chances must be quite high.'

'Oh, Anna, do try to be more cheerful. We'll all have a lovely day tomorrow.'

Well, she has survived the night and 'the great day' has arrived. Eve appears soon after morning coffee. She settles Anna in the wheelchair in a quiet alcove off the main lounge, making sure the maroon cushion (matching the curtains) at her back is plumped up, her shawl symmetrical, and her skirt smoothed over her knees. On the wall opposite is a large mirror with a gilt frame, slightly chipped in places. Anna rarely examines herself in a mirror these days, but in this position she has little choice. The mirror is barely a metre away and shows her entire body, in cruel detail.

She stares at her reflection. How tired she looks. And old – so very old, she realises with shock. Her face is small, almost child-like. The flesh, now pale and sallow, has loosened around the jaw, forming two soft jowls. The skin around her eyes has darkened, as if perpetually shadowed by fatigue. Yet, Anna notes with satis-faction, she remains scarcely lined. Always small, she seems to have shrunk into an almost gnome-like form, her body engulfed by the wheelchair. Her legs, discoloured and blotchy from poor circulation, dangle above the floor like a child's. Her hair has been set in neat waves. Anna is very particular about it – very particular about physical appearance in general. People these days seem happy to look totally ungroomed. Anna tuts out loud to herself at the thought.

'Mmm?' says Eve. Anna shakes her head. The hairdresser comes every Thursday and Anna rarely misses an appointment. Her thick, dark curls were once admired by all. Even now, she notices, much black hair shows through the white. She turns her head from one side to the other and looks round to Eve with a soft sigh.

'I'm getting so grey now.'

Eve laughs. 'Don't you think you're entitled to have some grey hair at a hundred?'

The only image of herself Anna allows to be displayed in her room is a studio photograph arranged as a present for Sam, soon after they first married. In it, Anna looks film-star beautiful; her hair is sculpted in Forties' style, her skin pale and smooth as milk. She gazes aslant at the camera from darkly sultry eyes, a faint, enigmatic smile on her lips. Even now, over seventy years later, it is how she likes to picture herself.

The staff fuss around Anna. Eve crouches by her mother's chair, always ready to be her interpreter. Anna knows she's on show, expected to be the life and soul of the party, but she can't hear, can't make out what people are asking her.

Doreen looms over Anna, stroking her hand.

'Are you having a nice time, Anna dear?' she shouts.

Anna smiles uncertainly up at her, glancing at Eve for reassurance, working out what response is needed.

'Very nice party, thank you,' she says. Or rather, 'sank you'. She's never lost her accent, even after all these years.

Doreen grins and nods. Behind her a nervous-looking young man is shifting from one foot to the other. Doreen stands up and grabs him by the arm. She pulls him down to the level of Anna's chair.

'Anna, this is Simon. He's a reporter with the local newspaper. They're doing an article about very old age.' She speaks slowly and enunciates every word clearly. Anna grits her teeth. As though talking to a half-wit. She frowns at Doreen.

'Simon would like to ask you a few questions, for the paper!'

Anna shrugs and turns to the young man.

He squats in front of Anna, notebook in hand. His knees

crackle. Even she can hear them. From beside Anna's chair, Doreen gesticulates to remind him to speak loudly.

'Hello, Mrs Lawrence. How does it feel to be a hundred years old?' he bellows.

Anna searches his face and considers the question.

'Well …' she says, 'I do feel very old. A hundred is *very* old, but so is ninety-nine, and ninety-eight. I'm not sure I feel much different just by being a hundred. In fact, it does not feel real to me. Of course I *know* I am a hundred, but it's as if it is happening to someone else.'

Simon scribbles furiously, then glances at her eagerly.

'Do you have any secrets of long life you would like to share with our readers?'

'It's no secret. One minute you are young – like you. You think you will always be young. Of course, young people cannot imagine ever being old. But time goes on and on. Suddenly you are not so young, and you come to realise you *will* be old one day too, if you are lucky enough to live. And now … well, to be a hundred is extraordinary, for me too. Really it is too long to live.'

Anna slumps back in her chair, breathing fast after this lengthy speech, as if exhausted. Simon has been writing with concentration. He looks up.

'So … so you don't have any health tips for others, who might want to … er … live as long as you?'

Anna stares at him.

'I used to walk a lot. I never learned to drive. My husband wanted to teach me, but I didn't want to learn. Maybe that helped. I walked everywhere – well into my eighties. But people didn't think so much about healthy eating when I was young. We ate anything we could and were glad of it. After the First World War, when the Allied Forces occupied Vienna, they allowed one child from each family to come to a soup kitchen to be fed. Of my sisters, I was the skinniest, so they sent me. I was only four or five years old. My sisters were so jealous! *T'ja*, we were all hungry.

4

But I was terribly ashamed, even at that age, to have to stand in line with all the poor children and accept charity – charity from the *enemy*! I hated that soup kitchen. Vah!' She pulls a face and shudders in horror, as if finding a disgusting, wriggling creature crawling on her body.

Anna pictures the hall with its queues of children, Kaethe pushing her forward, muttering in her ear: 'Smile at the gentlemen, say thank you.' There at the high table she could hardly see over, soldiers had ladled out hot soup into her proffered bowl, grinning and saying words she could not understand. She had glared at them, those foreign soldiers. She wouldn't smile, even though Kaethe had pinched her arm and hissed at her.

Anna looks at Simon. He shifts his gaze from her to Eve, as if unsure whether her revelations should be included in his article. He smiles and nods.

'You've always eaten a lot of fresh fruit and vegetables, haven't you, Mum?' Eve puts in loudly.

'Oh right, fresh fruit and vegetables.' Simon writes it down. 'OK. And what did you think about your birthday card from the Queen, Mrs Lawrence?'

'Well of course, it's what she does. It's a tradition. Once, maybe she wrote them all herself, when there were not so many people who lived to over a hundred. Now there are too many of us! I expect she has her assistants to help write and send them all. It doesn't mean much to me. I prefer the cards I was given by my family and by people who care for me.'

Simon appears disappointed by this reply. Anna is quick to occupy the pause in the questioning.

'Have you worked long for this local paper?' she asks.

'No, about three months actually. It's my first job after graduating.'

'And you hope to work for one of the bigger papers one day? The *Daily Mail*, or *The Guardian* perhaps?'

Simon laughs and seems to relax for the first time during the interview. 'Well, that would be very nice, but right now I'm happy to be working for my little local rag – and talking to you, of course.'

'What else do you want to know?'

'Where do you come from, Mrs Lawrence, if you don't mind me asking?'

'Where do I come from? That's a hard question. Originally, I come from Vienna, as I just said. Then the Nazis came to power and things got very difficult. We could not stay in Austria. So I escaped to Palestine with my first husband, Jakob.' Anna pauses, picturing their arrival at Haifa for a moment. She looks back to Simon. He is staring at her, his pencil frozen above his notebook.

'*Ja*, poor Jakob. That was a hard time, a bad time. Then later I met my second husband, Sam. Sam was an Englishman. An Englishman through and through.' Anna smiles and then sighs deeply. She feels Eve tapping her arm. Her eyes settle back on Simon.

'What did you say your name is? I didn't hear.'

'It's Simon.'

'*Simon*. Simon, it's a good name. I called my son Shimon just like you – my first son.' Anna focuses steadily on a spot on the wall beside her, as though an image of her son might suddenly appear there.

'Shimon was born long, long ago. But he was taken away. I could not keep him. I did not see him for many years. It is a terrible thing to be separated from your own child, terrible. As if a vital part of your own body is torn from you. I should never have agreed to be parted from him, but I had no choice, you see. So many years ago, so many years.' She leans forward towards Simon. 'It is strange to see your children grow old. That is one of the curses of being a hundred. No, it is not all wonderful, you know.'

Simon swallows audibly and shifts his position. Anna pauses

and glances at Eve, who strokes her mother's hand and nods encouragingly at her.

'Much later, after Shimon, came Ben. He was Sam and my first child together. He was born in England during the last months of the war. At the end of the war Sam was posted to Berlin, so then Ben and I moved to join him in Germany. To Germany! Just imagine – into the arms of the enemy! That's where Eve was born,' she says, looking at Eve again. 'We were in Germany for many years. We came to England when my husband retired.'

'You've had quite a disrupted life then, Mrs Lawrence.'

'Yes, you could certainly call it disrupted.'

Doreen appears with a glass of sherry for Anna, a drink she dislikes.

'I think that's quite enough questions!' Doreen says, patting Simon's shoulder. 'People are waiting. The mayor's arrived. We should move Anna into the main part of the lounge. We have to get on with the ceremonics – and everyone's dying for a slice of Anna's cake!'

Simon leaps to his feet. He bends over Anna's chair and gently shakes her hand.

'Thank you very much for talking so openly to me, Mrs Lawrence. I've really enjoyed meeting you. I'm sure people will be fascinated to read about your story.'

'Hah! For you it may be a story, Simon. For me, it's my life.'

He nods and backs towards the edge of the room. Anna is wheeled out of the alcove. Eve's brother Ben has been hovering near the doorway of the large residents' lounge with his wife, Nadia, and their three adult children, Charlie, Guy and Alma. Eve's husband Richard stands talking to their two sons, Mark and Adam. Milling around the adults' feet is a variously sized army of children and toddlers. Anna's beloved daughter-in-law crouches low, admiring a bead bracelet held up by one of the little girls. She turns and smiles warmly as Anna is pushed in, bringing a lump to Anna's throat. Alma holds the baby in her arms – Anna's latest great-grandchild.

'You look fantastic, Mum,' Ben says. 'Happy birthday!'

'Thank you, my darlings. It's lovely to see you all.'

She beams at her large family gathered around her. She searches the room anxiously. Are they all here? Not quite all, someone is missing. Where is he?

The children are ushered forward. Each child is embraced in turn, and each gives Anna his or her small present and card, watching intently as she struggles to unwrap it. She exclaims dutifully over every bar of soap and handkerchief, every photo frame and box of chocolates. Alma deposits the baby on Anna's lap. He looks round uncertainly at his great-grandmother, his lip quivering. Anna smiles at him and strokes his soft curls. The baby notices a piece of shiny wrapping paper on Anna's lap. He grabs it and becomes absorbed in crumpling it. The threatened tears are held at bay. Anna admires the baby's eyes and marvels at how advanced he is for four months. She allows Simon to photograph her for the paper, surrounded by her grandchildren and great-grandchildren. He promises copies for the family to keep.

A large platter is brought in with the cake, shaped as the figures of 100. A murmur of approval and anticipation rises from those residents who are sufficiently aware of the proceedings to notice. The cakes are ablaze with a hundred lit candles. A discordant rendering of 'Happy birthday to you' is sung while Anna blows out the candles, eagerly helped by the children. Small pieces of cake are distributed to all the residents and visitors. The children sit on the floor at Anna's feet, with their paper plates and exhortations not to make a mess. Every now and then she smiles at one of them or pats a head. How sweet they are, so innocent. She struggles with remembering exactly which child is which.

The voices murmur on and on. She watches her children and grandchildren talking to one another. Every now and then one of them catches her eye and smiles or gives her a little wave. Anna is unsettled. She scans the family, knowing it is incomplete, waiting. The young people have gathered in a group at one side of the room and are laughing together uproariously. Anna smiles to see them. Then she sighs. Sam should be here. If only he could have seen his grandchildren and great-grandchildren. How he would have loved them. Sam always loved to grow things, but he never knew what a wonderful family he had grown.

Glancing out of the tall Edwardian window, Anna notices the sweep of a rainbow glowing against the pale wet sky of late afternoon. It makes her think of her mother suddenly, her poor mother, so long gone. 'Find the rainbow, Anna,' she used to say, 'and then run towards it.' Just a feeling, like a dream, an echo, from all those years ago. As the light fades from the sky outside, so too does the rainbow, leaving Anna with a strange emptiness, a sadness. Many of the residents are nodding in their chairs, if not actually sleeping. The smaller children are growing restless. Anna is ready for the peace of her own room.

Chapter 2

1945

Sam and Anna arrive in England in March 1945. After nearly six years of war, the country is in a dreary and depressed state. The first thing Anna notices is the greyness, the dark and gloom. They spend a few nights in London, where Sam takes pleasure in pointing out the sights to her: St Paul's Cathedral, the Tower of London, Big Ben and the Houses of Parliament. They avoid the worst of the bombed areas. Almost constant rain gives the black-ened buildings an oily gloss.

Anna is thrilled to visit some of the famous places she has read about, but never dreamt of experiencing. Yet it's a relief to move out of London to Sam's brother and sister-in-law's home in Surrey. At least there are green fields and trees, and towering skies. After the intense light of the Middle East, the brilliance of the sunshine, everything here looks washed out and monochrome. Even on sunny days the sky appears hazy and milky rather than blue.

'If only we could go to Berlin *together*, Sam. Surely you could put in a request, in the circumstances? Why do we have to be apart, now of all times?' She strokes the solid curve of her belly.

Even as she says it, Anna has doubts. Could she really live in Germany? It's a ridiculous, horrible idea. Yet, how could she possibly *not* live wherever Sam is?

Ten days later, Sam goes ahead with the first waves of Allied troops to Berlin. Over the coming months he sends Anna long accounts of the devastation and hardship he encounters there:

… the scene greeting us was one of utter desolation and despair. Berlin is totally destroyed. I know you feel little sympathy for the Germans, and why should you? Yet one cannot help but feel compassion for these people, most of them innocent civilians – victims of the war and of their own regime. Some live in the remains of their ruined homes, without doors or windows, often without complete walls. Others simply live on the street. There is no fuel, almost no food, and no security. Our Russian allies behaved abominably – like Mongol invaders in fact. Women of all ages have been abused and humiliated, and often their only means of support now is to sell themselves to their very abusers, in exchange for scraps of food. Young children forage like rats in the ruins and fight over any filthy crusts they may find. Old people are abandoned and left to die. It breaks my heart – but one can't dwell on the individual tragedies. There is so much to do to get systems up and working again: water and food supplies, shelter, transport, education, and on and on …

Anna, in England, is left to the mercies of Sam's family, who offer her refuge dutifully, if perhaps reluctantly. Humphrey is all right. Tall and stooped like a much older man, despite being younger than Sam, Humphrey can be affectionate and funny. His blue eyes sparkle and his lips twitch when he makes some pointed comment and waits for a reaction. Anna does not always understand his humour; she supposes it to be of a very English, dry and ironic variety. She likes Humphrey and, though never completely sure of him, she believes he likes her.

Constance, on the other hand, is prickly and easily offended. Anna does not know exactly why Constance seems to find her so threatening; perhaps it is the child she is expecting? Yet

Constance has three beautiful daughters of her own. At ten and eight, the older two are away in a boarding school, only seeing their parents for occasional weekends and in the holidays. It seems a horrible practice to Anna. Why have children, only to send them away? The youngest daughter, a little girl of three, is largely in the care of a nanny, known in the family as Nanny Lawrence. The child is brought into the drawing room after tea, prettily dressed, to be admired and caressed briefly and then returned to the nursery. Looking at the little girl, Anna is reminded of Rachel and their times together in Haifa, her lap a void longing to be filled. After a while, little Camilla learns to come to her for hugs and silly games, until Anna is scolded by Nanny Lawrence for spoiling the child.

She tries hard to understand Constance, to learn her expectations and fulfil them. Certainly, Constance does not consider it *her* role to bridge the cultural gulf between them. As Sam's wife, it is for Anna to adjust to her new situation, to learn the rules. Constance sees herself as keeper of Humphrey's reputation as a respected GP. She is ever alert to any threat to his position in the community. Anna knows that despite nearly two months of guidance and schooling in social etiquette, Constance finds her a frustratingly slow pupil. How strange it is, this English world of respectability and suppressed outrage.

In Humphrey and Constance's library Anna finds a copy of *Alice in Wonderland*. She thinks as a children's story it will be simple and may help her with colloquial English. The language turns out to be far from simple, yet it fascinates Anna, parodying as it does this very world of saying one thing and meaning something quite different. As she soon learns, Constance is an expert in this field. When by chance they meet a neighbour or acquaintance in the street or in a shop, Constance seems so delighted to see her, so warm and friendly. She admires her outfit, enquires after the health of the husband, enthuses over the achievements of the children. Yet, a few moments later, when they go their separate ways, Constance begins a terrifying assassination. She 'wouldn't be seen dead in that suit'; the husband is definitely not 'top-drawer' (Anna has to ask Constance to explain these expressions); the children are ill-mannered and dull.

Anna is well aware that she makes Constance anxious, afraid that Humphrey may be shown up by his brother's strange foreign wife and her unpredictable ways. Anna does not believe Constance dislikes her. In her way, she seems quite fond of Anna, but it is the uneasy affection one might have for a half-trained dog, which though appealing, could at any moment slip its collar and run riot.

Constance and Humphrey continue to entertain whenever they can – 'after a fashion' as Constance puts it. Small dinner parties are a regular occurrence at the Lawrence household.

'It's important to try to uphold our pre-war standards,' Constance maintains to Anna as they prepare for one such evening.

Charles and Susan Jennings settle themselves at the table. Anna has met Susan before; Constance had taken her to a 'coffee morning' at the Jennings' house the previous week, where cups of weak coffee had been served, bitter with chicory. Susan is a blonde, middle-aged woman with a pale, washed-out complexion. She has a habit of shaking with little spasms of giggling whenever she makes a contribution to the conversation.

Her husband Charles is Humphrey's senior partner – a large, noisy, red-faced man. He sits on Anna's right. As usual, Constance insists on placing Anna at *her* right-hand side. Anna is aware that this is not to favour her; it is not intended as an honour. On the contrary, Constance feels the need to keep a sharp eye on her, perhaps give her a meaningful prod or surreptitious kick under the table, or whisper advice under her breath. When Anna absently strokes the growing sphere of her belly, Constance indicates her disapproval with an audible exhalation through clenched teeth, accompanied by a hard stare.

13

Everyone's attention is on Humphrey, carving a scrawny chicken bestowed on him by a grateful patient. Little gifts like this are not infrequent and are an important supplement to the rations. Charles Jennings leans close to Anna, speaking softly in her ear in a manner both confidential and flirtatious.

'You look most charming, my dear. Splendid dress. Brightens up this drab weather no end. Just what we all need.'

Anna smiles at his looming face, suddenly uncertain how to respond. She glances round at Constance, who purses her lips and gazes about the table. Is this another of the sarcastic and indirect remarks she finds so confusing? Suddenly she feels that her red dress – so painstakingly sewn on Yael's machine from a pair of cotton curtains in preparation for her pregnancy – stands out vividly and inappropriately. It is also more suited to the Palestinian climate. She rubs her bare arms. Since arriving in England Anna has suffered constantly from the cold, not so much outside – Sam's mother has given her a thick woollen coat of her own, and one can put on several layers – but in the damp, unheated houses.

'Honestly, I don't know how you two manage it,' Susan says, with a giggle. 'Even in these hard times you always put on a splendid table, with everything so smart and spick and span!'

'Spick and span, eh? I nearly had to come to the dinner table unshaven tonight!' Humphrey is passing plates to his guests, each with a tiny portion of carved chicken. 'Not a drop of hot water left.' Humphrey smiles at Anna in a knowing manner, like a kindly schoolteacher who has caught out a favourite pupil in an unexpected misdemeanour.

'Oh dear …?' Anna says sympathetically, even as she senses uneasily that she has not fully understood the significance of the remark. Constance frowns at Humphrey, shaking her head faintly. It is truly a marvel, Anna thinks, how Constance can maintain a rigid smile on her lips, while frowning with the rest of her face.

'I know you're still not used to just how scarce the hot water is here,' Humphrey blunders on. All eyes around the table are now alternating between Humphrey and Anna, as though following a tennis match. 'I mean, in ordinary times it's fine to fill the bathtub to the brim, but … er … right now, with fuel shortages … well, there's not much to go round, is there? But then, how should you know that, eh? No matter though, no matter.'

Humphrey's remarks hang in the air like a chill fog. Anna is unsure if she is expected to reply, but a hard knot of anger rises in her chest and hammers against her ribs.

'Humphrey, are you telling me that I used up all the hot water in my bath? Because I think that is very rude of you to say, when I am a guest in your house!'

The high timbre of Anna's voice remains, like an echo, repeating her last words to the gathering over and over. Humphrey looks aghast at her, his mouth frozen half-open.

'I dare say you're right … yes, quite right. I do apologise, Anna. No offence intended,' he says after a pause.

Constance takes Anna's hand in hers, as if she means to comfort her. Her plump fingers close around Anna's wrist in a steely grip.

Anna's heart is pounding, the sound of it surely filling the room. She longs for Sam. Where is he? Why has he left her with these people? An uncomfortable hiatus is smoothed by the entry of Jenny, the Lawrences' cook, carrying vegetable dishes that she serves to everyone in turn, oblivious to the atmosphere. Conversation proceeds jerkily for a time. Humphrey winks at Anna across the table. Of course she smiles back. She resolves to speak to him later about the water issue. People here seem to talk in such a roundabout way about important matters, circling the crucial point but never quite articulating it. She is sorry to have upset Humphrey. He seems to be so kindly disposed towards her. But is he? She desperately needs allies. Certainly, she does not want to disturb the newly restored calm. A murmur of conversation rises falteringly from the table.

'Funny lot, we British, aren't we, my dear?' Charles is leaning over to Anna amiably again. 'So how do you think you are going to like living in England, eh? What do you make of it?'

'Bloody awful weather,' she replies without hesitation.

Cutlery stilled, there follows a stunned silence. Anna understands instantly that she has committed another social sin. Charles and Humphrey exchange glances and explode into great snorts of laughter. Susan titters behind her napkin. Constance glares thunderously.

'Where exactly have you learned such an … idiomatic phrase, Anna?' Humphrey asks.

'From the milkman, Humphrey. That is what he said to me this morning, when I opened the door.' She glances round the table, hoping for some means to redeem the situation. 'I am trying hard to speak English as it is spoken.'

'Well done, Anna! Jolly good. You're certainly learning to speak English as it is spoken!'

'However,' Constance adds, 'it is important to learn from the right class of person, darling.'

* * *

To Anna's relief, Sam has arranged for her to go into a small private nursing home for the birth of the child. At first she wonders whether Humphrey, as a doctor, expects to attend to her himself – how dreadful that would be. But it turns out he has simply recommended the nursing home as the best in the area. Labour pains start one Sunday afternoon. Constance times the intervals efficiently. Anna's bag has been packed for some time. Humphrey drives her to the hospital. A receptionist greets them, explains that a room has been booked for Anna and asks if she can manage to walk there. Anna says she can.

'Better leave you in their capable hands, my dear. Just follow instructions and you'll be fine. Remember, it's all been done before. Natural process, and all that. All the best to you. Constance will be in to see you tomorrow, no doubt.' Humphrey kisses Anna uncertainly on the cheek and turns to go. For a moment Anna almost calls him back, begs him to stay with her.

She has a small private room, very plain, very white. She feels totally alone. A brisk midwife comes in to examine her. She washes her hands and returns to the bed.

'I was led to believe this was your first child, Mrs Lawrence.' She studies Anna's face with a quizzical frown.

'I'm not sure what you were told. I had … I lost a child. Some years ago.'

'Ah, yes. I understand.'

Anna looks at her. *No, you understand nothing of me.* The midwife comes back to examine her again every half hour or so. She offers little further conversation and even less comfort. The pains grow in strength and frequency and Anna is moved to a delivery room next door.

After an agonising, momentous struggle, a boy is born, a beautiful, perfect boy. As Anna holds him, breathes him in, and kisses him, over and over, the tears released become a flood, and will not stop. She is convulsed with weeping. She weeps for all the years gone by, for all that has happened and all that cannot be undone. The midwife clucks disapprovingly and urges her to stop – she should control herself for baby's sake. It might upset him. She has a fine child and should be grateful. She needs to be calm for baby.

Constance visits them the next day. She admires the baby and hugs Anna and tells her how proud and happy Sam would be. She mentions that she and Humphrey have taken some blankets and cooking utensils to the rented rooms to which Anna and the baby will be moving on leaving hospital. After she goes, Anna spends hours gazing at her sleeping son. The nurses come to show her how to change and bath him. They handle his small body with detached efficiency. The baby abandons himself to their firm hands. He stares at the ceiling light. When being bathed, his fragile limbs stiffen and then relax. Anna is told to 'put him down' immediately after his bath or feeding him, to establish a routine. As soon as the nurses leave the room, she picks the baby up and presses him to the hollow of her neck. She inhales his blissful smell. He nuzzles against her and roots around for her breast, his soft mouth open and urgent.

The following day Constance brings Mother to see her new grandson. Mother holds him and kisses his tiny fingers. She looks up at Anna and shakes her head, her expression anxious, as always.

'He's so like Samuel as a baby, dear, that same little worried face.'

She unwraps a parcel of exquisite tiny garments she has sewn and knitted. Anna leans forward and embraces her mother-in-law. Mother stiffens in her arms, looking at once alarmed and delighted. Constance says they have wondered what the baby will be called.

'Sam and I agreed Benjamin for a boy – Ben for short,' Anna says.

'Benjamin,' says Mother. 'That's unusual. Is it Jewish?'

Chapter 3

Sam

The behaviour and manner of Dr John Quentin Lawrence reflected the beliefs and attitudes of the Victorian era during which he was raised. Dr Lawrence was respected and trusted, but not greatly liked. He was regarded as a stern and severe man, who believed in hard work and frugality. He married Winifred Wainwright, a parson's daughter, not for her good looks – she was on the thin side with a long face – but for her humble and compliant demeanour. He knew he would be able to rely on her to make a good doctor's wife, and to uphold his values.

Despite her complete ignorance of the physical side of marriage until her wedding night, Winifred was pregnant with their first child. She woke early one morning with violent pains, which she knew to be contractions. She breathed quietly, so as not to wake her husband. She bit her lip and dug her fingernails into her palm. When the clock reached quarter to seven, she allowed herself to speak aloud.

'Good morning, John. The time for the child has come.'

Dr Lawrence opened his eyes and looked at his wife in confusion for a moment. Then he felt a brief flutter of excitement.

Dear God, let it be a son. Any further child can be a daughter if it must, but let this be my son. He remembered his list of home calls and sat up.

'I will ask Alice to fetch Mrs Roly to attend to you. Are you feeling quite well, my dear?' He was not in the habit of calling Winifred 'my dear'.

She gasped and doubled up, her body consumed with pain. There was something almost indecent about such a physical experience, one that was totally outside her control. After a few moments she straightened and flexed her shoulders.

'I believe I am. The pains are quite close together.'

Dr Lawrence regarded Winifred approvingly. It was just like her not to make a fuss.

'Good, good – then perhaps you won't have to endure them too long, Winnie.'

Dr Lawrence dressed quickly and rang for Alice. The girl could not conceal her excitement at the task she was given.

'Ooh, I'll run all the way to Mrs Roly's, sir.'

'All in good time, Alice. Before you go, kindly lay out some breakfast for me. I'm due at my first call shortly.'

Samuel James Lawrence was born some hours later, on 24th March 1902. After the last patient had left his evening surgery, Dr Lawrence paid his wife and first-born son a visit. The small east bedroom had been prepared as a lying-in room. Dr Lawrence was relieved to find that all was clean and neat, and quiet. Winifred was sitting up in bed, brushing her hair. Next to her, the infant was sleeping in a mahogany cradle in which, nearly forty years previously, Dr Lawrence himself had slept.

'Here he is, John,' Winifred whispered, 'here's our Samuel.'

Dr Lawrence peered into the cradle.

'Splendid. What a funny little fellow.'

* * *

Sam, his younger brothers Humphrey and Albert, and his sister Freda, grew up in the rambling house on the edge of the village of Stonethwaite in Cumberland. Their father's surgery occupied half the ground floor. During surgery hours, patients waited on hard wooden chairs in the hallway. There were two consulting rooms: one for Dr Lawrence, large enough for minor operations, and a smaller one for Dr Jasper, his junior partner.

At the back was a small dispensary, where Dr Lawrence made up pills and medicines. Stacked on one shelf were glass bottles of ominously coloured liquids: red, green, and brown, each sealed with a cork. Dr Lawrence was a great believer in the placebo effect for simple country people. These bottles contained nothing but sterilised water, some harmless colouring, and a little alcohol added as a 'pick-me-up'. His patients swore by them.

'Ah no, Doctor, not the green one; my Betty takes that. It's the red one 'as worked wonders for my rheumatism.'

Apart from the kitchen, the house was always cold, even in summer, the sun rarely having time to penetrate the thick stone walls before the chill of evening returned. On the bitterest winter nights a meagre fire smouldered in the sitting room grate. Bedroom fires were lit only on rare special occasions, such as when Freda shivered and quaked with scarlet fever. Winifred was in charge of the running of the house. It was a house looming with heavy dark furniture inherited from an earlier age. Carpets were worn and soft furnishings threadbare.

Sam had no memory of anything new ever being bought for the house. Even shoes were considered an extravagance, and were kept for as long as possible. As the eldest, Sam sometimes had new shoes bought for him, but only when his toes were firmly pressed against the tips. Shoes were patched and mended, their soles and heels reinforced with crescents of metal. When unarguably outgrown, Sam's shoes eventually passed to Humphrey, and finally to Albert. Sam's feet caused him problems for the rest of his life.

Meals were bland and simple, in accordance with Dr Lawrence's taste. He considered that excessive use of seasoning overstimulated the appetite and the senses, and was to be avoided. Each week, Winifred struggled with the domestic budget allowed by her husband. She made careful lists and opted for the cheaper cuts of meat, which were cooked at length in the Aga until reasonably tender, and stretched with turnips, potatoes, barley and suet dumplings. Certain items not absolutely essential were omitted from the shopping until the following week. She supplemented the family diet with produce from a large vegetable and fruit garden. It did not occur to Winifred to suggest that Dr Lawrence might have increased her household allowance. The children always left the table a little hungry.

While they were very small, the children were taught to read and write by their nanny in the nursery. Nanny Lawrence was a kindly spinster of middle years, from whom the children enjoyed occasional demonstrations of affection. When Sam was nine, a governess arrived and introduced him and Humphrey to the rudiments of history, mathematics and French. Two years later Nanny Lawrence disappeared, despite anguished tears shed by Albert and Freda, then aged six and five. At the same time, a tutor was engaged to prepare the older boys for their entrance examinations. He performed his task with rigour, caning Sam and Humphrey viciously across the knuckles for any lack of effort or application.

The austerity of home life prepared Sam well for conditions at boarding school. He expected neither comfort nor affection, and received none. The battlefields of France and Belgium were rapidly absorbing a generation of young men. Many of Sam's teachers were old men or survivors of the war, returning damaged and embittered, and resenting their pupils' untouched youth and opportunity.

Despite its harshness, Sam's childhood was not without pleasure. His father's work meant he was rarely present at home, except when occupied in the surgery. The children were expected to entertain themselves, when not actively engaged in schoolwork. They roamed the hills and country freely on foot and by bicycle, slabs of bread and cold tea packed into knapsacks. Sam often helped his mother in the vegetable garden. She was not a talkative woman, but he sensed her quiet fondness for him as they worked side by side, planting lines of potatoes, turnips and carrots.

'Well done, Samuel. By autumn we'll be enjoying these.'

When Sam reached the age of seventeen, Dr Lawrence called him into his study for a discussion about his future.

'Are you considering medicine, Samuel? I have contacts at St Thomas's, you know. I'm sure they'd take you on, as long as you don't make a mess of matriculation. It's a fine profession.'

'I don't think I'm really cut out to be a doctor, Father. Not like Humphrey.'

'*Not cut out for it?* I don't know about that. That seems a somewhat flippant way to refer to your future. You do realise we can't send you all to university, don't you? If you don't want to pursue medicine, have you thought about the other options? There's law or there's the army.'

Sam longed to escape the constraints of his life. He longed to see the wider world. In 1922, he became one of the youngest officers to graduate from Sandhurst. Dr Lawrence and Sam's godfather – an uncle in Ireland – shared in paying for his commission, with money long set aside for just such an eventuality.

His first posting was to Ireland. It was not the exotic setting he might have hoped for, but he liked the Irish, and recognised that history had dealt them a poor hand. His commanding officer warned him against this view.

'Be careful, Lawrence. It's a mistake to try to see both sides of the argument – or to consider the argument at all for that matter. Our job is to keep order, nothing more. Keep out of the politics.'

In Ireland Sam learned that great charm was not incompatible with extreme brutality. There was a spate of house burnings by the Black and Tans, after which the IRA considered what reprisals against the Protestants might be appropriate. IRA leaders of the local Brigade felt it would be unjust to burn the homes of people not involved directly in anti-Catholic acts. Instead they decided to target Leindown Castle, residence of Lord and Lady Tullycomb. Lord Tullycomb was a member of the British House of Lords and a determined opponent of Irish National aspirations. British officers sometimes stayed at the Castle, and officers from the local garrison – including Sam – were occasional visitors there.

The IRA also selected Leindown for its history of devout Unionism and its longstanding links with the British establishment. At the time of the attack, Lord Tullycomb was away in Scotland on a fishing trip. The only occupants of the Castle were Lady Tullycomb, her daughter Hester, and five servants. The Castle and most of its contents were burnt to the ground in the raid, but no one was harmed.

Sam participated in the subsequent military investigation. He was impressed by Lady Tullycomb's steadfast refusal to identify the attackers, saying only that they had 'behaved like gentlemen'. She informed the military that she and Hester had been allowed to identify some of their most treasured possessions, and then ten IRA men had been assigned to carry these objects out of the house. Two armchairs had also been taken outside for herself and Hester to sit in safety and comfort. Sam noted that these chairs were placed in the rose garden, where the women would be sheltered from the sight of their home being destroyed, and where the smell of burning might be masked by the fragrance of the blooms. He was ordered to remove these references from his report, his commanding officer being concerned that the true criminality of the act should not be disguised.

On another occasion, Sam was cycling back to his base following a match at the nearby tennis club, when he rounded a corner and stumbled upon an IRA ambush. A general – a highly decorated hero of the First World War – and his friend, a colonel, together with their wives, were driving in the other direction, in order to play tennis themselves. Seeing signs of an ambush ahead, and unable to turn the car around in time, the general accelerated the car in a desperate attempt to escape. The ambushers opened fire with revolvers, rifles and shotguns, killing the general and the colonel's wife instantly. The car swerved sideways and crashed into a ditch.

Sam was nearly upon them. He witnessed the event, but was unable to intervene or escape the notice of the attackers. He had no option but to continue cycling. As he reached the rebel road block, unarmed and vulnerable in his white shorts and shirt, he waved his tennis racket in the air. The IRA men, respecting a sportsman, shook their heads and allowed him through unharmed, before making their escape without further bloodshed.

Sam was able to summon help for the injured survivors of the ambush. He was genuinely surprised when his advance through the site of the attack was later referred to as an act of heroism. He had been confident that the rebels had nothing to gain by targeting him too and, in any case, felt he had no alternative but to proceed. Sam's gentle and courteous manner endeared him to all sides of the conflict. Over time he gained a reputation for being a fair and effective negotiator.

After two years, he made a brief visit home before leaving for India with his regiment. Freda was overjoyed to see her eldest brother. Humphrey had begun his medical studies in London, and Albert was still at school, prior to joining his brother at St. Thomas's Hospital.

The family had been invited to an evening with the Fairbairn sisters. Dr Lawrence disliked social gatherings. He regarded them as a regrettable but necessary extension of his working role. Winifred felt shy and self-conscious, worrying about the earth that refused to be prised from under her fingernails, and about her outdated gown. Freda was thrilled at any opportunity to leave the house and meet people. She had heard that the Misses Fairbairns' orphaned niece Charlotte was staying with them, and she hoped to befriend her. Sam regarded the evening as a bit of a bore, but he was quite happy to accompany his sister. Their parents joined the older guests in the drawing room, while Sam and Freda made their way to the sitting room, where younger people were gathered.

Though not vain or self-conscious, Sam was aware that he made quite an entrance; tall and slim in his lieutenant's uniform. After two years away from home, his shoulders had broadened and he had acquired a confident and easy-going manner.

He and Freda were introduced to Charlotte. She had a pale complexion and fair hair arranged on top of her head. She was wearing an azure blue dress, pulled in becomingly to her narrow waist with a darker blue satin band. Sam supposed she was pretty, yet there was a hardness about her. Her smile was quizzical rather than warm, as if she was about to say, 'What exactly do you mean by that?' Sam's attitude to women was one of gallantry rather than true connection, due perhaps to lack of exposure. He thought nothing critical of Charlotte; only he sensed that experience had made her suspicious of others. Perhaps it was an instinct to comfort and protect her, but he found himself strangely drawn to her.

'Do you ride, Miss Fairbairn? The weather is so fine at present – I wonder if you would like to go for a ride with me? Not too far, of course.'

She frowned. 'Distance is no object for Bunty, or for me.'

That prickly, challenging expression again.

'Bunty is your horse? I'm afraid I was thinking of my bicycle.'

Charlotte snorted. 'Never been on a bicycle in my life, and don't intend to try.'

Sam was not an expert horseman, but he had achieved some proficiency in Ireland. Charlotte's uncle lent him his horse, which was a little more frisky than he would have liked. Charlotte's

Bunty was a fine bay with a serene temperament. Over the coming week, they made several excursions together. Charlotte seemed to enjoy his company. She relaxed and started to laugh more, but there was little warmth in her manner. She remained distant and gave no signal that greater closeness would have been welcomed. Yet, by the time Sam was ready to leave for India, they had agreed to write to each other.

* * *

Sam was completely bewitched by India: the overwhelming heat, the noise, the colours, smells and tastes of it. He wrote to Charlotte of all he experienced. In particular, he told her of his trips to Kashmir: trekking on horseback through hills smelling of pine and rosemary, sleeping under canvas on a camp-bed made up by his batman Morris, and eating delicious fragrant food cooked over an open fire by Rahman Singh. He knew she would like to hear of his equestrian adventures, the sturdy little horses sure-footed on stony screes and steep mountain tracks.

Despite the detailed and vivid descriptions of his experiences, Sam thought little of Charlotte during the long voyage, and for the first weeks in Calcutta. At times he worried about not missing her, but he put it down to the distraction of adjusting to such an alien environment. His head was filled with one new impression after another – there was little room for anything else.

Gradually, he settled in to his rooms and took stock of his life. He became aware of an absence. It was not as if he were lonely; far from it, he was constantly in company. His fellow officers were a mixed bunch, as always, but he found comradeship with Ellis, St John, Cameron and Hailsham. His men liked and respected him. He enjoyed the knowledge that he had created a good rapport with them. His contact with the local people was equally positive. He was learning Urdu in order to communicate better with them. There were regular dinners and dances at the officers' mess, where he dallied with one or two young women: an English governess employed by a local Maharaja to tutor his children, and the older daughter of the District Commissioner. His senior officer, Major Wellbeck, warned him off.

'Take care, Lawrence. These girls are after husbands, remember. If that's what you want, fine. But make the proper approaches.'

Sam felt colour rising up his neck.

'If it's just a bit of hanky-panky you're after, there are always the native women. The adjutant can tell you which is a safe house, so to speak.'

Sam wrote beautiful letters, descriptive, expressive, poetic. As time went on, the tone of Charlotte's replies became a little softer. The emotional content of Sam's letters rose in intensity. He was deeply moved by them himself. They were so convincing. How much easier it was to put feelings into writing than to express them face to face.

After a year, he asked Charlotte if she would consider becoming his wife and joining him in India. She wrote back to affirm that she might consider such a proposal, and detailing her precise needs regarding sufficient stabling at their married quarters. She explained that as she had no father to ask the 'correct questions', she had to ask them herself. Namely, what exactly were Sam's prospects in terms of his likely career path and future earnings? He replied that he expected to be promoted to captain the following year, when he would be twenty-five. He was too modest to mention that his commanding officer had explained that such early promotion reflected Sam's exceptional potential. Charlotte suggested they wait until the following year to get married. Until that time they considered themselves engaged.

The following year, 1927, Sam returned home on three months' leave. His parents were delighted to see him, and pleased about the forthcoming marriage. For some weeks Sam and Charlotte embarked on a spending spree, which alarmed Doctor Lawrence and Winifred inordinately, but they came to accept that the young couple needed to equip an entire household. The army provided some essential basics, but further items of furniture, bedding, kitchen goods and clothing were assembled, ready to be boxed and shipped to India. Winifred's greatest sadness was that Charlotte rejected her offered gift of her mother's old wedding ring. Charlotte wanted to choose a new one for herself.

'But what about the expense, my dear?' asked Winifred.

'Hang the expense,' Charlotte replied.

Sam and Charlotte were married at Stonethwaite Parish Church. Humphrey was Sam's best man. As they stood shuffling from foot to foot at the altar, awaiting the bride's arrival, Sam was overcome with misgiving. He saw his father in the front row, sombre as always, staring straight ahead. Next to him his mother, red-eyed and clutching a handkerchief, tried to smile at Sam.

'Oh God, what have I done?' breathed Sam.

'*Courage, mon brave,*' whispered Humphrey.

After the celebration, Sam and Charlotte retired to his old room for their first night together as a married couple. A second single bed had been carried into the room and pushed up against Sam's narrow schoolboy bed. It did not surprise Sam that Charlotte recoiled when he reached for her that night.

'Not here,' she hissed, 'with your parents next door!'

He could understand her reluctance. It had been excruciatingly embarrassing saying goodnight to them and going upstairs together. But as he gazed at Charlotte's forbidding back, he wondered if they couldn't at least have hugged each other.

Early the next day they took the train to Southampton, where their ship was waiting. That night, in the privacy of their cabin, Charlotte was extremely tired from the journey. The second night she appeared so nervous and anxious that Sam tried to reassure her. He kissed her neck and chastely ran his fingers down her rigid shoulders and arms. Charlotte was an innocent girl, he told himself, shy and unschooled in the ways of the world. She had not had the supportive presence of a mother during her earlier years. What did he expect? He needed to give her time, to be patient.

He was patient for all the weeks of the voyage, and then tried hard to sustain patience when they moved into their bungalow. Charlotte was unhappy with the sleeping arrangements. She would have liked separate bedrooms. Sam's patience was running out. One evening he abandoned all his good intentions and shouted about his rights as a husband. He asked why she had married him: was it just for a ticket to a social position and a good life in India?

'If you absolutely insist, I suppose I have to agree, occasionally. But don't expect me to enjoy it.'

Sam's desire faded in direct proportion to the growth of his anger and frustration. It seemed clear that Charlotte's only true love was for horses. If he could have offered her impregnation with good Arabian stock, she might have considered the proposition. Children – *his* children – were out of the question.

It took six years of misery before his commanding officer would agree to a divorce.

'The army doesn't approve of divorce, Lawrence, especially not a rushed job. You don't want to destroy your career prospects completely.'

They lived at opposite ends of the house. On the surface, they kept up a semblance of normality. When attending balls at the officers' mess together, Charlotte sometimes said, 'I suppose you'd better give me your arm.'

In 1933, Charlotte returned to England. Two years later they were granted a decree nisi. Sam never contacted her, or heard from her again.

At thirty-three, Sam resigned himself to a solitary life, successful in his chosen career, but lacking personal attachments: a life devoid of warmth and affection. He created a beautiful garden around the bungalow. The servants were instructed to water the plants every evening, whether or not he was there. Alongside the hibiscus, orchids, oleander and bougainvillaea were roses and delphiniums, ceanothus and hydrangea. The garden was his greatest pleasure. He wished he could share it with his mother.

Sam remained in India for two more years, after which he was posted to Egypt, by then a major. It was a time of increasing unrest, as the quest for full independence – a cause for which Sam had some sympathy – grew in momentum. His visits to England were few, and many years apart. His parents were ageing. In 1940 his father died. Winifred, bereft, moved to Surrey to a cottage roughly equidistant from Freda and her husband's small house, and Humphrey and his wife's much larger one.

In 1942 Sam began a posting as a lieutenant colonel in Palestine. A man of extreme gentleness, his experience in work and in personal relations had been of continuous conflict: Ireland, India, his marriage, Egypt and now Palestine. At first he was drawn to the Arab cause. Gradually his respect and sympathy for the Jews grew. Surely all people deserved the right to live safely and freely, to have a homeland? Above all, he admired their determination to force the arid land into fertility, into prolific growth. He remembered his first CO's warning about seeing both sides of the argument. Yet he couldn't help believing both the Arabs and the Jews had a just cause.

A year later Anna Wiener, a Jewish refugee and a widow, was appointed as secretary to Sam and his fellow officers in the training section. He was immediately, miraculously attracted to her. She was as different from Charlotte as any woman could be: small, dark, intense, emotional and sharply intelligent. Sam recognised that Anna was traumatised and complex, her life one of even greater turmoil than his own. He knew they came from different countries and cultures, and that he should proceed with caution. He sensed mystery, perhaps danger, at her core. But any initial hesitancy was soon thrown aside. He could think of nothing, no one else. Rejected by the only other woman to whom he had reached out, it was a wonder to Sam that Anna loved him too, that she responded to his touch, that she chose to be with him, that she wanted to have children with him.

In March 1944 Sam and Anna were married at the British High Commission in Haifa.

27th October 1945, Berlin

My darling Anna,

It was wonderful to get your letter of 5th Oct, and the lovely photograph of Benjamin. What a splendid little fellow he is. He's grown so much since I was with you both; looks quite a little rugby player now (a rough, uncivilised and no doubt incomprehensible game played by British males – I'll tell you about it some time). What a lot of hair he has now – and how come he's inherited my red instead of your beautiful black hair? My only disappointment was that you didn't include a recent photo of you too though – the one of us both in Surrey is now hopelessly dog-eared (yes, another strange English expression!) from my constant fingering. Do please get Humphrey or Constance to take one of you, and send it to me.

I hope you are well and happy and enjoying life, despite Surrey's limitations and the dismal weather. Is the new accommodation working out? It has to be an improvement over the last place. What an unpleasant experience for you, and so unnecessary. I hope Mrs Wilson is an agreeable landlady and will be tolerant of any noise Benjamin might make. Remember, you're paying the rent and it is your home, and Ben's, for the time being. You should feel free to do as you please, and to come and go as you wish.

Are you missing me? I can't wait for us all to be together again – and to that end, I have been extremely busy since you wrote with your list of instructions and requirements(!) Of course I quite understand your insistence that we engage no

staff young enough to have been in the Hitler Youth. I think
you'll find that I've complied with your wishes. We now have
a cook, a nanny, and a gardener – and I'm working on a
suitable maid. Their credentials are as follows:

Cook: Frau Helga Stammel. Known as 'Maggi' (after the
Swiss soup firm). Aged 64 years. Previously very wealthy. Then
abandoned and divorced by her husband. Cooking not bad.

Nanny: Frau Selma Rausch. Aged 52 years. From Silesia.
Denounced for expressing anti-Nazi sentiments and impris-
oned during the war.

Gardener: Herr Eisen. Aged 68 years. Refugee from Eastern
Germany. Lost his entire family during the war. A silent man
– but wields a mean spade.

As you will see, the Germans have done a pretty good job
of destroying the lives of some of their own people too. I trust
they are old enough for you? At the moment Frau Rausch is
preparing the nursery and is on a 'retainer' until you and
Ben arrive. The others have started work – Maggi does her
best with the limited supplies. (I hope you are eating all right?)
I'm due to interview a couple of potential maids tomorrow.
Frau Rausch is going to help me make a selection.

I think you'll approve of the house. It's spacious and has
a very large garden (which pleases me, of course). With
Eisen's help we should have quite a crop of fruit and vegeta-
bles next year. I know the requisition business is not very
comfortable – but you may be surprised to hear that the
owner says she's delighted to have a British family in her
house. She reckons we'll take better care of it than the
Russians or Americans!

Meanwhile, the work proceeds quite well. We're making
progress organising the educational side of things. A little more
food is gradually getting through, but there are still terrible
shortages. Of course there's a huge black market trade, for
those who can afford it. At least transport is slowly improving.

I won't write more now – all news when you come. Oh God, I love those words – when you come!

Darling Anna – I miss you so much. I long to hold you, touch you, smell you. Not long now until we can all be together – a proper family. Speaking of families, are you surviving my dear relatives? Mother adores you – she wrote six pages about your last visit with Benjamin! Humphrey is a good sort. Don't take Constance's ways too much to heart. She's a bigot and a snob, but otherwise a treasure.

Take special care of yourself – and Ben – these next few weeks, and write again when you can.

All my love, as always,
Sam

PS. I was so glad to hear your suggestion of having a 'Naming Ceremony' for Ben when you get here. It's a wonderful idea. Let's make a real occasion of it – we'll have a party on the rations!

Chapter 4

Anna

Anna is born in 1914 just before the start of the First World War, a war that is to have a fundamental effect in shaping her early life. Anna's parents, Artur and Matilde Feldman, run a successful factory making clothes for both the 'ready-made' market in large stores, and for private customers. Despite having come from farming stock only a generation previously, Artur has a sharp brain for business. Matilde is from an educated, artistic and musical family. She has inherited a spontaneous flair for design. Her women's outfits and children's clothes are soon amongst the most sought after in fashionable Vienna. With their eldest daughter Esther, Artur and Matilde are able to move to a spacious apartment in Mariahilferstrasse, in the centre of the city.

However, challenging times lie ahead. With the break-up of the Austro-Hungarian Empire, eighty per cent of their market disappears. Profits plunge, but employees still need to be paid. Artur is a patriot; he loves Austria. Leaving Matilde to run the factory, he enlists and spends three years fighting for his country. By 1918 the Austrian economy is in ruins. Food is scarce. Despite their former affluence, the family is on the verge of starvation, as is much of the population of Vienna. There are now three young daughters to support. After the war is over, Allied occupiers set up soup kitchens to feed the most vulnerable. One child from each family is permitted to receive a hot meal each day.

Margaret, the youngest, is still being breast-fed. Anna, the middle child, is judged to be the puniest, the most deserving. She is taken to the feeding hall by Kaethe, the family's maid. Even at four, Anna senses the deep humiliation of defeat in being fed by British soldiers.

Worse than the deprivations, Matilde contracts the Spanish flu sweeping Europe. The virulent infection kills many neighbours. Matilde becomes very ill and develops encephalitis. She is not expected to survive, but somehow she does. The infection has destroyed vital areas of her brain. At thirty-four she is left with a form of Parkinson's disease. Year by year it deprives her of more abilities and strength, until she becomes bedridden, her body and limbs possessed by trembling, her speech a high monotone.

Life in the once fine apartment on Mariahilferstrasse centres on Matilde. She had been the mainstay of both the business and the family: shrewd with money, clever at stretching small amounts of food, and efficient at paperwork. Artur's priority is to fulfil his wife's needs as best he can. The children must not make noise. They cannot invite their friends home to play. Matilde must be kept comfortable and serene. Every evening Artur spends time with her after returning from work. He sits on her bed holding her hand and reports on the day's events, and Matilde makes suggestions regarding the business.

Gradually Artur rebuilds the firm. Less educated than his wife, nevertheless he has a way with people. Naturally charming, he is popular with both men and women, and is a successful salesman. The staff are loyal; they remember Artur and Matilde's support during the hard years. Slowly the business becomes profitable again.

Anna and her sisters live contented, protected lives. As their mother's health deteriorates, it is Kaethe who plays a central role in caring for and nurturing the children. Although Esther, Anna and Margaret would love to have a more active mother, who can play and read with them like many of their friends' mothers, Kaethe surrounds them with love and affection. For a few years their lives are relatively carefree. They attend a mixed private school, the majority of whose pupils come from homes as comfortable as theirs. The girls walk to school arm in arm with their friends, thinking only of fun and friendships. Lotte, Leila, Gretchen, Magdelene, Wilma, Sara and Monika – all are indistinguishable from one another.

The girls light candles for Hanukkah and then clip them onto the fir tree, to be lit on Christmas Eve. They wish each other a happy new year for the first of January, and again for Rosh Hashanah. Other than these enjoyable events, they are scarcely aware of who is Christian, who is Jewish. Artur is a pragmatic rather than a devout man. He rarely goes to temple, and then only to meet a business associate. Viennese society is not without its divisions, but these relate largely to identifying those who live in a less smart neighbourhood, or who are less well dressed, less well spoken, less witty.

Anna is pretty, petite, with black curls and dark eyes. She is hard working and diligent at school, her marks always in the top three of her class. She is equally good at sports: skiing, skating, swimming, basketball and gymnastics. She is regarded as sweet-natured and kind by the other girls, and polite by her teachers. Despite these many attributes, Anna is not priggish or conceited. She has a quick temper and a wicked sense of humour, which endears her to her friends. Despite her popularity, Anna has a more troubled side to her temperament. Perhaps the household's preoccupation with her mother's needs and illness induces in the growing child a tendency to occasional bouts of melancholic contemplation. From an early age, she keeps a diary in which she records 'days of sad thoughts'.

One day as they walk to the bakery together to buy the morning rolls, Anna, at the age of eight or nine years, astounds the down-to-earth Kaethe.

'Kaethe, why am I inside *this person* looking out?'

'Inside? Inside who? What are you talking about, child?'

'I mean, why am I *me*? I could have been anyone. Why was I born inside this body and not someone else's?'

'Well, now you're asking! That's not a question for poor Kaethe, but for God. And it's not something a little girl like you needs to worry about.'

'But I *do* worry about it! Sometimes I think how easily I could have been Laura or Sara, or a Hottentot living in the desert or an Eskimo girl in an igloo, or even … a … a boy!' Kaethe stops walking and puts an arm around Anna's shoulders.

'Oh my goodness! Oh dear me, a Hottentot? I think I like you just the way you are, *Liebchen* – and Mamma and Papa don't want a different little girl, they want you! Just be happy with who you are. There's no need to brood so much.'

Anna sighs. If only Kaethe would understand that it's not that she *wants* to be a different person, it's just that these questions are troubling. However, in the family, such a quest for answers is regarded as self-absorption, which is not to be encouraged. Despite these concerns, in the main Anna's childhood is as her parents would wish: contented and cheerful.

Over time her life begins to change, gradually at first, almost imperceptibly, but then with increasing momentum. Every day, her best friend Laura calls at Mariahilferstrasse, and they walk to school together giggling and whispering. One morning, when Anna is fifteen, Laura does not ring the bell. What can have happened? Anna worries that perhaps Laura is unwell. She is reluctant to leave without her. But it is already late, and Kaethe shoos her out of the apartment with her school bag and her morning snack. Anna walks alone to school. She drags her feet; walking on her own is no fun. In front of the school, clusters of pupils are talking together. There is Laura in the midst of a group of girls. She glances at Anna self-consciously. Anna smiles and waves at her friend.

'Laura, what happened? Did you forget this morning?'

Laura looks uncomfortable. She looks round at her friends and back to Anna. Then she purses her lips and pulls herself upright.

'*Mutti* says we don't mix with Jews.' She turns her back on Anna. The other girls snigger and turn away too.

Many of the girls join National Socialist youth groups. They troop off on hiking and camping trips in the Vienna Woods or into the mountains, rucksacks on their backs. They cook over open fires and sing songs in the evening. These trips seem such fun. Anna loves swimming and hiking and singing. She yearns to go too, but she and her remaining friends are not invited. In class it becomes noticeable that top marks are never given to Jewish pupils any more. Now Anna's results are never awarded more than 'average'.

'You must continue to work hard and achieve the best you can, whatever the results,' Matilde urges the girls. '*We* know how clever you are.'

Anna tries hard to concentrate on her schoolwork as before, but it is not always easy to feel the same motivation. Things do not improve as she progresses through school. The new intake of pupils is now entirely Christian. Soon after she matriculates, the teachers in her school let it be known that they are no longer prepared to teach any Jewish pupils. University courses and many professions are similarly out of bounds.

'We have to hope this is a temporary situation,' Anna's father says, but he seems unconvinced.

Anna begins working as a nanny and governess, first for a

number of families needing short-term support. Eventually she obtains permanent work for a wealthy Jewish family with two children. She is fond of the children, a boy of nine and a girl of six, and feels any experience will help her in the future. The children's mother, Karin, is pleased to have intelligent adult company. Her family lives in Budapest, and she rarely sees them. Life can be lonely for Karin at times, especially when her husband, Otto, is away on business trips. Otto runs the family business, dealing in wood products and machinery. He often has to travel to other cities, and sometimes to other countries. Karin enjoys accompanying Anna and the children on visits to the park, or trips to the hills to pick berries and mushrooms. The two young women soon become relaxed and companionable together.

Otto, on the other hand, appears more distant at first. Always polite and somewhat formal with Anna, he rarely initiates conversation with her. Yet Anna finds herself strangely aware of his presence. Sometimes when she glances in his direction, she notices him looking steadily at her. She cannot help admiring Otto's exceptional good looks. He has a strong forehead, high cheekbones, and a powerful, masculine jawline. His shiny dark hair and caramel-coloured skin look so smooth, almost as though polished. At times, in Otto's presence, Anna is alarmed to notice a strange sensation in the pit of her stomach: a softening, a feeling of falling, almost as though she were plunging downwards on the Riesenrad in the Prater Park. She is aware too of a disconcerting quivering of her fingers whenever she watches Otto, as if they long to reach out and caress the velvety warmth of his skin.

One day in the early summer, as the children scamper ahead, Karin tells Anna they will be going on holiday to Lugano in three weeks' time.

'How long will you be away?'

'How long will *we* be away, you mean! Of course you will have to come with us, Anna. We usually stay a month or so.'

'But surely you want time as a family? Time with Otto?'

'Yes, sometimes we may ask you to be with the children so he and I can have some time together. But, Anna, you must enjoy yourself too. It's so beautiful there. The hotel is right on the lakeside. We all love it and you will too – I know it. You will have your own room, and can spend plenty of time doing as you please. You might even meet some attractive young men!'

* * *

It is now around two years since Jakob Wiener started to call at the Feldmans' apartment. His mother and grandmother are old friends of Artur and Matilde. Anna and her sisters have known Jakob and his twin brother Paul since they were all small children. Their father has been dead since the boys were young. When Jakob and Paul approach their twenty-first birthdays, their mother and grandmother decide to give a party.

Anna loves clothes. She and Esther help one another plan their dresses. They spend hours making sketches of their plans for dress designs, which they show to Matilde. She has such an eye, her ideas and her suggestions always right, always tasteful. Soon they have made their choices. Esther, with her auburn hair and green eyes, looks striking in cream muslin. Anna decides on a pale turquoise material to set off her dark curls.

Margaret is uninterested in clothes. She is happy for her mother to select a dress for her. She has her straight brown hair cut short in the modern style. She joins the Communist Party. Despite her plainness, Margaret is popular with young men. She shows genuine interest in their views on any topic, although she does not always agree. She gazes up at them, absorbed in their arguments, transfixed by their opinions.

On the evening of the party, Jakob welcomes them all, his eyes on Anna. She is flattered by his interest. He is four years older than she is, and handsome. They dance most of the evening. He keeps returning to her. There is something proprietorial about

41

his hand at her back as he leads her onto the dance floor. She feels secure in his hands. Month after month, they spend every spare moment together, going walking, to the sports club and to coffee houses. Anna is excited to be introduced to concerts, the opera and the theatre. Artur is not a cultured man, and circumstances have not allowed his daughters access to such experiences. Anna enjoys the attention lavished on her.

One day her father calls her into his study.

'Anna, did you know Jakob came to speak to me this afternoon?'

'Oh?'

'Has he not talked to you of his plans?'

'What plans, Papa?'

'Jakob asked me for your hand today.'

'My hand? I think he might have asked *me* first!'

Artur frowns. 'He behaved very properly. Perhaps he wanted permission from your parents before he spoke to you. I believe he regards you as more of a challenge.'

'Why a challenge?'

'You are having a good time with Jakob, yes?'

Anna nods.

'But I don't get the impression that you are madly in love with him.'

'I'm ... very fond of him.'

'But?'

'It is when we go swimming together. Jakob has a good figure ... but he has hair on his shoulders.'

'What? *Hair on his shoulders?* You would reject a good man for such a reason? Then you are right not to marry – you are just a silly, immature girl, and not worthy of Jakob.'

Anna's lip trembles. 'Papa! I haven't said I'm rejecting him. I just ... need to be sure.'

'You certainly do. I am disappointed in you. Don't judge people by appearance alone, Anna. You'll find it's an unreliable way to assess a man's worth – much less important than you think. Jakob is a fine young man, steady and reliable, as his father was too. Talk to your mamma. You need to think seriously about this – and Jakob deserves an honest answer.'

Two months later Jakob solemnly presents Anna with an engagement ring: an emerald set in a star of small diamonds.

Chapter 5

Jakob

The marriage of Julia Kassel and Rudolf Wiener took place in Vienna in September 1895.

It was a grand affair; Rudolf's mother Paulina considered that nothing less would be appropriate for her only son. She regarded her prospective daughter-in-law as pleasingly compliant, but a trifle ordinary. Rudolf could surely have chosen a bride from one of Vienna's many wealthier families. He had, after all, attracted the attention of Count Bessendorf's beautiful youngest daughter Adele in the past, as well showing interest in Mitzi von Kahldorf, whose father had accumulated fabulous riches through international dealing in gold and diamonds.

The Kassel family was decent enough it was true – Julia's father an esteemed lawyer – but nevertheless, Paulina couldn't help feeling a lingering sense of disappointment. She was concerned that in their reduced circumstances after the untimely death of Rudolf's father, her son needed to take advantage of the best opportunities and connections available. It was hardly a time to marry for love! How helpful a clever businessman like Herr von Kahldorf could have been to a son-in-law's career.

But Rudolf, who had himself trained as a lawyer, wanted nothing more than to join Jakob Kassel's practice. He had no sense that this might have been beneath his capabilities. He even talked of wanting to represent the legal needs of the poor. Paulina realised it was time to have a serious talk with her son.

'Rudolf, you are a young man with strong principles, and of course that is very admirable. But a social conscience is a luxury you really cannot afford, my darling. No, I wish you would think more of ambition, of what you can achieve – especially with a little help.'

Rudolf, always closely attuned to his mother's feelings, was aware of her lack of enthusiasm for his marriage to Julia and it saddened him. He hoped in time she would discover Julia's virtues – that she was sensitive and gentle, thoughtful and clever. He would not be talked out of his marriage plans.

The newly-weds settled into a fine, spacious apartment in the centre of Vienna, only five minutes' walk from Paulina's home. Of course, it was not a distance Paulina ever considered walking herself: there were carriages for that. The tall windows of their apartment looked out over the green expanse of the Stadtpark, where Rudolf and Julia often strolled on fine Sundays.

Rudolf worried that his mother would be lonely following their marriage, but Julia was adamant about the importance of living independently. She understood Rudolf's concern – as the only son – for his mother's welfare, but she also knew that her mother-in-law was a forceful personality, who could quite easily dominate their lives. She visited Paulina regularly for coffee, and Paulina came for dinner with the young couple twice a week. Rudolf was pleased to observe a growing friendship between the two women.

Paulina prided herself on her good taste. She enjoyed discussing her ideas for colour schemes and soft furnishings for the apartment with Julia. Julia, who was secretly indifferent to her domestic environment, preferring to read or play the piano, was happy to allow Paulina a free hand with such decisions. Sometimes Paulina asked Julia to accompany her to one or other of her friends' homes. Sometimes, on warm days, they went for a carriage ride in the Ring Boulevard. Paulina encouraged her daughter-in-law to wear the outfits she had chosen for her on these expeditions. After all, one never knew who one might encounter.

Occasionally Julia invited her own mother and Paulina to come to tea together. Julia was irritated by Paulina's magnanimous and kindly manner towards her mother, as if generously bestowing attention upon an inferior, but she bit her tongue and made no comment. While Julia's mother dressed with careful effort and some anxiety for these occasions, Paulina's entire wardrobe was flawlessly fashionable and sophisticated.

'My dear Frau Kassel, how pretty you look in your flowered muslin. Like a breath of fresh country air!'

Paulina's tall, imposing figure moved from room to room, silk petticoats rustling like a soft breeze playing among the leaves in the trees. She glided so gracefully her feet appeared to be raised just a fraction above the floor by some unseen force. Julia's father Jakob nicknamed her 'The Countess'. It was a name of which Paulina would have approved.

Rudolf and Julia's marriage was one of fondness and companionship rather than great passion. This appeared to suit both of them. Rudolf progressed steadily in his career and gained a reputation for competence and reliability. Julia had time and freedom to pursue her own interests of painting and music. Together they enjoyed the theatre and concerts, and yearly holidays at the Baltic or in Italy, accompanied by Paulina.

The years passed and in 1910, just as they began to consider themselves on the verge of middle age, Julia discovered to everyone's surprise and delight that she was pregnant. Her slight body grew enormous and, on a warm spring night, healthy twin boys were born. Rudolf and Julia were overjoyed. They named one baby Paul to honour his paternal grandmother, and the other

Jakob after Julia's father. Paulina was astounded to find herself a grandmother, but she entered into the role with enthusiasm. Following the birth, she moved into her son and daughter-in-law's apartment.

'Just while the babies are so tiny. You must concentrate on caring for them, my dear Julia. And of course, you need rest. I will run the household for you.'

Julia made occasional protests to Rudolf, but they both knew Paulina was there to stay. She ruled all domestic aspects of the home. Within weeks the cook was making outraged representations to Julia.

'She dislikes the recipes I have used these many years, Frau Wiener. She tells me the dumplings are too heavy and that I overcook the meat. I cannot work like this.'

A new cook was engaged who understood Paulina's requirements and agreed to her regime from the start. Paul and Jakob's nursemaid and the housemaid knew better than to argue with her rulings.

'Make sure the boys have their woollen hats on unless the weather is hot, in which case they must wear their cotton sun bonnets. And see to it that their ears are always tucked back. We don't want children with bat ears.'

'Of course, *Gnädige Frau*.'

The little boys grew up secure in the knowledge that all three adults in their home worshipped them, but they learned that it was their grandmother who was the real force to be reckoned with. Paulina supervised every aspect of their lives: what they should eat and at what time, when they should go to bed or take a nap, how much fresh air and exercise they needed.

Julia took great pleasure in playing with the children and reading to them. When they were four or five, she taught them to read and began to teach them the piano. Rudolf spent an hour or so playing with Paul and Jakob when he returned from work, enjoying a little lively fun, and rough and tumble. Paulina approved of this for a time – she could deny little to her beloved Rudolf, and she believed growing boys needed the more robust intervention of a father – but at six o'clock precisely she summoned the nursemaid to give the children their bath and calm them down, ready for bed.

The boys were clever and diligent. They progressed well at the small private school they attended, for which Paulina paid. Paul and Jakob were not identical but, like many twins, they were very close. Of the two, Paul seemed the more light-hearted and sociable, while Jakob was a serious, emotional child. Paul had many friends. He was always at the centre of a large group, keeping the others entertained with his clowning. Jakob had a small number of close friends to whom he was fiercely loyal. Both boys mixed freely with both Jewish and Christian children. Jakob's best friend, Fritz Henkelmann, was from a Roman Catholic family.

In 1923, when the boys were thirteen, tragedy struck the family. Rudolf, like his father before him, had a sudden heart attack at his desk and died at the age of fifty-five. Bereavement affected Paulina and Julia differently. Distraught at the loss of her treasured only son at such a young age, Paulina determined to focus all her love and caring on her two precious grandsons. Grief galvanised her into action. Julia, on the other hand, appeared broken down, despondent, almost indifferent to anything life might still have had to offer. If she previously lacked assertiveness, she was now distinctly passive.

While Paulina became stronger, Julia grew weaker. In this way, the personalities of the two women complemented each other and paradoxically they grew closer. The first hurdle to be faced was a sudden and extreme reduction in income. Rudolf was an intelligent and resourceful lawyer, but an impractical businessman. His affairs were in a poor state. He had not ensured the financial or material security of his family. Paulina and Julia ploughed through files of bills and receipts, and boxes of accounts, all in Rudolf's impenetrable and spidery handwriting.

'We will have to dismiss the cook and manage the cooking ourselves,' Paulina announced, 'and now that we all live together here, I shall sell my own apartment.'

Julia made no comment about the fact that Paulina had already been living with the family since the boys were babies. She was happy for her mother-in-law to take command of the situation.

'The important thing is for Jakob and Paul to continue to receive the very best education, especially in these difficult times. That must be our priority.'

Julia nodded in agreement.

As Paul and Jakob progressed through their teens, one by one their Christian friends rejected them. Fritz Henkelmann's parents refused to receive Jakob in their home. At first, Fritz had no such reservations about calling at Jakob's house, although he did not reveal these visits to his mother and father. Gradually though, his visits became fewer. Away from their homes, Fritz remained a loyal friend to Jakob, and the two young men continued to meet in coffee houses, and to play football or go skiing together.

* * *

Paulina and Julia continued to entertain in a modest way. Their circle of friends had shrunk, with a gradual falling away, first of the most rich and grand, and then of almost all their Christian acquaintances. They had known Artur and Matilde Feldman and their daughters for many years. Both families had been through difficult times, and Paulina admired the way in which Artur had held his business together, despite his wife's illness. He had also shown great concern and support for the Wiener family since the death of Rudolf, who was his lawyer and friend.

Although the girls were not their social equals, Paulina considered Esther, Anna and Margaret quite charming. It was true that there was some concern about Margaret's leaning towards radical political activities as she grew older. There was even rumour of her having joined a naturists' club. However, Esther was strikingly attractive and Anna was pretty and sweet. The children had played together from time to time ever since they were quite small.

When Jakob left school he began a course in architecture, while his brother Paul followed their father in studying law. Jakob took his studies seriously, well aware that opportunities for higher education could be snatched away at any moment. Some of his Jewish friends talked of communism as a possible way forward. Out of interest, Jakob attended one or two meetings of the Communist Party. He noticed Margaret Feldman sitting in the hall, a couple of rows ahead, giving the speaker her rapt attention. She would have been barely fifteen. As they left the meeting, Jakob and Margaret were pushed together at the exit by the jostle of the crowd. They smiled at one another, and Jakob offered to accompany her home to Mariahilferstrasse.

* * *

The front door is opened by Margaret's sister Anna. Anna shakes her head and gives Margaret a look of exasperation when Jakob explains how they have met. How pretty Anna is, when she raises her eyebrows to Jakob with a wry smile, her hands on her hips. She thanks him for bringing Margaret back and apologises for not inviting him in at such a late hour.

Jakob is not a radical activist, but like many young people he is searching for answers to the growing inequalities in Viennese society, and especially the erosion of the rights of Jews. Disappointed by the speakers, he soon decides communism is not a solution he wishes to pursue, and attends no further meetings. Yet Jakob's spirits are raised by the encounter with Anna, and he looks forward to his forthcoming twenty-first birthday party, to which all three Feldman sisters will be coming.

Paul and Jakob's party is a great success. Paulina has sold some jewellery to ensure her grandsons' birthdays are marked in a way that befits them. It is a fine, glittering occasion. Paul dances energetically with all the prettiest girls present, and charms some of their mothers by asking them too to dance. Jakob does not allow his brother anywhere near Anna, protectively keeping her to himself. Paul accepts Jakob's possessiveness with his usual good humour. Jakob dances only with Anna, though of course he asks his mother and his grandmother to honour him with a waltz. Paulina is buoyed by the evening. It is quite like old times.

Jakob is entranced by Anna. For two years they spend every spare minute together. Due to new rulings of the government, he has had to leave his architecture course before completing it, and Anna is working as a governess and nanny, having been unable to attend university. They have discussed the future and agreed that it will be necessary to travel abroad if they are to have the opportunities they both want. Paulina has provided a modest allowance for her grandsons to allow them some independence. Jakob loves Anna's enthusiasm for every experience: theatres, concerts, riding, swimming, skiing. She enjoys his company and always seems delighted to see him. But Jakob worries that perhaps she does not love him with the same intensity he feels for her.

'She is still young,' Paulina reassures him. 'Give her time. Anna likes all of life's pleasures – that is clear. Make sure she has a good time with you, and don't put too much pressure on her.'

But it is not in Jakob's nature to concentrate on life's pleasures alone. He wants a commitment from Anna. He visits Artur Feldman to ask his permission to marry his middle daughter. Artur grips Jakob's arm affectionately and steers him into his study. Kaethe brings a tray of coffee. She leaves with a curtsey and a curious look at Jakob.

'And have you asked Anna to marry you, Jakob?'

'Well, not in so many words. I felt it best to ask you first. But I think we have both assumed we will always be together.'

Artur studies the earnest young man before him. Jakob's face

51

is tense. He licks his lips and blinks at Artur. His left knee jiggles a continuous nervous rhythm.

'That is very proper. But with Anna, I suggest it is best to assume nothing. She is still young of course.' Artur echoes Paulina's words.

Jakob is disappointed that Anna does not immediately leap at his proposal, but instead asks for time to consider it. It takes some weeks before she tells him that yes, she would like to marry him, and they become formally engaged. Jakob is overjoyed.

* * *

Some months after this, Jakob receives a note from Fritz Henkelmann, asking to meet in a coffee house known to both of them. It is nearly a year since they have seen one another.

'First of all, I have heard about your engagement. Many congratulations to you – you're a lucky man, Jakob. Anna is a lovely girl.'

'Thank you, Fritz. I *am* a lucky man, and I know it. The wedding may be a little while off, but I hope you will be my best man? I imagine we will have to leave Austria before much longer, with all the restrictions imposed by this poisonous government.'

Fritz scrutinises his friend silently, as the waiter brings a coffee pot and lays out their cups. He stirs his coffee thoughtfully. 'You should go soon, very soon.'

'Mmm. Well of course, it will take time to make all the arrangements.'

'No, Jakob. Do not delay.'

'Oh …?'

'Look. We've been friends for many years …'

'Yes?'

'I like you, Jakob – you know that. I like you and Anna.'

Jakob feels a growing sense of unease. 'What are you saying?'

'I want you to know that I am in total support of this

52

"poisonous government", as you put it. I am a fully-fledged member of the National Socialist Party, and I believe absolutely in their policies.'

Jakob laughs out loud for a moment, his laughter fading as he takes in his friend's humourless face.

'I don't believe it! Fritz, is this some kind of joke? Really I don't find it very funny, not funny at all.'

'It's no joke. I believe the Nazis are right: with the Jews' monopoly on large areas of trade and business, they are a major cause of the social and economic difficulties both Germany and Austria are suffering. We must eliminate the Jews in Austria and restore racial purity to our country. That is absolutely essential.'

Jakob feels sweat trickling down his spine. He shivers. '*Racial purity*! How can you talk like this? You know I am a Jew ... and Anna's family is also Jewish.'

'Of course I know it. That is why I wanted to speak to you.'

'You agree to the "elimination" of Jews, yet you call yourself my friend?'

'I said we had been friends for many years. I said I like you.'

'But our friendship is now at an end?'

'We cannot continue to be friends as before, that is certain, but I do care what happens to you. It is because of our friendship that I want to help you – you and Anna. I would not want harm to come to either of you.'

'This is absurd! You want all Jews driven out or ... what? Beaten up? Killed? Yet you feel some sympathy for me, some loyalty to me – a Jew!'

'That is exactly right. We must all make a distinction between what is personal and what is principle. Listen, Jakob, we could go on debating this round and round all evening, but I don't have much time. The fact is I have come to warn you.'

'Oh? Are you about to bring a brown-shirted mob round to beat us up?'

Fritz does not smile. He glances at his watch. 'Believe me, this really is no joke. You must leave Vienna, leave Austria. You and Anna must get out as soon as you can.' Fritz leans forward and lowers his voice. 'I have seen your name on a list, Jakob. Did you really think no one watches those communist gatherings? What a stupid thing to do. Now your name is on the list, and sooner or later they will come for you – and that little fool of a sister of Anna's.'

'Margaret ... but she's hardly more than a child.'

'That makes no difference. The important thing is don't delay. I may be able to help with papers, and I have some contacts, here and abroad. Make sure you go soon – and if you care for your families, try to get them out too.'

Jakob sits for a long time after Fritz has left, trying to calm the leaping of his heart and the trembling of his hands. He will have to persuade Anna to leave her home, her family to whom she is so deeply attached, and accompany him to a new land. Will she do it? They have talked of leaving, but never as an immediate intention. It was discussed as a vague possibility, almost as a fairy tale. How would Anna react? Would she even *believe* his account of his conversation with Fritz? He hardly believes it himself. Jakob resolves not to speak to Anna of what Fritz has told him, not yet at least. Instead he must find other means of persuading her of the necessity of leaving.

An unexpected opportunity to achieve this presents itself before very long, an opportunity Jakob does not welcome at all.

Chapter 6

It should have been a perfect day, away from the cares of work and routine; a picnic long planned for in the Vienna Woods. In the soft autumn sunshine, the air is fragrant with the scent of warm grass, late flowers and pine trees. But from the start, Anna's tension clouds the atmosphere. They sit on a log in a dappled clearing, their picnic bags unopened.

'Tell me what is wrong.'

'Oh, Jakob, it is hard, so hard. I'm so very sorry.'

'About what? You are frightening me. What's the matter? You must tell me, Anna.'

At last, staring at her hands in her lap, Anna tells Jakob what has happened. She has had an affair with Otto, her employer, the father of the children in her care.

Jakob's initial reaction is one of total disbelief – is it possible that Anna, pure, innocent Anna, would behave in this way? Gradually, disbelief gives way to fury. His anger is not directed at Anna so much as at Otto. Anna has to agree that Otto has exploited her: she young and trustful, he an older man of wealth and experience. She is deeply ashamed of her naivety, and even more ashamed of her treachery towards Karin, who has come to regard her as a friend. She had wanted to believe Otto's soothing assurances, while knowing in her heart they were not true. A pleasant diversion with a pretty young woman: that was all it was for him. He was confident that she would never make a fuss – it would ruin her reputation if it became known. No doubt it was not his first affair.

'Jakob … I'm so sorry,' she says again, putting her hand on his trembling arm. Jakob shakes her off and turns away. Anna covers her face with her hands. She does not tell him of her attraction to Otto's suave charm, his delicious brown skin. She does not tell him she had been overwhelmed by desire.

'Jakob. There is something else.'

There will be a child, she tells him. It is just the beginning, early days, but the signs are clear. There can be no doubt – she is sure. Jakob leaps to his feet, stands with his back to her, his hands clasped around his head, as though trying to block out the news. He makes a strange noise, something between a groan and a cry, and swings his upper body from side to side. She explains that she has not told Otto about the baby and does not intend to, ever. He would never acknowledge the child as his. Also, she does not want to hurt Karin, who has been so good to her and who knows nothing of the relationship.

'How could you, Anna, how could you? Oh God it's unbelievable, it's a *nightmare*. I can't understand how … how you could abandon all your moral standards.'

'I have no explanation. I can't understand it myself.'

How could the feelings be so strong, so totally consuming, as to overcome any thought of morality, of caution, any idea of possible consequences? Anna is frightened when she thinks about the inevitability of her journey into Otto's arms. She is even more frightened by the absence of such a pull towards Jakob.

Jakob says little for the rest of the day. They walk in silence through the wooded paths. The beauty of the gold and red leaves shimmering in the slanting sunshine appears to mock the dark mood between them. Then, as the sun grows low behind the trees, Jakob seems to reach a resolution. Grimly, he steers Anna to the train back to Vienna. They go to Emil's, their favourite coffee house. Emil knows them well. There are few other customers at this time. Emil comes from the kitchen to greet them, a white apron fastened around his generous middle. He looks closely at them and throws open his arms.

'Nah! Children, children – what's the matter? Such faces. A lovers' tiff already? Wait 'til you're married – plenty of time for quarrelling then.'

Jakob cannot respond in the same spirit. Unsmiling, he orders two coffees. Emil glances at Anna and shrugs theatrically. She smiles back half-heartedly and follows Jakob into one of the dark wooden booths.

'I can't accept this child as mine. It's not my child, not *our* child.'

'I understand.'

'But,' he continues, 'I can't let you … you cannot go through … an abortion.' He grasps each of Anna's wrists and holds them in front of him with violent force. He looks fiercely into her eyes. 'Do you still want to marry me?'

Anna feels as though a heavy stone is compressing the base of her throat, choking her. She looks back at him, and nods.

* * *

Jakob makes arrangements with military precision. Esther, Anna's older sister, and her new husband, Reuben, are the only ones involved. No one else must know.

'We will have to bring the date of our marriage forward.'

Anna struggles to stifle an involuntary gasp. The walls of the room seem to sway and then close in on her.

'And, we will have to emigrate to Palestine much sooner than we planned.'

A sense of panic worms up Anna's spine, touches the back of

her neck. Does she even *like* Jakob? He is so solemn, so strict. She breathes in deeply.

'It's not such a big deal,' he says. 'We'd have to go anyway – there's nothing for us here any more. It's just a change in the timing. Others are doing the same.'

It is true. Esther and Reuben are planning to go to America, and Margaret to England. Immediately after their marriage, Jakob explains, they will travel to Switzerland. It should be possible to find temporary jobs in Zurich. He has one or two contacts. He will sort out their papers – and of course Fritz has offered to help. Until they leave, normal life must go on as far as the families are concerned. Artur is already displeased that Anna has left her job. He is suspicious too, knowing how ambivalent she had felt about marriage to Jakob.

'Marriage is a big commitment, Anna. You are quite sure? Why such a great rush all of a sudden?'

'I'm sure, Papa.'

'Otto and Karin like you. What possible reason is there to give up a good position at a time like this? You young people have no stamina.'

'There were problems, Papa.'

She wishes she could tell her father the truth.

'Problems, problems – you think no one else has problems? Have you even thought about your mother and how this will upset her?'

* * *

Although Jakob has not been able to complete his architectural training, he is offered a position as a clerk in a firm of Zurich architects. He has no option but to accept it, though Anna knows he finds it beneath him. She is able to present testimonials from her work as a nanny and governess, including – to her great shame – a glowing one from Karin. These enable her to find a job as an assistant at a kindergarten. Jakob also makes the necessary arrangements with a discreet maternity clinic in Zurich.

Esther and Reuben visit Switzerland from time to time, on the pretext of 'walking expeditions'. Esther's visits mean everything to Anna; she misses her parents desperately – it will be many months before she can see them again. Jakob and Anna live simply in a clean but modest apartment block. They rent one small room, and share a tiny kitchen and bathroom with four other families. They spend little, saving as much as possible for the journey ahead.

The year 1935 is an exceptionally hot summer and Anna becomes tired and depressed by the final month, when she has to give up her job. Despite having agreed readily to the baby's adoption at first, as the time draws near, she is taken over by a sick foreboding. She tries not to visualise the baby as a child, but rather as the unfortunate by-product of a mistake. Yet as her belly grows, the baby makes its presence felt more and more, kicking and turning. Sometimes a part of its body pushes against the wall of her stomach. She finds herself responding involuntarily, by stroking what must be a foot, or a tiny elbow, and smiling. She stops hastily if she notices Jakob watching her. Anna dreads the birth. As long as she is pregnant, the child inside her is hers alone.

Anna grows increasingly quiet and withdrawn as the birth draws near. Finally, one night, she gently touches Jakob awake and whispers, 'It's coming.'

She is wheeled into a delivery room, while Jakob is told to wait outside, his face pale and drawn. At this most monumental event of her life, they are separate. It is the beginning of a pattern that will continue for years to come, one she is powerless to alter.

Anna screams. Jakob, alone outside, is agonised by sounds he is unable to interpret fully. He leaps to his feet, his heart pounding unevenly, his fists clenched. Every now and then one of the nurses leaves the room to tell Jakob that all is going as it should, all is well.

At last the struggle is over. Jakob hears a thin wailing sound. He leans against the closed door, sobbing. The sound that comes next is more disturbing, a strange primitive howling, like a wild animal in extreme pain. The door is flung open and the noise envelops Jakob. He realises it comes from Anna. A nurse scurries past him, holding a small bundle. She pauses in front of Jakob, revealing a tiny monkey-like face in the white shawl.

Jakob tries everything. He brings Anna small delicacies to try to tempt her to eat, suggests outings to the mountains or to Bodensee, even tries being stern with her. She remains distant, silent, wan. They have agreed never to speak of the events of the past months. She is grateful for that. Sometimes at night she wakes trembling and sweating.

'Shhh,' Jakob whispers. He holds her and strokes her hair until the shaking subsides and her breathing steadies.

'I'm sorry to disturb you,' is all she can say.

By the end of the summer, they are ready to leave for Haifa. Esther and Reuben have gone to make their new lives in America, their parting an agony for Anna. Will she ever see them again? Jakob is calmer than before. For him, the worst is now over. It is a matter of gradual recovery. He is confident that in time their new life will absorb them and blot out the past.

Before making their way south to Brindisi, they stop in Vienna for a few days to see their families. They try to convince them of the increasingly precarious situation, to persuade them too to leave.

'We are too old to move to a new country,' Jakob's mother and grandmother say complacently. 'That is for young people.'

They do not truly believe the most ferocious policies of the Nazi government will ever materialise – 'not here in Vienna'. They cannot contemplate change to their comfortable and privileged lives.

Anna's father is more realistic. He has other reasons for resisting change.

'Your mother is not well enough to make such a journey. She would not survive it – and I will never leave while she lives, never.'

Anna sits on her mother's bed, struggling to keep tears under control.

'Anna, Anna, you are so pale. Are you not well?'

'I'm fine, Mamma, fine. Just a little stomach upset.'

Matilde clutches Anna's hand and presses it to her chest.

'Be happy in this new land, my precious girl. You will have a good life, I am sure of it. Remember what I have always told you: look for the rainbow – the beautiful rainbow – and run towards it! You will find happiness. I will not see you again – not in this life – my dearest Anna, I know that, but you will be here in my heart, always.'

'Nonsense, Mamma, of course we will see each other again, you'll see.'

* * *

Jakob lies on the deck, where he has fallen into an exhausted sleep. Anna reaches out to stroke his cheek, then withdraws her hand. She studies Jakob's face. It is still a handsome face; shadowed with several days' growth of beard, so out of character for a fastidious man like him. There are lines between his brows and deep hollows at the sides of his mouth. He looks gaunt. Even in sleep his expression is one of anguish.

Later, in the growing heat of the following morning, they stand at the ship's rail and watch as a British naval frigate approaches. The British are so close that the white shirts of their uniforms are clearly visible. A roar of protest rises from the gathered refugees. A woman near Anna lifts her baby high in the air over the side of the ship. The little boy thinks it is a game. He kicks his legs and laughs.

'I will throw my son into the sea rather than return!' the woman screams.

'Please stay calm,' shouts the British officer. 'We must check your ship – we will not harm anyone. You should be able to land.'

The mother lowers her baby. She hugs and kisses him, sobbing uncontrollably.

On this occasion, the British are primarily interested in checking the vessel for weapons. Their feet clatter down the iron steps and stomp through the hold. A few officers set up a table on deck and passengers are required to line up. Individual papers are given a cursory glance, and their owners an intimidating glare, as if to warn them that the British are not to be meddled with, and then all are waved on impatiently. When the ship is finally permitted to proceed, the refugees stand mute and drained on the deck.

'Look, Anna, the Carmel hills,' Jakob whispers, pointing at the hazy rise of the land. Low houses cluster around the harbour and straggle back among olive and cypress groves. A faint hum of vehicles and voices grows louder as they approach the shore. The air is warm, an exotic mix of unfamiliar smells drifting back and forth like gentle waves on a beach.

In her hand Anna holds a small piece of paper, crumpled and damp: a precious scrap on which an address is written.

* * *

It is a whitewashed two-storey house, its plaster crumbling, the wooden door bleached grey-white by the sun. The shutters at the windows hang unevenly. They knock cautiously. After a few moments the door creaks open a crack and a woman holding a small black-haired girl on her hip peers out.

'Yael? We are Anna and Jakob.'

The woman scrutinises their faces, then smiles broadly, puts the child down and swings the door open.

'Come in, come in. You are welcome here. Say "*shalom*" to Anna and Jakob, Rachel.'

The little girl smiles shyly from behind her mother's legs. Anna crouches down and says, '*Shalom*, Rachel.'

'Ah, very good! Already you speak Hebrew!'

'If we can get by with just "*shalom*", then yes.'

'One word will soon become many,' Yael continues in Yiddish. 'Now come, follow me.'

She leads them up a steep, dark staircase and along a passage. There is a small cooking area along one wall: a black stove, a sink with a metal drainer, a shelf on the wall with plates and dishes, some pans of varying size dangling from hooks beneath the shelf.

Yael opens a door and dazzling sunshine engulfs them. As their eyes adjust, Jakob and Anna put their meagre bundles on the floor and look around a large room, almost painfully bright. The walls are white. The wooden floorboards have been scrubbed so hard they are bleached pale, almost white. There is a small ward-robe, a simple table and two chairs, all made of wood. The bed is old and it, too, is wooden-framed. The mattress sinks a little, but looks clean. They exchange glances. Yael watches.

'Ah, you have no bedding! I should have thought. Look, don't worry, it's fine. I will lend you some sheets and pillows until you can get some of your own.'

Jakob shifts uncomfortably.

'No, no, thank you. We will manage with just our clothes for now. It's warm enough.'

'Pshh – nonsense! You have to have sheets.' Yael studies Jakob's face. 'Well anyway, I will get them and you can use them or not, as you please.'

She returns a short while later with a pile of bedding. Rachel carries a small tray with some bread, olives, and a pale mixture in a bowl. Yael explains it is a local dish made of mashed up beans and oil. There is also a small bowl containing some coins.

'Just until you can get some local money yourselves.'

Yael begins to usher Rachel out of the room.

'Thank you, Yael. You are very kind.'

She pauses and looks steadily at Anna, her eyes dark and penetrating.

'We all arrive here with nothing. Now rest, you must be tired, both of you.'

They eat the food hungrily. It restores their spirits. They unpack, their minimal belongings looking forlorn in the empty space of the cupboard. They make up the bed with Yael's sheets.

'We will use them for now, just so that we don't offend her. As soon as we earn some money, we'll buy our own.'

'She seemed perfectly happy to lend us what we need. Surely there is no shame in that, Jakob? Sometimes people get pleasure from helping.'

Jakob frowns and shakes his head. 'You can be so naive, Anna. If we accept help from others, we are immediately in their debt. It puts them in a position of power over us. I'd have thought you, of all people, would realise that.'

A hot rage rises in Anna's chest. She bites her lip. Will their lives always be like this?

Later they walk together along the sea front. Their ramshackle ship has already disappeared, but there is an array of small boats moored in the harbour, mostly fishing boats. They turn away and explore the streets rising behind Yael's house. Nothing in Anna's life has prepared her for this place; everything is so different, so foreign. People stare at them, as though knowing they do not belong. She can't tell who might be friendly, who a threat. The air itself feels alien, thick with heat and unrecognisable smells. She thinks of the apartment in Mariahilferstrasse, with its smell of furniture polish, fresh ground coffee and good familiar food. She thinks of Kaethe, wholesome and pink in her starched apron, of Mamma lying pale in her bed.

One narrow street leads to another. Some have rough cobbles, others compressed mud, which covers their feet in a thin film of dust as they walk. The houses lead directly from the streets and alleys. People stand in doorways and watch who passes. Anna feels many pairs of eyes following them as they walk. Despite the evening sun, little light penetrates the alleys, shaded by buildings of clay or stone on either side. Somewhere in the distance a muezzin calls people to prayer, his voice plaintive in the still air.

They come across a bakery, open even at the late hour. The baker's apron is floury and stained. Sweat darkens his armpits and glistens on his face. He scoops large flat loaves from the sides of the oven with a huge wooden shovel and places them on shelves, their dry crusts scraping on the surface.

'Do you think the food is clean?' murmurs Jakob.

'It's been baked in the oven. Bread is bread everywhere.'

They buy a loaf, and a bag of peaches, for the morning.

The next day Anna returns the tray to the kitchen. Yael insists she sits down. She makes two small cups of thick strong coffee, and joins Anna at the table. She is a stocky woman, with a broad face and fine slanting eyes. Anna guesses she is eight or ten years older than herself. Yael talks slowly and steadily; about how she and her elderly parents came to Palestine some fifteen years previously to escape anti-Semitism following the revolution in Russia. She met her husband David in Palestine. He was a 'Sabra', born on a kibbutz. Now they are all dead, she says, and she has only Rachel. Anna nods but does not feel able to ask more about her husband's death. Yael sits resting her chin on her hand, looking at Anna as they talk.

'Everyone in Palestine has a story to tell,' she says, 'and most of them are tragic – why else would they leave their homes and struggle to this place?' The child, Rachel, creeps cautiously towards Anna and stands gazing at her. Anna reaches out and gently draws her in to stand leaning on her lap. She strokes the smooth skin of the little girl's arm and feels the comfort of her weight against her.

Anna tells Yael of her home in Vienna, of her parents, and her work as a governess and nanny; how she would like to work with children if possible. But they agree that as she speaks almost no Hebrew, this is out of the question. She did learn some English at school. Yael suggests Anna might try to get a job at Spinney's, a British-owned department store, where many of the customers are English. She knows a woman who works as a floor manager, and could introduce Anna to her. Anna eagerly agrees.

* * *

Maya Rosenberg looks her up and down doubtfully.

'Do you have a black or grey dress, no tears or patches? It can have a white collar, but no other colours. Also some clean, plain shoes, in black or grey. They must be smart but also comfortable; we're on our feet all day.'

'Yes, yes, of course,' Anna blurts. She does a quick mental calculation. Her only dress is black. It is very old and worn, but perhaps it will do. She has no black or grey shoes. Her only shoes are the pair she is wearing now. They are brown, faded and very shabby.

Mrs Rosenberg agrees to take Anna on as a sales assistant for a two-month trial, provided she looks the part. She can start the following day. Anna is thrilled and appalled in equal measure.

'What can I do for shoes?' she wails at Yael. They gaze down at her feet.

'Hmm. You can't wear mine, your feet are smaller. I have an idea – come.'

Yael takes Rachel by the hand and links her arm in Anna's. She leads her to a dark and cramped shop deep in the old quarter. Shoes of every size and type hang at the window and on the walls, and stand stacked on the counter. The smell of leather and polish reminds Anna of her father and his self-imposed nightly task of cleaning the family's shoes. Yael greets the shoemaker in

Arabic and engages him in a lengthy conversation. He leans over the counter and studies Anna's shoes, scratching his head. He gestures to her to take them off and hand them over. She looks uncertainly at Yael. Yael nods impatiently and gesticulates as the shoemaker has done. Anna places her shoes on the counter and stands in her bare feet. The man hands her a pair of coarse rope sandals. Yael pushes her out of the shop.

'There,' she beams. 'No problem!'

'What do you mean? I can't wear these!'

'No, no, no! Don't worry. Just put them on for now, to go home. Tonight, we come back. He'll fix your shoes. He's a good man. You'll see.'

That evening, Yael and Anna work on the finishing touches to her work outfit at the kitchen table. Rachel leans against her mother's shoulder, watching. Jakob returns from his own search for work, to find them giggling like schoolgirls together.

'See here, Jakob,' says Yael, holding up the shoes, miraculously restored and gleaming black, 'how smart your wife will be tomorrow!'

Jakob strokes Rachel's head, but does not smile.

'How did you pay for them?' he asks Anna quietly.

'We only had to pay the shoemaker for his work – just three shekels.'

'You had that?'

'It was a *loan*, Jakob,' Yael says. 'Soon you'll both be earning.'

Jakob sighs and goes up to their room, his feet thumping on the wooden stairs. Yael and Anna exchange glances.

The following morning at Spinney's, Anna presents herself neat and businesslike. As well as the shoes, she wears her black dress, clean and pressed, and softened by a little white lace gathered at the neck, cut from an old dress of Yael's. Maya Rosenberg walks a slow circuit around Anna and nods her approval.

Over the next two months, Anna works hard at her English, which is scarcely more than school English at first. Somehow she seems to get by. The polite formality of her relationship with customers suits her. It makes no personal demands on her; they remain strangers. The main thing seems to be to listen to their needs and to compliment them on their choices. She learns to make non-committal comments, which customers can interpret to suit themselves.

'It shows off your figure perfectly, Madam.'

'That colour brings out the blue of your eyes.'

'I understand this style is popular in London at present.'

Anna keeps her eyes on the customer's image in the mirror – the fine cut of the dress, the beautiful peach colour, the sapphire blue, soft ochre, maroon, or turquoise like the depths of the Mediterranean. She avoids looking at her own drab reflection, as black and dreary as mourning.

After the trial period, Mrs Rosenberg informs her that she is liked by the customers, and her work is satisfactory. She is offered a permanent position. Meanwhile, Jakob finds a bookkeeping post with a building firm. In addition, he spends three evenings a week studying to complete his architectural qualifications. He also works part-time on a voluntary basis in an architectural firm, to broaden his practical experience. He is always tired, but pleased that they are making their way in their new world.

Their wages together enable them to pay Yael the modest rent and buy a little food. Of course, they have repaid her small loan. A few weeks later they manage to buy some cheap bedding from a street stall. To Jakob it symbolises newfound independence.

* * *

After they have been in Palestine for a year, Jakob suggests that maybe they should have a child. They have never talked about it before; the idea takes Anna by surprise.

'A child?'

Jakob is offended. 'Perhaps you don't want *our* child?'

'Of course I do, Jakob. It's just that … well … do you think we can afford it?'

Yet, the more she considers it, the more she is drawn to the idea of a baby. Perhaps a child will bring some joy into their lives, perhaps even help to bind them together. The months pass and no baby comes. Jakob and she rarely talk about it, and he never openly refers to the events of previous years. He suggests she visits a doctor. The doctor, a kindly Jewish man in his sixties, assures them he can find no physical reason preventing her from becoming pregnant. It is important to relax, he tells them; stress can work against conception. Anna firmly believes that she is to blame for her childlessness – that it is a punishment.

She becomes extremely fond of little Rachel. Sometimes when she returns from work, they play together or she reads Rachel a story in the warm courtyard at the back of the house. She loves to feel the soft weight of the child's body on her lap, the fusty smell of her hair, the smoothness of her little limbs. Sometimes Yael watches from the doorway, noting the tenderness with which Anna holds her child, the fervour of her kisses. Often she makes Anna a cup of coffee and sits with her in the yard. One day she invites Anna into her kitchen, where she has laid some clothes out on the table: two dresses, a skirt and a blouse. She suggests Anna could borrow her machine and alter them to fit.

'You are always so kind, Yael, but I can't accept,' Anna says, thinking of Jakob. She caresses the fragile material of a cream-coloured dress. It slips through her fingers like water.

'What's kind? Should I throw them away? I can't wear them any longer – look at me.' Yael pats the curve of her stomach and hips. 'If you're really worried about accepting them, you could help me with a little sewing in exchange – I'm no good at it.'

From this time, Anna is often in Yael's little parlour. She sits at the treadle, taking in one of the new dresses, altering or repairing a garment for Yael or Rachel, or making curtains to brighten the old house. Slowly, Yael and Anna grow closer. For the first time she feels able to trust Yael enough to speak of the past. Yael listens and nods. Sometimes she strokes Anna's arm affectionately, or hugs her. Sometimes she talks of her own life in her pragmatic, matter-of-fact manner; how her husband David was killed by Arabs as he patrolled the kibbutz, how Yael found out she was pregnant with Rachel only after David's death.

'Do you hate them?' Anna asks.

'Hate them? Hate who?'

'The Arabs.'

Yael frowns and considers this question. 'No, I don't hate them. They believe this is their land, just as we do. We are all just looking for a place in the world, a place we belong – a safe haven. Of course I hate what they did to David, but actually, as individuals, I often prefer Arabs to Jews. They are not so rigid, not so tight-arsed and self-righteous! Look at Jakob!'

Anna looks at Yael in shock, and they both laugh.

'I'm sorry, Anna. Jakob is a fine man, and he worships you, but does he have to be so miserable, so serious all the time? Does he have no sense of fun?'

'I think I am responsible for destroying whatever sense of fun Jakob once had.'

Yael grabs Anna's wrist and holds it firmly.

'Don't ever say that! You cannot be responsible for another person's temperament. Don't take that on to yourself.'

'Jakob is talking of returning to Austria to bring our parents out.'

'What! Is he mad? You know what is happening back there – and he wants to go back?'

Acquaintances from Vienna have arrived in Haifa recently with stories of cruelty, tragedy and terrible hardship. They brought a letter from Jakob's mother and grandmother, a letter crying out with fear and sorrow. His twin brother Paul was shot dead while resisting arrest. Julia and Paulina now have no means of support or protection. They are terrified and barely surviving.

Many neighbours have been taken away or have simply disappeared. Anna's mother died just as the Nazis marched into Vienna. Her father is still there, hiding, with some help from former employees, Christians, but it is becoming more and more dangerous.

'Bastards!' Yael spits. 'Nazi pigs! Don't let him go, Anna. It's suicide.'

'Do you think I haven't told him? You know how stubborn he is.'

* * *

Anna tells Jakob she is taking on a part-time job coaching a schoolgirl, a doctor's daughter, in English.

'I thought your own English was not so good.'

'It's improved a lot since I started at Spinney's – certainly good enough to help a ten-year-old child with her schoolwork. I can go after work, on one of the evenings you're studying.'

She does not mention that the family lives in the Arab quarter in Wadi Ara, or that she needs to travel by local bus to reach their home. She loves the adventure of the bus journey: its rattling, vibrating fragility, the heat and dust, the chatter and laughter of her fellow passengers and the smell of garlic, spices, and hot human bodies. At first they stare at her quizzically, but after a few weeks Anna is greeted like an old friend by regulars, a seat always offered to her. Often her neighbour presses a piece of bread with black olives wrapped in paper into her lap, saying, '*Yalla, yalla.*'

Dr Khan's house is a modest two-storey building of sandstone blocks around a cool courtyard. It is the height of summer, and Anna is shown to a table in the courtyard, shaded by two drooping olive trees. The child, Shafia, is brought to meet her by her mother Rahima. Shafia smiles shyly at Anna. She is small for her age. Anna gestures to her to sit beside her, and says slowly in English, 'Come, Shafia, sit here.'

Shafia's smile broadens and she whispers, 'yes.'

Rahima places a tray of tea on the table beside Anna, and gestures for her to help herself. They start with greetings: hello, good afternoon, how are you? My name is Anna, what is your name? Shafia is a quick learner. She works eagerly at the homework Anna leaves for her to complete before her next visit. Dr Khan and Rahima are delighted with Shafia's progress.

After two months of lessons, Anna notices a disturbing itching. She consults her own doctor. To Anna's horror, he tells her she has body lice, and provides a lotion to be used for a week, day and night. Her clothes and bedding have to be boiled.

'Why didn't you tell me you were going on a bus? What do you expect travelling with local people? I can't believe you'd be so naive.' Jakob has little sympathy.

'They are good people, just poor.'

'Why are you so secretive, Anna?' he complains.

She dreads having to explain to the Khan family that her husband is not happy with her travelling so far to the lessons, but in the event, Dr Khan himself tells her he feels it would be safer for her not to come any more. He has many Jewish patients who value his gentle, polite manner and his medical expertise, but he has been warned off by Arab nationalists who consider him a Jew-lover, disloyal to his own people. Dr Khan is concerned that Anna herself may be regarded with suspicion, and does not want to put her at any risk. Anna finds it hard to believe that any of the friendly, hospitable people, such as those who welcomed her on the bus, could really wish her any harm. She is deeply pained by Shafia's sad, disappointed face, when she explains that she cannot come again.

* * *

In September 1939, despite all Anna's objections, Jakob insists on making the journey back to Vienna. Anna and Yael pack his small case with warm clothes for the imminent winter in Europe. What little money can be spared is sewn painstakingly into the linings of his jackets. Yael brings him a gold necklace and earrings belonging to her grandmother. Jakob shakes his head.

'Yael, I can't …'

'Jakob, you must. Bribes are all that might keep you alive.'

Somehow Jakob makes his way back to Vienna. Anna receives a short letter from him a few months after his arrival. The remaining family members are alive and in reasonable health. He writes cryptically of 'shortages' and the 'necessary move' to a different part of the city. This letter is followed by total silence for a year and a half. Anna is nearly mad with anxiety, her life suspended. Then out of the blue a brief note arrives, posted in Italy, from Fritz Henkelmann, Jakob's Roman Catholic former school friend. It reads:

'Dear Anna, Sincere condolences. Jakob, mother and grandmother have all passed away. Artur transported. Bless you. Fritz H.'

More than two years later Anna learns that Jakob, his mother and grandmother had been transported by train to Auschwitz. The women died in the gas chambers immediately after arrival. As a fit young man, Jakob was selected for work duties in the camp, and survived for many months. Weakened by starvation, he died of typhus, probably late in 1941 or early in 1942.

Anna is inconsolable, wild with grief. She does not know what to do with herself. What is she doing here, alive, alone? What future is there?

'It is all my fault.' She looks at Yael. 'I didn't even love him, not as I should have.'

'Don't be ridiculous,' Yael responds fiercely. 'Did you bring Hitler to power? Did you build the death camps? Did you force Jakob to return to Austria? No, you tried to stop him.'

Yael pulls Anna to the window. Outside, as often, a gaunt, haunted-looking man, a neighbour, is on his knees in the central square, tending the flowers. Anna has greeted him often and received a polite nod in response. Otherwise he has never spoken.

'What do you see?'

'I see old Boris, in the garden ...'

'"Old Boris". He looks like an old man, doesn't he, but actually he's younger than me. Let me tell you about Boris. The Nazis made him watch while they put his young sons in a barrel stuck with nails and rolled them down a hill over and over again, for their own amusement and entertainment. He's lost his parents, his wife, and his children, and why? Because he committed the crime as a Christian of marrying a Jew, and allowing his children to be brought up as Jews. He was a doctor – a paediatrician – but he refused to experiment on Jewish babies for the Nazis. So they tortured him and killed everyone he loved. That's what they do, Anna. *It wasn't his fault.* Jakob's death isn't your fault. Now you can do one thing only, like the rest of us. Like Boris. *Live!* Live as best you can. It's what Jakob would have wanted.'

Anna is desperate for news of her father. It is only years later that she discovers that Artur, ever resourceful and a natural survivor, bribed a guard to turn a blind eye, and escaped by jumping from a train. After a long and perilous journey on foot, he made his way over the border to Yugoslavia, where he was helped by partisans. He eventually reached England, exhausted, with nothing but the clothes he was wearing. He was offered refuge by Quakers, given food, clothes and shelter, and in time was reunited with his youngest daughter Margaret and her family.

* * *

Slowly, time passes and some of the acuteness of pain is blunted. Anna settles into a routine, and eventually even a degree of contentment. After several years in Palestine, she is still not acclimatised to the extreme heat of summer. During the hot weather, she leaves the house in the relative cool of the early morning and walks to the city centre. During the long lunch hours she sits in a shady park reading, or studying to improve her English and Hebrew.

On one occasion, a colleague at work, a manager in the menswear department, asks her out for a drink. Anna agrees to meet him the following evening, but then regrets her decision.

'I'll have to tell him I've changed my mind, that I can't go.'

'Why not? What's he called? Is he hideous or what?' asks Yael.

'His name is Ariel Fiedler, and no, he's not hideous – he's quite good-looking. But I feel nothing for him. I wouldn't know what to say to him.'

'Nonsense! Are you going to live like a nun for the rest of your life?'

'Probably.'

'Don't be ridiculous! He's just asked you to join him for a drink, not a wild night of passionate lovemaking.'

'Why don't you go instead?'

'Because he hasn't asked me – he's asked you.'

Rachel has been watching Anna and her mother's exchange.

'He probably likes you because you're pretty, Anna,' she says. 'You should go out with him. Maybe you'd have a nice time.'

'There you are,' says Yael. 'Out of the mouths of babes!'

* * *

One evening, Yael brings home a length of fine black material and some pieces of cream cotton and lace.

'Look here, turn it to the light. See how it gleams when the sun shines on it.'

Anna looks, and touches. 'Where did you get it? How did you pay for it?'

'Now don't you turn into Jakob! I got it in the market, and I bargained for it. It's for you. Are you going to go on wearing your work dress for ever? Have you looked at it lately? I'm surprised Maya hasn't said anything.'

It is true. The black dress Anna was once so proud of is now irreparably old and faded, the fabric rough and pilled. How is it that she has worn it for so long without noticing? She picks up the new material and strokes its softness, seeing in her mind the exact cut of the new dress, how it would fit her waist, skim her hips and then hang crisply to the hem. The treadle, which has lain unused in the kitchen cupboard for two years, is soon heaving and whirring by the window.

After work, Anna begins attending an evening class in shorthand and typing. She loves it. She buys a second-hand typewriter on which to practise. She and Rachel have fun setting each other silly sentences or nonsense words to type. Anna's fingers quickly learn to interpret the letters automatically, as a pianist's interpret written notes. The appearance and growth of text in response to her unconscious tapping seems almost magical.

The British Army has advertised for shorthand typists. After all her time at Spinney's, Anna feels the need for a change, a new direction. The new dress will do just as well in a different job. She is interviewed by a brisk but not unfriendly female officer.

'Your speeds are quite impressive, Mrs Wiener, but your English is not yet perfect, is it?'

'No, but I do understand almost everything. And I am continuing to study English, and Hebrew.'

'Hebrew won't help much here. You do realise that not all your countrymen will approve of you working for the British Army?'

'Yes, I understand.'

'Very well. You could begin next week.'

Anna's new responsibilities are to provide administrative support for four senior officer instructors in the Training sector. The office is large and light, and contains four desks, the condition of each reflecting the personality of its user: Major Hamilton-Thomas's is stacked with papers in meaningful piles,

Major Blythe's as obsessively neat as a parade ground, Lt Colonel Hampson's as untidy and tousled as a rook's nest, and Colonel Lawrence's ordered with careful logic. They are friendly and welcoming, and always appreciative of her contribution. Anna enjoys the light-hearted and very masculine banter, at first just between the men but gradually including her too, even though she does not always understand the subtleties of their humour. She comes to know and like all four men, but after a time she becomes aware in particular of Colonel Sam Lawrence. His eyes seem to follow her round the room, not in a predatory way, but with great interest.

Chapter 7

1946

London musters one of its foulest days of enveloping yellow-grey smog for their departure, as if wanting to squeeze them bodily from its streets. Anna is quite willing to be expelled, but in the station gusts of steam and smuts add to the vile air and she worries about Ben's breathing. She pulls his little scarf up to cover his nose and mouth. He immediately yanks it down with a happy chuckle, thinking she is playing peekaboo with him. Constance shakes her head and laughs. She has accompanied them from Surrey to Waterloo. Anna is grateful for that. She and Constance have finally come to a tentative understanding of one another, Constance as close to extending friendship as she can be.

'Did you think that wretched porter looked reliable? He seemed a bit slow-witted to me. I hope to goodness he's put your luggage on the right train. Anna, are you sure Sam knows what time you're due to arrive?'

'Yes, of course. Really, Constance, don't worry. You know what he's like about organising me. I've enough instructions to fill a book: exactly where to be and at what time; what to eat and what not; even what to tip the taxi driver!'

'Such a long journey. Benjamin will be very tired, and you too, poor girl, by the time you get there.'

'He'll go to sleep on the train. Anyway, it'll be worth it to be with Sam again.'

'I bet he can't wait to see you both.' She pauses and looks at Anna. 'It's not going to be easy though, is it? Living in Germany, I mean. Have you thought about it much?'

'I've thought of little else these last few weeks. Sometimes I'm terrified. I guess it'll help that I speak German.'

'Yes, I wasn't just thinking of how you'll get on with the Germans. Army life is strange too. Some of those army wives are a pretty rum lot.'

'Sam said some of them expect to take on their husband's rank themselves!'

'Exactly, and you'll be Mrs Brigadier. They may not like a … foreigner … in that position.'

'Mmm. Well, I'll just have to do my best. You know I'm not used to these British social hierarchies.'

'Well, I don't suppose they'll appreciate your socialist ideals much either, darling. I'd keep quiet about all that.'

They embrace with genuine warmth. Constance kisses Ben.

'Goodbye, little sweetie. We'll miss you.'

Ben smiles uncomprehendingly and waves his hand. Anna's throat contracts and tears prick her eyes. To her surprise, Constance's large blue eyes are swimming too. She sniffs and dabs at them with her handkerchief.

'Do write and let us know how you get on,' she says stiffly.

* * *

The house, built around the turn of the century, stands large and solid, surrounded by an expansive overgrown garden. The walls have once been rendered white, but now the surface is patchy and stained in places. In the centre, a massive oak front door is guarded by two pretentious columns. To one side, tall windows punctuate the walls, which descend in stepped sections from the roof to a ground-level room. On the other side, the house rises more sharply to three storeys. The steeply angled tiled roofs of traditional German style look in good condition. A driveway curves symmetrically with rampant trees and shrubs beyond, swaying wildly in the wind. The frontage has an air of gracious living, now faded and worn. Great flakes of sleet sting their necks and faces, melting wetly on contact with their skin. She takes a deep breath. Sam holds her firmly round the waist.

'All right?'

'Yes,' she says. 'Into battle.'

Inside, Ben squirms in Anna's arms, impatient to explore. She presses her face into the soft, warm tufts at the back of his neck, absorbing the comfort of his smell, then puts him down on the floor. He immediately crawls away, and then sits up uncertainly. Looking round and realising he is in unfamiliar territory, he heads rapidly back towards his father.

'Da-da, da-da.'

Sam crouches down to him.

Anna gazes about the spacious hallway. Black and cream tiles cover the floor. Most are in good condition, only a few chipped or broken, and the surface looks scrubbed clean. The ceiling is high and domed, encrusted with decorative plasterwork, stained from cigarette smoke but otherwise undamaged. A broad staircase branches into two at the first landing, each sweeping round and upwards. The deep maroon carpet looks scarcely trodden. The wooden banisters are polished to a rich chestnut shine. Anna frowns. After Palestine's functional simplicity, its determined egalitarianism, and England's dreary shabbiness, who still lives in such opulence?

Reading her face, Sam turns to murmur in her ear. 'Senior party official …'

She nods bitterly. Of course. Why should they not take over the house? Retribution is fine. She believes in retribution. The vanquishing forces claim their rights in requisitioned property. A searing aggression towards all Germans rises in her, a hatred pounding at her head like fever. Let them lose their homes, let them lose everything, let them suffer.

Sam strides onwards, Ben in his arms. A narrow passageway at the side of the hall leads to a large kitchen. They open the door and step inside. Three faces turn towards them, anxious, searching. As Sam and Anna approach them, all three stand up. Anna pauses, denying them her attention. Let them wait. She takes stock of the room. It is light and warm. A large black stove dominates one side, logs stacked neatly beside it. A wooden drying rack hangs above the stove, several towels dangling from its rails. Wooden cupboards span the other wall, and two large white sinks stand beneath the window. All the walls and woodwork are cream, freshly repainted.

Anna turns slowly to look at the people in the room, now watching her apprehensively. They have been sitting around a large scrubbed wooden table in the centre of the room. Nearest to Anna is a small solidly built woman of indeterminate age. She wears a frayed grey dress, heavily mended, with a pink apron tied at the waist. Her thin hair is cropped short and of a faded reddish colour, peppered with grey. Her face is almost colourless, the skin stretched over broad Slavic cheekbones. Her eyes are dark, alert and shining. As Anna approaches her, the woman looks straight into her face with an openness and directness she can't help liking, despite the hard knot of rage clutching her heart.

'Frau Selma Rausch,' Sam says, as though announcing guests at a formal ball. 'A nanny for this young man.'

Anna studies the woman for a long time and Frau Rausch holds her gaze unflinchingly. Will she share the care of her son with this woman? Will she trust the life of her child to this *German*

81

woman? Hesitantly, reluctantly, Anna holds out her hand. Frau Rausch looks at the hand before her, and then clasps it eagerly, shaking it vigorously and smiling.

'*Willkommen, Gnädige Frau, willkommen!*'

Who does she think she is, welcoming me to my own house? Anna's anger is not easily relinquished, but the woman's face is so frank and so full of undisguised pleasure that slowly, the lump in her chest softens and she returns the smile, just faintly. She finds herself patting the woman's hand. Frau Rausch's smile widens in response. She nods her head and pats Anna's hand herself.

Anna withdraws her hand and moves on to greet the next figure, a tall, painfully thin woman with white hair screwed into an untidy bun. A bleached overall hangs loosely over bony shoulders. Her worn face looks as though the skin has somehow been sucked inwards until it clings tightly to the fragile bone structure, creating an intricate delta of fine wrinkles. Her expression is impassive, distant, her eyes listless. She looks barely alive.

'Frau Helga Stammel – known as Maggi,' says Sam. 'Our new cook. It'll take all Maggi's imagination to make something edible of the rations.'

Anna recalls some of the information Sam has provided about each member of staff and feels an involuntary surge of compassion. Frau Stammel has lost everything, even her identity. The loathing she had expected to feel, the satisfaction in the misfortune of these Germans, begins to evaporate.

'Frau Stammel, Maggi, you will have a safe home here.'

Maggi continues to study the floor at her feet. '*Danke,*' she whispers. Thank you.

Anna turns her attention to the third figure, a girl of no more than seventeen. Instantly her mood changes. The sturdy young woman with her fresh, milky complexion, and fair hair pulled into two thick plaits, looks as Aryan as Brunhilde: a living example of Nazi Youth. Her features are not fine, but those of a healthy country girl. Like Maggi, she wears a white overall, buttoned demurely to the neck, but straining at the bust and hips. Furious, Anna turns to Sam.

'Who is this? I told you – no young ones, no Hitler Youth!'

The girl stares fearfully at her, her blue eyes wide. She begins to tremble violently. Sam puts Ben on the floor, and places an avuncular hand on her shoulder.

'This is Hannelore, our maid,' he says soothingly. He leads Anna a few paces away and talks quietly, his eyes on Hannelore.

'At fifteen she was required to bear a child for the Führer. The father was a seventeen-year-old soldier on leave from the front. It turned out they rather liked each other. They might even have married, but he was killed on the Eastern Front before the baby was born. Then the Red Army came ...' Sam pauses in his account and looks at Anna meaningfully.

'Hannelore did what she could ... what she had to ... to survive. She was thrown out of the family home by her father. An aunt is helping to care for the child. He's now eighteen months old, am I right? Eighteen *Monate*?' Sam raises his voice for these last sentences, and puts up fingers, signalling 'eighteen'.

Hannelore nods. Sam beams like a proud teacher showing off his prize pupil.

'See how she's learning to understand English! Good girl!'

Anna feels faint. 'All right, Hannelore,' she says, 'but I need to speak to you in a minute.' She turns to Sam. 'What about the gardener?'

Sam steers her towards the window. A very tall man with white hair and beard stands stiffly by a wheelbarrow in a pathway of the garden, as though on parade, waiting to be inspected. The man sees Anna at the window and briefly raises his hat. Then he turns and pushes the wheelbarrow slowly round the corner of the house.

'Herr Eisen,' says Sam with a grin.

'Yes, I remember. Herr Eisen doesn't talk.'

'No, but he and I are getting the garden sorted out. Should be lots of fruit and vegetables by next summer.'

Sam looks so pleased with himself that Anna has to hug him, although she supposes one shouldn't do that in front of the servants.

'Frau Rausch,' she calls, picking Ben up from the floor, 'would you please look after Benjamin for a little while?'

'Yes, gladly, Frau Lawrence.'

'Ben, this is Selma. Sel-ma.'

'Del-la!' says Ben, 'Del-la,' so creating a new name, which is always to remain with Selma.

'*Ja*, Della!' she says. She reaches for the child, kisses him, and bears him away. The others begin to disperse.

'Hannelore, please come with me a moment.'

The girl freezes. Anna opens some of the unfamiliar doors and finds a small salon behind one. She beckons Hannelore to follow, and closes the door behind them.

'Come and sit down, Hannelore. Don't be frightened.' Anna speaks in German, hoping the girl will feel more at ease with her own language.

Hannelore sits uncertainly on the edge of a chair, wringing her hands. Anna takes her hands and holds them gently.

'Hannelore, I'm sorry, but you cannot dress this way if you are to work for us.'

The girl looks at her in confusion, fingering a sleeve. 'But, Frau Lawrence, I have washed and pressed it. It is completely clean!'

'Yes, the overall is fine,' Anna says quietly, 'but … I can see that you are wearing nothing else. You have no underwear on.'

Hannelore begins to sob. 'Please *Gn-Gnädige Frau*. I have none … nothing.'

'You have nothing to be ashamed of, Hannelore.'

'The Russians took everything we had. I had just rags. My aunt brought me here. The Herr Brigadier was so good to take me in.

Frau Stammel was also very kind – she gave me this.' She grasps the hem of the white overall. 'I had to feed my baby … and there was so little food.'

'What is your baby's name?'

Hannelore gives a tearful smile. 'I call him Mekki. After his father, Mikael.'

'He is a lucky boy to have such a good mother. Will you bring him to see me, and to play with Benjamin?'

The girl nods eagerly.

'Now tell me, Hannelore, can you sew?'

'Oh yes, Frau Lawrence. My grandmother taught me. But I have no needle or thread …'

'Don't worry,' Anna interrupts. 'We will find some cloth, and needles and thread. You can use my sewing machine. A very good friend gave it to me, when I also needed clothes to wear.'

* * *

Next morning, after Sam and his driver Max have left for work, there is a loud knocking at the front door. Hannelore comes to find Anna. She tells her that a lady is asking to see her, a German lady. Anna settles Ben on her hip and carries him into the hallway. A tall, imposing figure is strolling around. She appears to be studying her surroundings with great interest and confidence.

'Ah, good morning, Frau Lawrence,' she says as Anna approaches, extending her hand. Immediately the skin on Anna's neck begins to crawl. Who is this woman, who knows her name and behaves so presumptuously?

'Yes? What do you want?' She ignores the woman's outstretched hand.

'I am Frau Hartmeyer. This is my house, I am the owner.'

'Frau Hartmeyer, you may have been the owner of this house, but the British Army has requisitioned it. So for the present, it is *my* house and not yours.'

The woman smiles without humour and bends her head to one side, as if conceding a point. She tickles Ben briefly under his chin.

'Yes, yes, of course you are right. And may I tell you how pleased I am that a respectable *English* family will have the care of my house.' She emphasises the word as if to indicate that she knows Anna is not English. Anna shifts Ben to her other hip.

'We have only just moved in and I am very busy. I ask you again, what do you want?'

'Of course. You will want to arrange the house to suit yourself and your family. It is simply this, Frau Lawrence. In the rush to vacate the house, I left one or two small boxes in the attic. Would you allow me to take them away? They are of no use to you – just some old books and pictures.'

Anna says she will speak to her husband and asks the woman to come back on Saturday at eleven o'clock. There is something oddly unsettling about the incident.

* * *

'I didn't like her, Sam,' Anna tells him that evening.

'Oh, she's probably all right,' he says amiably. 'Can't be easy giving up your home to strangers.'

'No, especially to Jews!'

'Oh, come on, don't so suspicious. We'll have a look at her boxes, and if all's well we can give them back to her. That'll probably be the last we see of her.'

The following evening Sam brings two dusty wooden crates down from the attic. Although it feels intrusive, they examine all the contents. Sure enough, they contain innocuous items such as family recipes, photograph albums and envelopes of loose photos, a few ornaments and household objects. Anna flicks through the albums. She pauses over one showing a younger Frau Hartmeyer holding a baby, a little boy, and wonders momentarily what might have become of him. Is he a grown man? Is he still alive, or might he have been killed in the war?

A few days later, at the appointed time, Sam and Anna hand the boxes over to Frau Hartmeyer and she seems very satisfied. She asks if she might take some plants from the garden: a few rose bushes and small fruit trees. Sam tells her firmly that this is not part of the agreement. She will be offered a third of any fruit that ripens. She expresses gratitude for this offer. Anna feels more than a little regretful that she condemned the woman so readily. Perhaps she is not so bad; she is a mother after all, like herself.

A week later, Anna wakes early one morning. Sam is still deeply asleep. A reluctant dawn is just starting to show through the curtains. Something draws her to the window. Pulling the curtain aside, she sees a woman digging furiously at the roots of a young redcurrant bush. Behind her is a large wheelbarrow, already half full of plants and shrubs. Anna rushes back to the bed and shakes Sam. It generally takes him a while to waken.

'Sam, Sam! Frau Hartmeyer is in the garden. She's stealing some plants!'

At these words, Sam's eyes open wide. He stares at Anna for a moment, and then leaps out of bed, grabs his dressing gown and pounds down the stairs. Sam's German is far from perfect, but he makes his meaning quite plain. A gentle, polite man who rarely loses his temper, it takes an attack on his garden to bring out the tiger in him.

'*Nein! Nein!*' he yells. '*Raus! Raus! Sofort raus!*' No! No! Out! Out! Get out immediately!

Anna hears Frau Hartmeyer's whining tones in response.

'My plants! I am only taking what belongs to me.'

Anna clamps her hand over her mouth. Her chest convulses with suppressed laughter. Gasping, she watches at the window as Sam tips everything out of the wheelbarrow, and pushes it and Frau Hartmeyer towards the gate. As she passes under the window, Frau Hartmeyer looks upwards and spits, twice, in Anna's direction.

* * *

Sometimes, Anna accompanies Sam on his wanderings through the garden. She tries hard to show interest when he talks of the roses, peonies, lupins and geraniums – he loves the garden so much. Yes, the flowers are pretty and colourful, but her interest is really engaged only when he speaks of potatoes and onions, of cherry trees, strawberries, gooseberries or tomatoes. After all, these are *food*, and therefore of intrinsic value.

In her imagination, Sam's passionate interest in the garden seems a quaint and lovable trait, typical of a traditional Englishman. One of his greatest pleasures at the end of a day's work is to change out of his uniform and into old brown corduroy trousers and a patched sweater, to spend an hour or two pruning and clipping, strolling between the beds of flowers and shrubs or discussing with Herr Eisen his latest idea for some corner of the ground as yet unplanted. It is the two men's common absorption with plants that enables Sam to communicate with Herr Eisen, who remains silent with almost all others.

'What has Herr Eisen told you about his family? What actually happened to them?'

Sam looks at Anna in surprise. 'I've never asked him. He hasn't said anything.'

'But you seem to spend hours talking.'

Sam rubs his temple thoughtfully. 'We talk about the quality of the soil, how much sunshine the east side gets as opposed to the west, what size crop of potatoes to expect, and whether to plant spinach or green beans ...'

Anna gives him a push. Sam grins, and then looks reflective.

'You know, I suppose my conversations with Herr Eisen remind me of my relationship with Mother long ago. We were often silent too – just working side by side in the garden for hours – but it felt easy, comfortable.'

'It's a shame we're so far away from Mother.'

'Yes, we must try to get her to come for a visit,' Sam says.

'I'd like her to come too, and she'd love to spend some time with Ben.'

'Will you write to her? I think she'd be more likely to come if the invitation comes from you. You know she's never set foot outside England.'

'I'll write tonight.'

That evening, as Anna bends over her letter, Sam kisses the back of her neck.

'You know, Maggi is really a quite remarkable woman. She's started coming outside when I'm gardening – she seems interested in anything to do with it. I think she must miss having a garden of her own.'

Sam slumps in the armchair, stretching his long legs to the fire, the usual cigarette drooping from his lips. Anna turns to frown at him.

'Yes – and it's not just the vegetables and fruit as you might expect.' Sam looks at her meaningfully.

She smiles back and raises her eyebrows.

'No, whatever I show her: flowers, shrubs, trees – even the compost! I think she has a real flair for horticulture.'

Anna is intrigued by Sam's report of Maggi's fascination for the garden. Somehow it does not ring true. Maggi has proved herself a reliable and competent cook, but she continues to be quiet and withdrawn, rarely showing animation over anything – except perhaps cigarettes, on which she relies heavily. Through the army, Sam and Anna have access to regular supplies of cigarettes, and give each member of the household a weekly allowance. Those who do not smoke are able to use them to barter for food or other items.

The following evening, when Sam goes outside as usual, Anna

watches from an upstairs window. As he had described, Maggi walks closely behind Sam, stopping when he stops, gazing into his face with rapt attention and nodding eagerly as he indicates the mixed borders with expansive gestures of his arms. Perhaps he is right and Maggi really has developed a special interest in the garden? Sam flicks his cigarette end onto the path and ambles on. In an instant Maggi reaches down, picks up the stub, prises the still-glowing end off with her nail and stuffs it into her apron pocket. She hurries after Sam, and keeping pace with him, resumes her nodding and smiling. The drone of Sam's deep voice drifts up through the warm evening air, punctuated occasionally by Maggi's soft responses.

'*Ja, ja, natürlich, Herr Brigadier.*'

Anna watches them thoughtfully. The following day she finds Maggi laying the dining table for lunch.

'Good morning, Maggi.' Maggi raises her eyes with her usual haunted look.

'Good morning, Frau Lawrence,' she mumbles.

'I need to speak to you, Maggi.'

'Yes of course, Frau Lawrence, perhaps after lunch? I will just go and finish preparing it.' Maggi looks down uneasily and begins to shuffle towards the door.

'That can wait a few minutes – please come and sit down.'

Maggi follows meekly as Anna pulls out two chairs from the table.

Maggi lowers herself and examines her bony fingers, twisting her hands, as though searching for some fault.

Anna takes a deep breath. 'Are you all right, Maggi?'

'All right, Frau Lawrence?'

'Do you have … everything you need …?' Anna breaks off, unsure how to continue.

Maggi stares out of the window beside her.

'I mean, do you have enough money?'

'Ah, money. The world thinks so much of money, does it not,

Frau Lawrence? Once I had a lot of money, now I have almost none. No matter. Nothing matters any more. What use is money now anyway? There is nothing to buy, nothing I want.'

This is the longest speech Anna has ever heard from Maggi. She takes another juddering breath.

'Nothing, except cigarettes, perhaps?'

Maggi looks at Anna directly for the first time. Her expression changes. A faint frown clouds her forehead. A pulse throbs in the delicate skin of her temple. Her jaw trembles for a moment.

'You have been very good to me, Frau Lawrence, you and the Herr Brigadier, very good.'

'Maggi, we could give you five more cigarettes a day if that would help, and perhaps a little coffee, which you could exchange …?'

Maggi looks down again. She shakes her head and twists her apron in her lap, as though struggling with some great inner pain. Her eyes fill with tears. Anna is horrified. She reaches out and touches Maggi's hands.

'I'm sorry we can't do more – there are others to consider too, and the allowance won't stretch further.'

Maggi withdraws her hands and plunges them into her apron pocket, then extends them to Anna. In the palm of her hand she holds out two cigarette stubs and two whole cigarettes.

'Look what I have come to! Frau Lawrence, what have I come to?' Her voice becomes an anguished wail. 'I must leave you. I must go from your house.'

'Leave? But why, Maggi? Where would you go?'

'There! Look at that! Look how low I have sunk.' Maggi's extended hand is shaking a little. 'You offer me kindness and generosity, and how do I repay you?'

Anna stares at the two proffered cigarettes in Maggi's outstretched hand. She glances across at the silver cigarette box on the sideboard, used to offer to occasional guests, and from which Sam extracts his after-dinner smoke. A flutter of anger wakes in her chest, turning into a pounding fury. She looks at the agonised face before her. The pity she felt a few minutes earlier dissipates.

'You took cigarettes? You *stole* our cigarettes!' Anna's voice rises to a shrill crescendo. 'You stole from us? I wasn't sure about you … any of you. But I made up my mind to trust you. We took you into our house, our *home*, Maggi. We tried to treat you well – and you stole from us?'

Maggi's breath comes in short gasps. She closes her eyes and clutches either side of her face with her hands. 'Yes. It is terrible. I will go, Frau Lawrence. I will leave your house,' she whispers. 'Immediately, if you wish.'

Anna hesitates. A confused panic takes hold of her. 'No, no, not yet. I will speak to Brigadier Lawrence.'

Maggi's face closes. Anna is reminded of the wraith-like figure she encountered in their kitchen when she first arrived in Berlin. A figure that stood before her, yet appeared not quite alive, not quite within this world or of it. At that time her doubts had been overcome by pity.

'You must not go yet,' she says slowly.

Maggi raises dull eyes to Anna's face.

'Every morning I wake and wonder that I am still alive, that the sun still shines, and the birds still sing. Why, Frau Lawrence? What for?'

Later that day, Sam looks at Anna in disbelief. He shakes his head.

'For Christ's sake, Anna! What the hell do we care about a few wretched cigarettes?'

'It's not the cigarettes … it's about trust. It felt like … a betrayal of trust. Oh God. Oh God, Sam. What have I done?'

'I guarantee, you could trust Maggi with Ben's life.'

'I did begin by offering her five extra cigarettes a day …'

Sam draws her to him. 'Well, that's more like you. Let's see what we can do to make sure she gets a few more bloody cigarettes. You know the story of her life. You know what the woman has been through, don't you?'

* * *

Helga Baumann was born near Frankfurt in 1881 into a family of great wealth and privilege. The cherished only child of Ernst and Lilli Baumann, she grew up adored and indulged. Her father was the owner and managing director of Reischaft, a successful engineering firm. At the age of thirty-seven, Helga's mother became gravely ill. Ernst engaged the most renowned and most expensive doctor he could find. When the learned man diagnosed leukaemia, Ernst dismissed him and turned to another physician. The diagnosis was the same.

Ernst's great wealth could do nothing to halt the relentless progression of the disease. He was by nature a warm and generous man. Financial success meant little to him if not shared with those he loved. He had always enjoyed spoiling his wife, whom he adored. Emotionally inarticulate, he expressed the romantic leanings of his heart by showering extravagant presents on Lilli. It was as though he believed he could hold her fate at bay by concentrating on life's pleasures. Lilli desperately wanted to talk to Ernst about a future she knew did not include her. In particular, she wanted to discuss the future of their daughter Helga, aged fourteen – a vulnerable age, Lilli felt. But Ernst refused all mention of what he called 'gloomy thoughts'.

'*Hush, hush, mein Liebling,*' he would croon, caressing the increasingly fragile bones of Lilli's shoulders and fastening another sparkling jewel around her neck.

'Look how pretty you are. We will all be happy again, when you are better, just as always.'

Lilli did manage to speak to Helga, explaining the inevitable, and stroking her hair as she held the sobbing child gently to her chest.

'You and Papa will have to take good care of each other, *Schätzel*,' she told Helga.

Lilli died surrounded by delicate silk dresses and shawls, boxes of jewellery and soft fur stoles. All this unworn finery passed to Helga, who treasured it only for its connection with her mother. Over the coming years, Ernst occupied himself with his business and with the welfare of his daughter. He never remarried. Helga became the sole focus of his affection. Despite her father's generosity, Helga was modest by nature. She inherited good taste from her mother, and wore the finest designs and materials. Her slender frame showed them off to good effect. Helga was admired for her bland, blonde beauty and quiet charm. Her father's riches added to her attractions and, by the time she was twenty, Helga had her pick of suitors.

One of them was Klaus Stammel. A handsome, clever young man with a confident manner and an eye for good business opportunities, Klaus came from very different stock to Helga. His father had been head gamekeeper on the estates of Baron von Rubenhof. When the gamekeeper was killed by the Baron's eldest son in a hunting accident, the old man felt great sorrow at the loss of one of his most loyal employees. It pained him particularly that his own son's carelessness had caused the death.

He assuaged his conscience by supporting the grieving widow, and paying for young Klaus to benefit from the best education. Growing up in his mother's modest cottage, yet surrounded by affluence, stimulated an intense longing in the growing boy, a longing for a lifestyle that always seemed just out of reach. Rather than feeling any sense of gratitude to his benefactor, Klaus seethed with bitter resentment. He was determined to make his own way in the world, whatever the cost.

Klaus began his career as a junior accountant at Reischaft, where his sharp brain and business acumen soon came to the attention of senior staff. He rose rapidly to become a senior accountant, and then junior director by the age of thirty. Ernst

Baumann also noticed the ascent of the promising and ambitious young man. He admired his energy and drive, perhaps seeing in him something of his younger self. He invited Klaus to dinner on St Martin's Feast, together with three other directors and their wives. Ernst observed that Klaus looked steadily at his daughter throughout dinner, and that she smiled back at him, a flush rising in her pale cheeks.

After dinner the guests assembled outside in the drive, while a procession of villagers tramped past bearing lanterns. Helga had a basket of sweets and fruits, which she threw to the children as they passed. They caught them with shrieks of laughter, and waved their thanks to Helga. Klaus made his way to her side. Her face glowed in the light of the flickering candles.

'Isn't it wonderful!' she exclaimed, looking up at him and shuddering slightly.

'It is indeed wonderful, Fräulein Helga,' said Klaus, 'but I see that you are cold.'

He took off his jacket and wrapped it around Helga's shoulders, gently pulling her hair out from under the collar. Throughout the coming months of courtship, Klaus was respectful of Ernst as his employer and as the father of his beloved. Within a year, in 1906, Klaus and Helga were married.

Ernst Baumann readily took his new son-in-law into his family, into his business, and into his heart. He rejoiced in his daughter's union with Klaus, and at the prospect of grandchildren. The thought of how pleased Lilli would have been gave Ernst great comfort.

Helga was blissfully happy. She was wildly in love with Klaus, and he was attentive to her in every way.

Klaus too was happy with the direction his life was taking. Now at last he was able to live the life of the rich he always envied and aspired to: a fine house with servants, exotic holidays, balls and parties, handmade clothes, and the latest motor cars.

Knowing how much pleasure her husband took in the material

things in life, Helga was content to allow herself to enjoy the trappings of prosperity too. After all, such wealth was a great good fortune and privilege, which surely ought to be appreciated, celebrated even. Helga loved to go shopping, even if an underlying sense of excessive frivolity caused her some unease. Just as an artist is skilled in applying colour and line, and a musician has a talent for tone and melody, so Helga acknowledged her natural instinct for style and good taste, whether for clothes and shoes, or furnishing and decorating their fine home. She felt it would be wrong not to use such a gift to good effect.

The top stores and dressmaking salons in Frankfurt vied for Frau Stammel's business. She pored over drawings of the latest Paris fashions, always judging which would suit her figure and complexion but, above all, which would please Klaus most.

Helga was not by nature sociable, but she took great trouble in arranging dinners and soirées for the most wealthy, influential and respected of their neighbours. Klaus took a close interest in the proposed guest lists and often made some suggestions or alterations.

'Why bother with old Doctor and Mrs Weltlieb? He'll be retiring soon anyway.'

'Yes, but they've been such good friends to Papa all these years, *Liebling*, so supportive to him when Mamma died.'

'Perhaps another time then. I think we should ask Wilhelm Klüger and his new wife. His bank has growing international connections which could be very useful to us.'

'Very important then – and maybe his wife is pretty?' Helga smiled coyly at Klaus.

'You will outshine her, as always.'

These evenings were always something of an ordeal for Helga, although she was regarded as the most charming of hostesses. Her greatest pleasure was really to stay alone with Klaus at their beautiful house in the Harz Mountains, where life was so simple. In the early days of their marriage they would slip away frequently for a long weekend or a few romantic days together. In the summer they would sometimes spend a week, or even two, relaxing there together. Helga loved the peace and solitude, just the two of them together, with only a local woman and a country girl coming in to cook and clean for a few hours each day. They were free to walk in the hills, bathe in freezing streams, sit in front of a log fire, and luxuriate in making love late into the morning in their rumpled feather bed, laughing wickedly as they contemplated the possibility of the cook appearing early and walking in on them.

Truly, their lives seemed perfect. Ernst enjoyed the company of his son-in-law, with whom he could discuss a wide range of issues, especially those related to business. Helga, in expectation of becoming a mother before long, concerned herself with supervising the running of domestic aspects of the house and estate, in particular with the employment of servants, whom she regarded almost as part of the family, in contrast to Klaus's more pragmatic approach.

'Really, *Liebling*, don't you think it is time to replace Hohenbaum with someone younger? He can scarcely bend, let alone *dig*, and he walks at the pace of a tortoise.'

'Oh, but dear old Herr Hohenbaum has been here for as long as I can remember. He loves the garden. Let's just get a lad from the village to help him with the heavy work.'

Klaus shook his head and smiled indulgently at her as if to say, only you, my love, could be so soft-hearted, and so impractical.

The years went by and, to Helga's great sorrow, no child appeared. Every month raised new hopes, only to end in disappointment. Klaus was aware of Helga's longing, but did not himself appear greatly distressed by the absence of children and never reproached her. In time she noticed that he spent more and more time at the factory or on business trips. She worried about him; he worked so hard, it couldn't be good for him. Visits to the mountains had become ever rarer – Klaus could spare hardly even a day or two to leave his responsibilities behind.

One autumn evening Klaus told her he needed to be in Berlin for two days to negotiate a deal with one of their partner firms.

'Must you go, *Liebling*? I thought we might spend a few days in the mountain house together. We haven't been for ages. You've been working so hard lately. Why does it always have to be *you* who goes? Why not send Stapelfeldt?'

'Ah, if only I could – but you know I can't trust anyone else with these important contracts.' Klaus stroked her hair, and kissed the nape of her neck. 'We will make a trip to the house together next month, I promise.'

Helga experienced a sense of emptiness when Klaus was away, a darkness and foreboding which threatened to overwhelm her. She forced herself to fight against it. How ridiculous, she told herself, when there was so much she could be doing and, after all, it was only for a couple of days. Perhaps a new dress would raise her spirits. She didn't really need it, but it might please Klaus. There was little else she needed, but some shopping might distract her from melancholy thoughts. So, on the spur of the moment, she asked the driver to take her into Frankfurt. Helga spent most of the day searching out small trinkets and luxuries to wrap for the staff at Christmas time. It delighted her to think of their pleasure in opening their small gifts.

Having completed her purchases, she strolled near the River Main in the late afternoon sunshine. How pleasant it was to feel the warmth on her face. How fortunate it was that she had decided to come to the city. There was so much to enjoy in life. It didn't do to brood and become downhearted.

A row of old steep-roofed houses overlooked the river. As she stood smoking a cigarette and watching the barges pass by, Helga heard a woman's laughter from across the street. She turned absently to look in the direction of the voice. A tall man emerged from a doorway, with a young woman on his arm. Deeply shocked, she realised the man was Klaus.

Gasping for breath, her heart pounding, Helga retreated into the shadow of a tree. No, it couldn't be Klaus; she must be mistaken.

But it was Klaus. He helped the girl into a car and they drove off together. Helga hurried to her meeting place with the driver and returned home. She debated with herself whether to mention this sighting to Klaus, and decided she must. What was he doing in Frankfurt instead of Berlin? There must be a logical explanation. It would be dishonest to keep such anxieties to herself. Yet, her earlier lighter mood had been replaced by one of great foreboding. She could not eat, she could not settle. She paced the floor restlessly and then retreated to her bedroom. The sound of Klaus returning caused her heart to pound uncontrollably and she was almost overcome by nausea. He, on the other hand, appeared in high spirits and greeted her affectionately.

'You seem rather pale tonight, my sweetheart, and so quiet. Are you unwell?'

'No, no. Perhaps a slight headache, that's all.'

She heard him singing to himself as he showered. She sat frozen at her dressing table. As he returned to the bedroom, Helga drew a deep breath.

'Klaus, I thought you said you were in Berlin these last two days?'

She brushed her hair with a trembling hand, watching her husband's startled look in the mirror.

'Yes, and so?' he said gruffly.

'I saw you in Frankfurt today.'

His face, turning grey, reflected a succession of thoughts, like the shadows of clouds passing over a field. He paced the floor for a moment.

'Ah, so now my wife finds it necessary to spy on me!'

'No, no, of course not, my dearest. I decided to go shopping.

I just happened to see you there.' Helga paused. 'You were with a young lady.'

Klaus strode over to her and put his arms around her, smiling at her in the mirror.

'Yes, *Liebling*, of course, of course. I didn't think I needed to tell you. It's not very interesting. There was a change of plan at the last minute – I had to sort things out at the Frankfurt branch instead of Berlin. Yes, a tricky job – but so tedious! Took me all of the two days, I can tell you. You must have seen the typist I had just engaged to take minutes – a pretty girl, don't you think?'

Klaus tilted his head to one side boyishly and grinned his special charming grin at her. How handsome he was still. Helga smiled back at him and nuzzled her head against his chest. She did not ask why he had to trouble himself with such a lowly task as hiring a typist. Nor did she ask why he did not return home for two nights, when Frankfurt was only an hour and a half away.

* * *

Over time, Helga developed her own interests, which Klaus did not share. It hurt her that sometimes he appeared to scorn her activities. Helga fulfilled her yearning for children to some degree through charitable work. With her own generous inheritance, she set up a trust endowing two schools in nearby poor areas. The children received not only education and books, but also a substantial midday meal. Klaus regarded his wife's benevolence as pointless and wasteful. It was not as if the beneficiaries were even employees of the firm – there were no advantages to the business.

For years Klaus had neglected his elderly and now retired mother, ashamed of her humble background, her coarse clothes and crude speech. It was Helga who re-established contact with her mother-in-law. Despite her husband's protests that his mother was perfectly content in her tiny cottage, Helga found her a small, comfortable house near their own home, and engaged a house-keeper to care for her.

The years passed and Ernst Baumann became too old and frail to continue at Reischaft. He was comforted by the knowledge that his son-in-law was there to take control of the business. He was confident that Klaus would continue to run the firm effi-ciently, with the welfare of its staff – and of course, that of his adored daughter – in mind too. In 1931 Ernst died, leaving everything to Klaus. He felt no anxiety for Helga; Klaus would continue to care for her. He went to his grave, and to his beloved Lilli, with a contented and untroubled heart.

Always flirtatious and still attractive, Klaus no longer bothered to hide his adventures. He had a series of younger mistresses. Helga was aware of these liaisons and they distressed her greatly, but she was afraid that overt objections might cause Klaus to leave her altogether. Without her father's protection, her position was becoming increasingly vulnerable. She began to smoke more heavily, and frequently sought comfort in solitary drinking. Klaus was disgusted by these habits. Over the years Helga aged less well than Klaus. Her slim body had become thin and angular; her fine pale skin lined and papery. More and more, their lives diverged.

Under Klaus's direction, Reischaft grew and expanded. During the 1930s, as Hitler's government built up its military forces, the firm flourished. Klaus expressed himself in favour of the regime under which he was prospering. He joined the Nazi Party. In public he praised their firm government and definite policies. In private he sneered at what he regarded as an unreliable and ill-educated bunch.

Helga was less careful about openly expressing her antipathy to the Nazi Party. She detested Hitler, whom she regarded as a mannerless boor and a nonentity. The growth of anti-Semitism appalled her. While Klaus was quite prepared to drop their Jewish friends and acquaintances, Helga remained stoically loyal. She agonised over how to help them: those who were trying to leave

101

Germany, and those who chose to or were obliged to remain behind. She grieved particularly over the Jewish children, many of whom she had got to know in her schools. First it was decreed that they were to be refused admission. Then they were forced to leave – who knew where to? – together with their families. Helga thought of their pinched faces and dark eyes as they clung to their parents, clutching pathetic bags of belongings or favourite toys. She despaired of her own impotence to help.

* * *

One morning in 1943, when he was sixty-six, Klaus came into Helga's day room, looking uncharacteristically uncomfortable. He would not sit down. Even before he spoke, Helga's hands flew up to her face, as if to protect herself from a blow.

'My dear Helga,' he said, 'I will come straight to the point. This may come as a shock to you, but I have come to tell you that I want a divorce.'

'A divorce! But why? Why now?' She gasped, afraid she would faint.

'You must agree, we have not been close for many years. I'm not saying this is totally your fault ... but there it is.'

'I must agree? What if I do not agree?'

'I do not want to hurt you any more than necessary, but really you have no choice. You have not produced children for me, or ... er ... for the Führer. I'm sure you know that under the infertility laws, I can divorce you immediately. I will be marrying Carla, my ... fiancée.'

'Oh, Carla? And how old is Carla?'

'Really, Helga, that is no business of yours. It happens that Carla is thirty. She is very eager to have children. Of course, I too long for children – and Germany needs children.'

'This longing seems to have developed only recently, Klaus.'

'Now, Helga, there is no need for any unpleasantness. I have considered your welfare in this situation at all times. I want to tell you that it was my wish for you to have the house in the Harz Mountains to keep for yourself.' Klaus paused to gauge the effect of this generosity on Helga.

'Yes, I know you've always been fond of it. But, of course, Carla pointed out to me that this was not in the spirit of party policy – and after considering the matter, I had to agree. Furthermore, we realised we might well need this house if our marriage is blessed with children.'

Stunned, Helga could take in little more of what Klaus was saying. She walked slowly from the room as if in a dream, a nightmare. She put up no further arguments and made no fuss. She did not want to see Klaus again, and he was relieved to keep out of her way. Within the week, she left the house she had grown up in and loved so much, never to return. Her sole possessions were one small suitcase and two thousand Reichsmarks. She wandered from one cheap lodging house to another, numbing her pain with alcohol and cigarettes. By 1945, only a few Marks remained, and by that time they were almost worthless.

Helga was saved from total destitution by her own former cook, Lena, now retired and living on the outskirts of her home town of Berlin. Lena had lost both her sons to the war. Her husband, a butcher, was sent to the Russian front at the age of fifty-nine. As German manpower became seriously depleted, the military recruited boys as young as twelve and men up to sixty years of age into the Volkssturm. Lena's husband was killed late in 1944. Her house, badly damaged in the relentless bombing, was little more than a shell. When Helga knocked at her door, Lena gave her refuge and taught her the only thing she knew about: how to cook. There were few ingredients available on which to practise. The two women formed a close bond in their mutual loneliness and distress. They scratched a living in what remained of Lena's house. Many nights they retreated to the freezing cellar, where they huddled under a heavy table, embracing one another for comfort and warmth, as bombs screamed and crashed nearby, and rubble and dust drifted downwards all around them like a cloud of spring petals.

Helga regularly made soups from whatever she could obtain: a handful of bones begged from a friendly butcher, a few potatoes, some shrivelled vegetables, wild mushrooms, nettles or sorrel. Lena jokingly nicknamed Helga 'Maggi', after the soup firm.

Maggi became her new name. Helga liked it. Helga no longer existed – she did not deserve to. She would never again be Helga. Maggi was the name she brought to the Lawrence household, when she joined them in 1945 to take up her position of family cook. It was the name by which she would be known for the remainder of her life.

Chapter 8

The Officers' Wives Group holds fortnightly coffee mornings or 'bring and buy' sales, events which Anna dreads and detests. The women take it in turns to host these occasions. As a Brigadier's wife, not only is she required to participate during such gatherings, she is expected to take a lead as well. Reminiscent of her experiences with Constance in Surrey, there is a precise etiquette, a code of behaviour, a series of expectations, about which all the women, except Anna, appear to be fiercely aware. There is an assumption that she must also understand the rules; as the wife of a Brigadier, how could she not?

Much of the system, she later learns, centres on rank. At the latest gathering, Anna commits a faux pas in relation to the observance of the hierarchy. She finds herself drawn to one or two women over and above others. Surely that is only natural, she believes, everyone likes some people better than others, and logically, some people less than others. In particular, Nancy Jordan is someone with whom she feels she could become friends. Nancy, about Anna's age and with toddler twins of Ben's age, is warm, friendly and unpretentious. She has a straightforward wit and intelligence. Anna feels a growing affection for her.

As the women gather to say their goodbyes and thank Betty

Swinburn for her hospitality, Anna grasps Nancy's hands and invites her to come for coffee the following week, and to bring her children to play with Ben. This is overheard by several women, including Betty, who gives Anna a dark look.

Mother has been staying with them for three months. Anna is thankful for her mother-in-law's company, and particularly glad to be able to talk to her about the officers' wives. She fights back rising tears. She stands up and paces the distance from the coffee table to the window and back again.

'It's so difficult, Winnie. I never will feel a part of their group, I'll never belong. I don't know if I even want to. I just seem to get everything wrong. If I behave coolly they think I'm snooty. If I try to be friendly it upsets them even more! Honestly, I wonder if I should just give up and not bother to go to their rotten gatherings.'

'Well no, no. You mustn't do that, my dear. That would just isolate you – it would put you in a very lonely position. And, it could harm Samuel too.'

'Sam? What's it got to do with Sam?'

'Everything.' Mother takes Anna's hand and draws her down onto the sofa beside her. 'Tell me, who is Betty Swinburn's husband?'

'Ted? He's a Brigadier, like Sam. A small man, a bit stuffy and pompous. I'm not sure Sam likes him much.'

Mother looks thoughtful. 'Hmm. And Nancy Jordan's husband?'

'He's called Stephen. Captain Stephen Jordan. He's friendly and funny – yes, he's awfully nice.'

'Aha. How *nice* he is, is neither here nor there. What matters is that he is a *mere Captain*, and your invitation to his wife deeply offended Betty Swinburn. She's bound to feel you should favour *her*, as a fellow Brigadier's wife. After you've done justice to her, she might allow you to move on to the Colonels' wives, and then perhaps the Majors' wives – all before you even consider inviting Nancy.'

'You mean they're jealous?'

'Indeed they are, dear girl.'

'But how idiotic! What do I care what rank their husbands are? Can't I choose my own friends? Surely I can see whomever I want, whenever I want? Must I be dictated to by a bunch of snobbish women?' Tears of fury course down Anna's cheeks.

'Anna, darling. It has taken the British Army two hundred years to establish a strict hierarchical order, to which these women are adhering. You may regard it as idiotic, and you're probably right, but you can't expect to undermine the system on which a whole institution depends – some might say a whole *nation* depends – and not cause serious ructions!'

Mother hands Anna a handkerchief. Anna blows her nose and shakes her head. She grins and gives a deep chuckle.

'What power! I thought I was simply asking a pleasant woman and her children to come round for an afternoon. I had no idea I was undermining the whole British nation!'

* * *

For weeks Anna has remained at home, scarcely venturing beyond the garden walls. She strolls around the large garden with Ben toddling ahead. There's plenty to interest *him*. He veers off to examine a flower, a tree or a dip in the path, often returning with a beetle, a worm or a pebble clutched in his hand to show her. The agony of being so restrained and limited by her surroundings begins to impel Anna to venture further afield. She pushes Ben in his pushchair half a mile along their leafy road, one day turning left, another day to the right. After a week she is longing to extend her walks. She is ready to scream with frustration and boredom. Should she be a prisoner in her own home?

Anna's restlessness is disquieting for Sam too; it makes him nervous. He writes a list of streets and nearby areas that he feels are relatively safe for her to walk in, provided she takes Mother or Della for company. He draws detailed maps of their district of Berlin, with certain routes and sections marked ominously in red: those he regards as potentially dangerous and to be avoided.

'It's just while there are such appalling shortages – and the police aren't fully up and running yet. It's still the law of the jungle out there and I don't want you taking any risks, especially at the moment.' Sam runs his hand tenderly over the expanding curve of her stomach.

Anna protests, but is secretly glad of Sam's protection. Her desire to explore freely conflicts with a natural cautiousness, and her lingering distrust of the local population. She comments that it's almost as though a yellow star suddenly appears emblazoned on her sleeve the moment she steps outside the safety of the house. Sam tries to reassure her that this particular fear is irrational.

'No one here knows anything about your background. Their most likely assumption will be that you're English – an English army wife.'

'I'm not so sure. Maybe I don't look very English. After all, Frau Hartmeyer clearly knew – or guessed. And as soon as I open my mouth they'll *know* I'm not English.'

As a precaution, Sam advises her to dress simply outside and not to carry large bags, which could invite attention. Instead he makes up a small paper package containing four cigarettes and a large pebble for added weight.

'Carry this at all times in your pocket or handbag,' he instructs her. 'In the unlikely event that you are accosted by a dubious character, shout '*cigarettes!*' and throw the package as far away from you as you can, preferably into a heap of rubble or some bushes. Then, while they go after it, you make a rapid escape.'

Anna looks doubtful. Somehow, this plan does not make her feel any more secure. When she explains it to Della, her response is to smile wryly and sing a line of a slightly bawdy popular song:

'*T'ja, dann kann man's laufen lernen, wenn man auch ni't*

will …!' 'Oh yes, then you'll learn to run fast, even if you don't intend to …!'

What a joy it is to walk. They find a park, muddy and neglected, but rich in shrubs and trees. Anna lifts Ben out of the pushchair so that he can run and run as he loves to do, like a tiny energetic gnome in his bright green siren suit. Della takes his hand and draws it gently over the bark of tree trunks to feel the different textures: the silky surface of silver birch, the rough oak, and the crinkled bark of beech, as dry and grey as the limb of an elephant. Ben runs laughing from one trunk to another to feel them again and again. They find some rusting swings and Della holds him on, while he shrieks and kicks his feet in delight.

The park should be full of children enjoying themselves, Anna thinks. Sometimes, she even has the feeling that a small child's face is peeping wistfully out at them from a bush or behind a tree. But when she stares at the spot, there is nothing, just clusters of leaves creating patches of dark shadow; the three of them are alone. Della clasps Ben under his arms and swings him round and round in a circle, while his laughter fills the deserted space.

'You are so good with him, Della.'

'And you are a fine mother.' Della links her arm with Anna's and looks thoughtful. 'I have always been very fond of young children, Frau Lawrence.'

'Have you never wanted children of your own, Della?' Anna asks.

* * *

Selma Rausch was born on a farm in Silesia in Eastern Germany in 1893, the youngest of three children. The farm was set among gentle hills and mixed woodland, rich with wild berries, mushrooms, chestnut and hazelnut trees. The soil was good: dark, rich and fertile. Selma's father Aloysius was a simple man, an illiterate peasant farmer, but also a wily businessman. Every autumn his neighbours rushed to sell any surplus crops, their eyes fixed on instant gain. It was what they had always done. A little money in the bank, or under the mattress, to stave off hunger in lean times. Aloysius, however, kept back a proportion of his grain and potatoes every year. He stored it in the driest part of his barns.

One year, when an unusually stormy spring brought torrential rain and floods, newly planted crops throughout the area were destroyed. Most of the peasants lost the bulk of their plantings and had no further seed in reserve. There was fear of a famine in the coming autumn and winter. Aloysius, however, had his large store of seed corn and potatoes, plenty for himself and for his neighbours. He was a reasonable man. He did not overcharge, although the neighbours were desperate to replace their ruined crops. Those who could pay did so. For the others, he got his daughter Selma to write up an agreement. They would pay as they could the following year, with some extra as interest. Everyone was satisfied. Aloysius became one of the most prosperous farmers in his region.

Aloysius wanted his children to have the education he never had himself. Each in turn walked the five kilometres to the nearest village school. Selma's older sister Gerta trudged towards her education, showing little interest in learning, but much interest in the farmers' sons, who sweated and sighed over their books and struggled to fit their large boots under the desks. She left school at the age of twelve to help her mother in the house and her father on the farm. Gerta was admired for her healthy complexion and robust good looks. By sixteen she was married to a neighbour's son, returning home for visits, often with another plump baby in her arms.

Selma's brother Peter was also a reluctant student. He longed to leave his books behind and join his father in the fields. After many arguments and some threats, Aloysius had to agree that Peter's stolid brain and massive hands were more suited to the plough than the pen.

It was Selma who carried the mantle of her father's educational ambitions. She took to school with enthusiasm and application. Her teachers pronounced her to be a clever child, and encouraged Aloysius and his wife Magda to allow her to remain in school as long as possible.

Until the age of thirteen, Selma was joyfully happy. She skipped home from school with a different book every day, which she eagerly showed her uncomprehending parents. This did not exempt her from what her mother considered to be proper work. Before school, Selma rose early, often before dawn, and milked the cows. She beat and shook the feather beds and hung them out of the windows to air. She swept the floor, washed the morning dishes and fed the hens. After returning home, she scrubbed the stone floor of the kitchen, and helped Magda make bread and prepare the evening meal. Then she was allowed to devote her time to completing homework and reading. It never occurred to Selma to complain.

When Selma approached the age of fourteen, her mother Magda began to lose her speech. At first it became slurred, as though she had drunk too much beer. Soon she could not speak at all. Her eyes widened with fear and frustration as she pointed and gargled towards Selma, trying to get a message across.

'I'm sorry, Selma,' Aloysius said one night, 'I know how you love school, but Mutti needs someone at home with her.'

Selma made no objection – how could she do anything other than care for her own dear mother? Gradually Magda's limbs became weak and wasted. She could walk only by holding on to the furniture, her face contorted with effort. She began to drop dishes as she attempted to wash them. Aloysius was deeply worried about his wife; he sensed a desperate fate. Despite the expense, he sent Peter in the cart to fetch the doctor from the nearest small town. It was the first time a doctor had set foot in the house. His visit was not encouraging. He informed the family that Magda had a serious wasting disease. It would only get worse.

She would become bedridden. She was unlikely to survive the year.

Selma devoted herself to her mother. She took over all of Magda's tasks. She washed her gently morning and evening. She cooked the family meal, then mashed some in a little dish and attempted to feed it to Magda. Magda coughed and choked. Selma patiently fed her thin soup and water with a tiny spoon. Soon Magda could no longer swallow even water without choking. When Aloysius returned from his work on the farm, he went to see his wife lying pale and helpless in bed. A man of few words, he took her hand and patted it awkwardly. Then he shook his head impotently and left the room. Just before Christmas, Magda was released from the agony of her suffering.

There was no question of Selma returning to school. She remained at the farm, taking on the role of woman of the house. In many ways her life suited her. She was spirited and independently minded. Her father appreciated her contribution to the household, and largely left her to pursue her own interests in her own time. Selma was short and stocky in build, with a broad face and high cheekbones. She was not unattractive to men and, over the years, had several lovers. She made love enthusiastically and without inhibition. Growing up on the farm, the coupling of men and women was as natural to her as breathing. She did not expect to marry, nor did she especially wish to.

Selma's brother Peter had been courting Else, the daughter of a local forester. In 1925 they were married, and Peter brought Else to live on the farm. Selma was pleased to have another woman for company, but Else was jealous of her sister-in-law and resented her position in the household. Else was surly and unfriendly, and found any opportunity to complain to Peter about Selma.

'She wants to be in charge – more like a mother-in-law than a sister-in-law.'

'Of course, of course,' said Peter impassively. 'Since Mutti died, she has to be both.'

Else was lazy by nature, and soon realised that it was in her own interests to allow Selma to take charge of the domestic running of the house. When Else became pregnant, she began to value Selma's hard work and support even more. In 1927, Peter and Else's son Heinrich was born, with the help of a midwife from the village. Selma squeezed Else's hand and spoke words of encouragement throughout. It was a long and difficult birth – Else's pelvis was narrow – but all was well in the end. It was Selma who cut the cord, wiped the baby clean and swaddled him tightly, as if he was in a cocoon. He gazed into her face with mysterious deep blue eyes.

'Look, Else, look!' said Selma, placing the baby in Else's arms. 'What a perfect son you have!'

Else leaned against the pillows and smiled. 'I think I could manage a little coffee now, Selma.'

The whole family was delighted. The birth of a child seemed to restore some life and joy after the trauma of Magda's illness and death. Aloysius took great pleasure in his small grandson, his thick fingers gently stroking the infant's tender cheek.

Selma adored her nephew. She loved to watch his chubby, pink limbs waving and kicking, as he lay on a rug. Heinrich learned to associate his aunt with fun and attention. He smiled broadly whenever she approached. He chuckled when she tickled him and sang to him. Else was happy to allow Selma to take on much of his care; she had little patience with children. When Peter returned after working, Else would take Heini onto her lap, but he would strain round to see Selma, and reach his little arms out to her.

Heinrich was a beautiful child, with fair hair that became almost white in the summer sun. He grew brown and healthy running about on the farm. Selma took him to see the animals and told him the names of trees and plants growing in the woods. She told him stories and read little books to him. She helped him to hold a pencil and begin to make scribbles on scraps of paper.

She never grew tired of his infant fascination with stones or insects or snails.

In 1932, when Heinrich was five years old, Else became pregnant again. An enormous belly protruded from her narrow hips. She went past her time – a week, and then two weeks. Selma called the midwife. The midwife was concerned; the baby had grown very big. It was in the breech position. She pressed and manipulated and squeezed Else. Her waters cascaded over the bed and onto the floor. Else screamed. At last labour started. For twelve hours Else shrieked and struggled, and the midwife pushed and pulled. Selma wiped Else's brow and hugged her sister-in-law. Else was exhausted; her strength had left her. Finally the midwife inserted her hand, grasped the baby's feet and pulled him out by force. He was blue and limp. The midwife handed the tiny body to Selma. She wrapped him in a towel and gently tried to rub life into him. He gave a small shudder and died.

Else's womb had ruptured. She was haemorrhaging heavily, the bed a mess of blood. Her face was white and terrified. Her last words to Selma were, 'Look after my Heini.'

* * *

Anna listens to Della's account in fascination. She hugs her. They continue their explorations of the city together. Their suburb is quiet and the streets often empty. The pavements, still littered with rubble, stones and bricks from bomb damage, are impassable in places. When they do encounter other people, they have to stand aside to let them pass. Some greet them politely, others stare or look away.

Once, a young child, perhaps four or five years old, thin and underdressed for the cold wind, steps out of a building, hand outstretched towards them.

'*Bitte etwas zu essen.*' 'Something to eat please.'

The little boy's face is pale and pleading. Who is caring for him? Why is he begging, all alone? They have nothing with them. '*Wir haben heute nichts. Komm wieder morgen.*' 'We have nothing today. Come here again tomorrow.'

The next day, and often after that, they bring chunks of bread, but they never see the child again. If only they could find him and take him home for a big bowl of nourishing soup. Anna longs to put her arms around the little boy. She weeps when she tells Sam about him.

After several expeditions without incident, Anna's confidence grows and she becomes bold enough to extend their walks further still. To Ben's delight, they find a bridge over which trains pass from time to time. He whoops with excitement whenever one rumbles and huffs into view, and shouts, 'Puffer tain! Puffer tain!'

One day, as they walk past a row of heavily bombed apartment buildings, a man emerges suddenly from a doorway. He is unshaven but clean, wearing a hat and a long military coat. He raises his hat. The man is middle-aged and well-spoken, and addresses them politely in English. He asks them to come and look; he has things that will be of interest to them, and especially the dear child. Della pulls at Anna's sleeve.

'Let us go home, Frau Lawrence.'

Anna hesitates. She is intrigued by the man. 'What is it you have?'

'Everything a lady could wish for, Madam. Food, nice clothes, shoes, books and toys for the little man. Come and see. You don't have to go right inside – just stand in the doorway and you will see.'

'Come, *Gnädige Frau*. Let us go back home. It is nearly Ben's lunchtime.'

'You stay here with Ben, Della. I'll just peep through the doorway. Just for one moment.'

Della looks about her anxiously. The man leads Anna to the building, keeping a discreet distance between them.

'Thank you, Madam, for doing me the honour. Do be careful here. Watch your footing.'

Anna supports herself against the doorframe and looks inside. As her eyes become accustomed to the gloom of the unlit room, she gasps in astonishment. The floor and walls are crammed with food of every type: tins and jars lining the shelves, chocolate bars in piles, sausages stacked at one side, joints of bacon hanging from the ceiling, blocks of cheese and butter, paper bags of flour and beans.

'All this food ...' she whispers, haunted by the face of the half-starved child in the street.

The man excuses himself and squeezes past her. He tips a large box towards her, to reveal the contents.

'Lovely clothes, Madam. Silk stockings for you. And see here, ladies' shoes – and shoes for the little boy. I have beautiful cloth for dresses or suits, thread for sewing. Look at these colours, and here this soft blanket, just right for the baby, am I right?' He glances at Anna's stomach, tilting his head respectfully. 'Even some bottles of wine. Good wine from France. Perhaps your husband likes a glass or two, Madam?'

A rage, a fury, rises volcanically in Anna, constricting her breathing and colouring her face with suffusing heat.

'You are selling all this stuff – *on the black market*?! Where did you get it from?'

'No, no, no black market. Just a little business – supply and demand, nothing more. I have been fortunate enough to come by some of these items over time, and I like to make them available to those who need them.'

'Your compatriots need them! Many children are hungry. You are not making them available to *them*, are you? You're just lining your own pockets!'

'Oh no, Madam, I *am* making these things available. Certainly I am.'

'At a price, you mean!'

'Well, of course, everything has its price.' The man shrugs apologetically. 'Has anything caught your eye? I am happy to deliver to your home if you wish.'

'No, nothing. Absolutely not!' Anna glares at the man, then turns and stumbles away from the building, towards Della, who is watching for her in great agitation.

* * *

'Bastard!' shouts Sam, when Anna and Della tell him of their adventure. 'Self-serving bastard. Taking advantage of his own people's misfortune. I'll speak to the MPs. We'll have to see if we can put a stop to his exploits.'

'Most of his stuff was American, Sam.'

'I bet it was!'

'I was so afraid for Frau Lawrence, Herr Brigadier, so afraid,' Della says. 'A man who could do such wicked things, could do … anything.'

'Yes, indeed. Thank you for protecting her, Della.'

As they have done so many times before, Anna and Sam wonder at and give thanks for their extreme good fortune in having found Della and included her in their household and family.

* * *

After Else's death, Selma fulfilled her pledge willingly. The following year, she walked with Heini the five kilometres for his first day at school. He clutched a paper cone filled with sweets, made by his aunt. No such treasure accompanied Selma nor her brother and sister on their first days at school. Selma took Heini the route she herself had walked alone at the same age. She hurried home and rushed through the cooking and washing, the cleaning out of the cowshed and tending the vegetable bed. Then she walked over an hour back to school in the afternoon for the journey home together. Only after a year did she feel confident enough to allow Heini to walk by himself.

Like Selma, Heini had a natural curiosity and enjoyed learning. She bought him a book with pictures of wild birds, and together they observed and noted down sparrow hawks, willow warblers, green woodpeckers, nuthatch, and others. Selma pointed out poisonous mushrooms to be avoided. Heini loved the red curve of the fly agaric, with its white spots. How could something so beautiful be poisonous, he asked Selma. She explained that the bright colours were nature's warning. She showed Heini how to distinguish the edible field mushrooms, boletus and chanterelles, which they gathered and added to stews and omelettes at home.

Beyond the farm, the wider world was changing. Dark and threatening clouds were gathering. Even in their quiet valley the country people knew of the Führer and the National Socialist Party, but country life went on much as before. The cows continued to need milking, the crops had to be sown and reaped. Seasons followed, one after the other. Aloysius had grown old and feeble. He and Peter took little interest in politics.

'What does it matter who is in charge? People will always need bread and meat and milk. That doesn't change,' Aloysius said.

Yet noticeable changes were taking place. A new younger teacher, Herr Keller, had replaced kind old Herr Rubenstein. Sometimes the children stayed longer at school for hiking, singing and marching. Heini enjoyed these activities greatly. People had always known that some of their neighbours – Yitzak the shoe-maker, Leon the fish-seller and old Tante Sara the tailor – were Jews, but it meant little: simply that their ways were different. Now the Jewish families were being looked on with suspicion. Aloysius spent more time at home, and sometimes listened to an old wireless he had bought. The Führer's strident voice filled the farmhouse. Heini sat motionless, his ear close to the sound, his eyes staring into the distance. Selma shook her head.

'So much hatred, *Vati*,' she said. 'Let's find some music instead.'

Aloysius was happy to let her turn the knob. His thick fingers were too clumsy to work the controls.

When he was ten years old, Heini announced that Herr Keller had allowed him to join the junior section of the Hitler Youth Movement. He was very proud. Even though he was still a little boy, he would give his service to the Führer and to his country. Selma was worried. She talked to her brother. Peter regarded his son's membership with calm indifference.

'It means nothing, Selma,' he assured her. 'All the children have joined. It's a game for them – no different to Boy Scouts. They just like to feel part of a group.'

Selma was not convinced. She took Heini to pick blueberries in the hills. As they walked, she tried to talk to him in terms he would understand.

'Heini, you must think carefully about some of the things Herr Hitler is saying. Sometimes even grown-ups say bad things. Sometimes they tell lies, if it helps them achieve what they want.'

Heini gazed at her with his clear blue eyes. 'I *love* Herr Hitler,' he said. 'He does not tell lies. He loves all true German children. He needs us to help build a strong country – that is what we will do together. It is wonderful. Look, Tante Selma, here are some good berries!'

In the autumn, Aloysius climbed a rise behind the house. He walked slowly. These days, walking uphill was a struggle for him. He steadied himself by holding on to a young birch tree, and looked out over his beloved fields. A terrible pain clutched his heart. As the sun retreated behind the hills, Selma went to look for her father. She found him lying stiff on the ground, one hand spread towards the land below, as if to say, 'Look at this good earth I have created with my labour.' She was relieved to see a gentle smile on his face.

Peter was now in complete charge of the farm. He had little time to think of anything else. Aloysius was buried next to Magda in the churchyard. Selma mourned her father greatly, but her immediate attention was taken up by worrying events nearby. The shoemaker's shop was attacked in the night. The glass window was smashed and shoes, leather and tools strewn around the street. A white star was crudely painted on the door, together with the word '*Juden*'. Yitzak and his wife were beaten and humiliated. Within weeks, the few Jewish families in the area had disappeared. The following year, war was declared. Many young men in the valley volunteered as soldiers. Selma was thankful that Peter, now fifty, was too old to be called up and Heini, at twelve, was too young.

However, she was disturbed when, two years later, her nephew became a full member of the Hitler Youth Movement, together with many of his school friends. Heini, who until so recently had worshipped his aunt, had become sullen and argumentative with her. He was furious when she continued to express negative views of Hitler and the government.

'Why can't you see that he is Germany's salvation?' he railed. 'Why must you criticise him?'

'Because I believe he is vindictive and cruel, and that he can only do great harm to Germany. Look at what has happened to the Jews already.'

'Tante Selma, don't say such things! Don't you understand that the Jews are the cause of all the problems and poverty in Germany? The Führer has made that quite clear.'

'You must not believe him, Heini. The Jews are victims, only victims.'

Her nephew pushed his lips into a deep scowl and stormed out of the house. It was a scene frequently repeated over the coming year. One morning in 1942, there was violent knocking at the door. Fifteen-year-old Heini opened it. Seeing two Gestapo men, his eyes flicked inwards to the kitchen, where Selma was kneading bread dough. Heini bit his knuckles, pushed past the men and ran out into the yard.

The Gestapo told Selma they had come to arrest her. They

told her they had information that she was a traitor. She was allowed to bring one bundle of spare clothes. Then she was dragged roughly from the house into a car, where two more men were waiting. Heini was skulking by the side of the barn. He covered his eyes with his hands and pressed his forehead to the wall of the barn. Selma looked at him as the car swung out of the farmyard, but he did not turn around. She did not see the tears that streamed down his cheeks. She recalled how years before as a little boy if Heini was scolded – which was rare – he would hide his face in his hands and turn away in distress.

* * *

Selma was taken to a transit camp. Together with fifty or sixty other women, she was herded into a large cell. There were no beds and the toilet facilities consisted of two buckets. Over the coming month the women were sorted and categorised. There were no trials. As an opponent of the regime, Selma was classed as a political prisoner. She was transferred to Boizenburg, a satellite camp of Neuengamme. It was a concentration camp for German political prisoners, communists, Gypsies, homosexuals and other enemies of the state.

Selma arrived in late November 1942 with a group of fellow prisoners. The camp guards screamed at them as they stood and swayed in the cold wind. They had not eaten for two days. They would have to work, they were told. Those who did not work hard could expect no food. The newcomers were stripped, shaved and sprayed. They were each given a stiff cotton uniform. Selma's uniform had a red triangle on the sleeve, to indicate her deviant political views. She was assigned to a hut. It was about fifty metres long and eight metres wide. There were one hundred sets of three-tier wooden bunks in two rows along the length. The stench of sweat, urine and faeces was overwhelming. Selma thought the cowshed at home smelled much better.

A prisoner showed the newcomers to their bunks. They were lucky, she told them; some inmates had died that week and there were vacant beds. In some huts there were already two prisoners sharing a bunk. They were shown the toilet and washing facilities: four taps and four latrines per hut. You learned to be quick, Selma was told. You had to be – access to the sanitary block was morning and evening only, before 'breakfast' and the 'evening meal', and you couldn't miss food for anything.

Over the coming two years Selma worked fourteen hours a day in the munitions workshop. It was heavy and tedious work, but Selma considered herself fortunate. The food was meagre: a thin gruel and tiny crust of bread in the morning, a watery soup and another crust in the evening. At least she was sturdy and healthy on arrival. Many of the women had been transferred from other camps and were already frail.

Selma befriended some of the other prisoners. She supported those who were ill or desperate as best she could. One by one, the weaker women died from exhaustion, starvation and untreated illness. A typhus epidemic carried away nearly half the hut. Despite this, more and more prisoners arrived. They were crammed in, two, sometimes three, to a bed. By the time she was released in 1945, Selma had lost more than a third of her body weight. Her kidneys were permanently damaged by the inadequate toilet regime. Her spirit was unbroken.

As her health improved, Selma decided there was nothing for her in Silesia. She had not heard of her brother Peter or of Heinrich in three years. The Red Cross helped her make her way to Berlin, where she had a good friend, another survivor of the camp. Through the Red Cross she received a letter from Peter, written in his large, uneven hand. He was so happy to hear she was alive and in reasonable health. He had tried to visit her in Boizenburg, but was not permitted, nor was she allowed to write to her. He was fit and well and had remarried. All was well on the farm. It was now part of a collective.

Heini deeply regretted his denouncement of his aunt, whom he loved very much. Still a patriot, he had joined up at seventeen, but it was during the final campaign that he realised Selma had been right all along – Hitler had betrayed the German people. Heini was killed on the eastern front in 1945, just before the war ended and just before his eighteenth birthday.

In Berlin, Selma searched for work. Through the Red Cross she heard of an English family looking for a cook, a maid, and a nanny.

'Do you speak any English?' the woman asked her.

'A little,' said Selma, searching her memory for words learned nearly fifty years previously.

'And which position do you wish to apply for?'

Selma thought about this for a minute and replied, 'I have some experience looking after children.'

* * *

Anna finds herself greatly disturbed by the incident with the black-marketeer. But most of all, the face of the hungry little boy in the street haunts her. A day or two later, she suggests to Sam they hold a Christmas party for needy local children.

'Good idea,' he replies. 'I expect Della can help sort out some deserving children for you.'

'But there are so many poor children in Berlin, Frau Lawrence. How should we choose them?'

'I know, Della, I know. We can't feed them all, of course. Oh, if only we could find that little beggar boy. Let's just pick ten or twelve children who live nearby. Maybe ask the laundry lady and the coal man? Oh, and maybe we could ask at the shop on Herte Strasse.'

'The poorest families will not be able to buy at the shop, *Gnädige Frau.*'

'No, you're right. Well, see who you can find. But remember

to tell them it's a special party this year, just for Christmas and to cheer the children up – not a regular event.'

It does not take long for Della to identify potential guests for the Christmas party. The remaining preparations take much longer. Over several weeks small portions of spare rations are put aside: flour, sugar, butter, and eggs. Both Anna and Sam are adamant that they will not engage in black-marketeering, but they are prepared to sanction a few minor exchanges for this particular event, using their own supplies. Maggi is given some extra butter and coffee to barter. She returns from the nearby market with a paper sack full of oranges. The oranges are small and gnarled, but Della examines them in wonder, turning them over and over in her hands, breathing in their exotic scent.

'It's wonderful, a miracle!'

'Maggi, did you really manage to get all these for that bit of coffee?' Anna asks.

Maggi hesitates, looking anxious. 'I hope I did right, *Gnädige Frau* – I … I used some of my cigarettes too. *My own* allowance of cigarettes,' she adds.

Anna puts her arm around Maggi's shoulders and squeezes.

'Thank you Maggi, how clever of you. The children will be so happy.'

Mother has the good idea of gathering worn-out woollens from anyone prepared to contribute. Soon she has collected a large bag full of moth-eaten, outgrown and discarded jerseys. She gets great satisfaction from supervising Anna and Della to wash the clothes, and then unpick and rewind the wool. The three women spend every spare moment knitting the wool into bright, warm mittens.

* * *

The morning of Christmas Eve dawns clear and bitterly cold. There is much to do before three o'clock. Herr Eisen brings extra wood for the fires, and the stove is stoked up with coal. The large hall is hung with paper chains, laboriously cut from old wrapping paper and magazines, and stuck together by Hannelore. Mekki and Ben watch with interest. They toddle back and forth selecting coloured strips for Hannelore to slot through the last link in the chain and paste together into a loop. She presses the two ends of the chain together, and gets Mekki and Ben to count to ten to allow the glue to dry.

A tall fir tree stands at the half-landing, decorated with dangling balls of tissue paper and wooden figures, carefully carved and painted by Herr Eisen. Mother has brought a box of old tinsel with her from England, the slender strips pressed between two pieces of card and preserved over the years – Sam says he is sure he remembers it being used at home in Cumberland. The tinsel is smoothed and draped over the branches of the tree to add some festive sparkle. Sam brings a stepladder and clips metal candleholders to the firmest horizontal branches, and pushes a small red candle into each. Ben claps his hands and points at the wondrous edifice.

'Tee! Tee!' he exclaims in delight.

In the adjoining dining room the long table is covered first with an oilcloth and then with an old green curtain. Herr Eisen has brought wooden benches for the children to sit on. Anna insisted they should sit at the table. They should be served properly, not have to line up as in a soup kitchen to receive their food. A plate and cup is placed for each child. Anna counts them.

'Twenty-two! I thought we were inviting twelve? And Hannelore's Mekki, and Ben would make fourteen.'

'Herr Brigadier thought we should expect a few extra ones who may have heard about the party, Frau Lawrence,' says Della.

'Extra ones? I hope we have enough food.'

'We've had years of stretching the rations,' says Mother. 'Surely we can manage a few extra mouths.'

At three o'clock the front doorbell starts to ring. Anna and

Sam welcome the first guests: a brother and sister aged about eight and six years, Gustav and Lena. They hover on the doorstep.

'My friend Sasha would like to come too,' says Gustav. A small, grimy boy steps forward out of the shadow of a laurel bush. A gap-toothed smile illuminates his face.

'Come in, Sasha, come in all of you, and welcome,' says Sam.

Next come three little sisters. Their mother has cut up an old net curtain and made each child a lacy 'party dress', fastened around their narrow waists with a piece of string. Anna is delighted to recognise the little boy from the street, brought by a gaunt-looking woman. She envelops him in a hug and assures his mother he will be sent home with some extra food. Then two small brothers arrive, wearing outgrown trousers barely reaching their bony knees, more like shorts. Their father apologises for their shaved heads.

'Lice,' he explains.

Mother utters an involuntary groan. Anna strokes the boys' prickly heads and crouches to welcome them. The hall starts to fill up. Ben and Mekki are racing around the hall chasing each other and shrieking excitedly. Several of the young visitors join in the game. Mother sighs.

'Samuel, I think you're going to have to exert some authority and take charge here, if we are to avoid total bedlam.'

At last the doorbell ceases its ringing. There are twenty children including Mekki and Ben. Sam balances on his stepladder and uses a long taper to light all the candles on the tree. The children watch entranced. Sam issues them with stern warnings not to get too close to the blazing tree. Then he puts a record on the phonogram. American dance music fills the hall. The children are astounded. They crowd around the phonogram to listen, laughing with delight.

Sam organises games, instructing the guests in a mixture of

126

bellowed English, pidgin German, and exaggerated mime. Those old enough to participate soon get the hang of 'musical statues' and 'musical bumps'. Winners are given a caramel, which they stuff into their mouths immediately, with a look of ecstasy. Anna engineers the results, making sure each child receives at least one sweet, even the smallest, who have no idea how to play and simply mill about joyfully. After several more games, Maggi and Hannelore announce that tea is ready for the children. Eagerly, they begin to head towards the dining room. Mother bars their way. She surveys the gaggle of grimy urchin faces.

'First, you must all come to the kitchen to wash your hands!'

Clean, and quietened by the appearance of food, the small guests are seated at the dining table one by one, each in front of a plate. On every plate is a thick slice of bread, generously buttered, a fat sausage and a small wrinkled apple.

'Look, Alma,' a girl remarks to her sister, '*white* bread!'

One little boy is overcome at the sight and bursts into tears. Anna immediately tries to take him on her knee to comfort him, but he clings to the bench, terrified that his unguarded food might disappear. Hannelore and Della circle the table with jugs, offering each child milk or orange squash to drink. Several sniff the squash or dip their fingers in, having never tasted it before. The children fall upon the food. Mother is horrified to observe the pace at which food is crammed into small mouths. Someone will surely choke! She speaks no German, but asks Anna the word for 'slowly'. She crouches by each child speaking softly and encouragingly.

'*Langsam, langsam.*'

They nod and smile at her as much as their bulging cheeks allow, and take no notice. When each plate is empty – it does not take long – Maggi brings in a cake, fragrant with a scattering of dried fruit, marzipan, melted butter and vanilla sugar. Each child receives a piece the size of two fingers. Awed silence descends on the table as they eat.

Sam, meanwhile, has disappeared. As Anna accompanies the children back to the hall, they notice a shadowy figure sitting in an unlit corner behind the stairs. Excited, and even fearful, they pause and whispers circulate.

'Saint Nikolas! *It's Saint Nikolas!*'

The boldest approach more closely. The figure looks amiable enough with his red robe and hat, and his thick white beard curling down towards his rounded stomach. More children creep cautiously towards him.

'Does he have sticks?' asks one small boy. They know Saint Nikolas is reputed to have an assistant who keeps a bundle of sticks for chastising children who have misbehaved during the year.

'No. You must have all been good,' says Anna. 'See, he has no sticks. Let's all sing to welcome him.'

She leads them in singing '*Stille Nacht*'. The sweetness of the voices rises up and fills the hall. Della blows her nose loudly.

'That was lovely. Now, one more time – and this time *everyone* must sing!'

Then Anna puts her arm around Erich, one of the bigger boys, and gently coaxes him towards Saint Nikolas. He steps forward bravely, grinning at his friends – but jumps back in alarm when Saint Nikolas speaks and moves.

'Ho ho, Erich!' he says. 'Come, come here, good boy.'

The young visitors are quite unperturbed by Saint Nikolas's broken German, but Ben is not fooled. On hearing the voice he shouts, 'Dada! Dada!'

Saint Nikolas plunges his hand into his sack and withdraws a small paper bag, which he hands to the trembling Erich. The boy grabs it and retreats to the safety of the crowd. The other children watch with awe as he examines the contents of his bag: a small carved spinning top, a pair of striped woollen mittens, an orange, and a tiny bar of American chocolate. Now greatly emboldened, they jostle to be next in line to receive their gifts. When all the bags have been distributed, Saint Nikolas gets up and waves to the children.

'Goodbye, children! Happy Christmas to you all.'

'Goodbye, Saint Nikolas! Happy Christmas!'

Then he shuffles through the hallway and disappears into the kitchen. The children are chattering like sparrows as they compare their gifts. Anna notices Herr Eisen at the kitchen door, watching them spin their new wooden tops. It is the first time she has seen him smile.

* * *

Slowly winter recedes. One mild day in early spring Della tucks Ben into the big old pram and settles him in a sheltered corner of the back garden for his afternoon rest. Half an hour later she goes to check on him and utters a piercing shriek, which brings Anna and Mother running out.

'He is gone, Frau Lawrence, Ben is gone!'

They scour every corner of the garden, and then discover, to their horror, a side gate slightly open. Has Ben wandered off alone or, even more terrible, has someone come in and abducted him? Anna is distraught. She clasps her head in her hands and screams.

'My boy. My baby!' She sobs, 'Where is my boy? I can't lose him, not *him*!'

Mother is clutching her, holding her up, as if fearing she might collapse completely.

'Telephone Sam to come at once,' she says, her voice cracking.

Anna rings Sam at his base and he returns within ten minutes. Max drives the car at such speed that gravel is flung to all sides in the front drive. A military lorry follows moments later and half a dozen soldiers jump down, men of action ready to form a search party. Anna is white-faced and wild-eyed. Della is weeping uncontrollably.

'What have I done? What have I done? I should not have left him. Oh, God in heaven!'

Mother is trying hard to remain positive and strong for Anna, but is close to breaking down herself. Her hand is clamped over her mouth, as though stifling a scream that would otherwise escape unchecked.

The soldiers set off on another search of the garden, but find nothing. Sam takes charge. They must widen the search. He orders two of the men to pursue the southward direction, two to go northwards, and two to follow the street leading westwards.

Just as the soldiers clatter through the house to begin their expedition, a large lorry draws up in the drive: the coal lorry. A huge coalman hops down from his cab, whistling cheerfully. He scoops a small green figure from the seat and, holding him on his shoulder, strides towards the door. The coalman's blackened face breaks into a dazzling white grin.

'Found him heading off towards the railway bridge. Toddling along the middle of the road! Thought I'd seen him here when I delivered last time. By, but he's a long way from home, I thought to meself. A right little wanderer. He's all right though. Just said he wanted to see the trains.'

'Puffer tains,' adds Ben, happily stroking his new friend's face. Anna rushes to the coalman, her face grim. She grabs hold of Ben, yanking him from the man's grasp.

'Ben! You naughty boy! How could you frighten me like that? Don't you ever, *ever* wander off like that again!' Her voice breaks into sobs.

Ben gapes at his mother. His face collapses and he starts to wail loudly. Della gently prises him from Anna's arms and wipes his coal-stained face, now laced by rivers of tears. Anna flings herself at the coalman and embraces him, weeping into his blackened chest.

'Oh bless you, bless you! Thank you for bringing my baby back.'

The coalman pats her back awkwardly and looks at Sam with a shrug.

* * *

Two weeks later Anna wakes screaming in the middle of the night. Sam holds her tightly to him, stroking her. She is sobbing and shaking.

'Shhh. Shhh, my sweetheart. It's all right. Just a bad dream. Everything's all right.'

'They took him! They took my baby!' she shrieks. Drops of perspiration glisten on her forehead. Her eyes are wild.

'I know, I know, darling. We thought we'd lost him. But we've got him back. He's quite safe. You were dreaming.'

She stares at him uncomprehendingly for a moment, then sinks back into the pillow.

* * *

Sam kisses Anna gently, careful not to crush the baby in her arms. He hands her a leather box.

'What is it?'

'Open it and see.'

Inside, a necklace of creamy pearls nestles in deep blue silk.

'You're spoiling me, Sam.'

'They're only cultured ones I'm afraid. Anyway, you deserve to be spoiled. No one else has given me a beautiful daughter.'

'I should hope not!'

'She seems awfully greedy for such a small person.' Sam strokes the baby's dark head as she nuzzles at Anna's breast. His touch stimulates a jerk of the tiny arms and another spasm of vigorous and noisy sucking.

'Hungry, not greedy. Her purpose in life is to grow.'

'Mmm. Must be rather nice to have to do nothing but eat and sleep. I wouldn't mind having a go myself.'

'Shhh! Sister will have you thrown out if she hears. She's very fierce, you know.'

'All Sisters are fierce. It's *their* purpose in life.'

* * *

The following day Della and Mother bring Ben to the hospital to see his new sister. He clutches Patricia, his worn stuffed elephant and sucks his thumb. They peer into the cot at the sleeping baby.

'Oh!' exclaims Della, shaking her head. 'Oh no, it's not possible! Such a tiny creature, so little! How can a human being be so small?'

'Hold her,' says Anna. 'She won't break.'

Hesitantly, Della lifts the baby out of the cot. 'So tiny,' she breathes.

'Baby … play?' asks Ben.

'When she's a bit bigger, Ben, not yet.'

'Baby name?'

'She's called Eve,' says Anna, stroking his cheek.

'Evening?'

'Just Eve.'

'Eve. That's a lovely name,' says Mother. 'Do you like it, Ben?'

Ben frowns and hugs Patricia closer. 'Ben … like … Patissa,' he says.

* * *

Max drives Mother and Anna to the station, while at home Della has sole charge of both children for the first time.

In the car Anna looks at Mother, thinking how fond she has become of her mother-in-law, how she will miss her company. Anna had felt drawn to her from the start, but now, she feels, they are truly close, deeply connected. Their relationship has become so important to her: part mother-daughter, part friendship, part sisterly.

Anna remembers the time years ago when Sam had taken her to visit his mother in her small house in Sussex – the first time she had met Mother. Sam's brother Humphrey had also been there. She can picture Mother's anxious, uncertain look, how she had deferred to Humphrey when asked a question, as though not trusting herself to give the correct response.

'Early signs of senile dementia,' Humphrey had said, and Sam had believed him, saying Humphrey was an experienced medical man, and must know about such things. Yet after Humphrey had gone home, when Anna talked quietly to her, Mother had become perfectly lucid, relating anecdotes about Sam's childhood and family life in Cumberland to amuse and interest her new daughter-in-law.

Later, Sam suggested it was as though Mother had recognised instinctively how Anna would bring to his life all that her own had lacked. In all the years of his childhood, Sam told her, he could not recall ever seeing his father touching Mother, nor uttering a single affectionate word. Anna felt so sad for Mother, and said how cruel – but Sam said his father was not cruel, simply a product of his age and background, the Victorian era.

Mother's life had been one of hard work and self-sacrifice. She knew no pleasure other than the satisfaction she derived from caring for her children and from her many acts of charity. Theirs was not a house of laughter. Yet Sam's father would have been appalled at any suggestion that he was unkind or that he had been anything other than a good husband. When he died it seemed to be too late for Mother to change the habits and standards imposed by all those years. She lived simply and frugally, only very occasionally breaking free of her sombre aura to laugh uproariously, riotously. Humphrey asserted this behaviour was confirmation of his diagnosis, but Anna believed Mother laughed for genuine reasons.

It is a pleasure they share; Anna too loves to laugh out loud. Mother's sense of humour had been suppressed for so long, and now would not be held back any longer.

On the platform Anna hugs her with great warmth.

'I so wish you could stay longer, Winnie. Must you really go? I'm going to miss you very, very much. When will you come back?'

'Dear Anna, I shall miss you too – all of you. But I must go back to my own house. And Freda needs me to pick the boys up from school on Tuesdays and Thursdays now that she's started her little job.'

Anna turns aside.

'No, no, darling. Don't cry. You're doing so well here. It will get easier – I know it will. And don't you take those wretched army women to heart. Sam's very proud of you. He adores you. And you've got your beautiful babies. Della will help you. What a good woman she is, isn't she? I'll be back, maybe in the summer holidays, if you'll have me. Now dry your eyes. Stiff upper lip, remember. That's the British way.'

The seat identified, the luggage loaded, the train is about to go. It can't be prevented. Anna has to leave Mother. They press hands together on the window. The train starts to creak slowly into motion, like a great lumbering dragon, exuding huge gusts of steam. In a moment, Mother's smiling face has gone. Anna watches the train snaking into the distance, growing smaller and smaller, until it disappears. She turns and walks back along the platform, alone.

Chapter 9

'Give this to Max's wife as soon as you arrive,' Anna says. She hands Eve the cloth shoulder bag, now fat and heavy and oddly bulging. It reminds Eve of Mr Steiner's boa constrictor after eating a large meal of rabbit and mouse. Mr Steiner is American. His boa constrictor is called Walter, which is a typically American name. Walter doesn't eat very often, so he is very hungry when he does. He opens his mouth as wide as a cave and swallows lots of enormous pieces of meat. Even so he's not very scary; he's not dangerous like a poisonous snake. He's more like a pet dog. Eve thinks about how Walter had slithered sneakily onto Mr Steiner's special armchair, and then sulked when he was shooed off it. Remembering about Walter makes her smile to herself.

'Eve, are you listening? You're to give these things to Max's wife straightaway. And don't forget to call her Frau Braun.'

'I know, Mamma, I won't forget. When is Max coming?'

'Just as soon as he gets here!' Anna snaps. 'There's no use hopping from one foot to the other like a flea – he won't come any quicker. Why don't you go and wait out in the driveway? But be sure to come and tell me before you leave.'

Anna turns and walks towards the sink. Eve wonders if she's in a bad mood again. She frowns and sticks her tongue out at her mother's receding back. She slides along the kitchen table towards Maggi, pushes her finger into her bowl and tries to load it with the soft gooey biscuit mix, but Maggi smacks her hand away.

'Tsh! Wait until it's cooked!'

Eve sticks her tongue out at Maggi too, and then starts to run from the kitchen. Maggi lifts her wooden spoon and pretends to be fierce. Eve gives a joyful shriek.

'Are you being a nuisance again?' Anna calls from the sink, but she doesn't sound very cross this time.

Outside Eve shuffles two lines in the gravel with her feet, but the stones get stuck in her sandals and poke into her feet, making little dents that hurt. She sits on the front steps and picks out the stones with her finger. The sun burns through her dress into her back. She wasn't allowed to wear shorts to visit Max's house, so she has to wear her sundress. Today is hot, just as she likes best, and the stone steps feel warm and dry and rough against her bare legs. She finds a good stick for drawing shapes in the gravel. She writes her name: E – V – E. If only Max would come. She draws a house, a tree, and a dog in the gravel, and then suddenly Max comes riding round the corner on his big, black bicycle. The wheels make a lovely, scraping sound on the drive and Max is whistling the tune of 'I love to go a-wandering'.

'Max!' she shouts, jumping up to greet him.

'*Hallo, kleines Kaninchen*' – 'Hello, little rabbit,' he says, swerving the bicycle dramatically to a stop in front of her. Little stones spray into the air. Eve reaches her arms up for him to lift her.

'One minute, one minute,' he says. 'What about telling Mamma we are going?'

Eve runs as fast as she can, her feet crunching on the gravel, back towards the kitchen door. She shouts from the doorway into the gloom.

'Mamma! He's here, Max is here! We're going!'

'Wait, Eve! The bag!' Anna calls from inside. She brings the bag and hands it to Eve. Eve puts her arms out to hug Anna, but her mother pushes her impatiently towards the door.

'Hurry now. Don't keep Max waiting.'

Anna and Maggi come out of the dark kitchen, shading their eyes in the bright sunshine. A good smell of baking follows them out. Maggi is wiping her hands on a cloth.

'It's very good of you to take her, Max, on your day off,' Anna says.

'Not at all, *Gnädige Frau*. It'll be a pleasure for the whole family.'

'Make sure you behave yourself, Eve,' Anna says, looking stern.

Max hoists Eve up onto the place where the handlebars join the crossbar of the bicycle. He has fastened his jacket to form a kind of cushion, so that the bars do not dig into her legs too much. He starts to push the bike away from the house.

'Max!' calls Anna. He stops and turns to her. She hesitates. 'Oh, nothing ... just ... just, you will bring her back safely?'

He smiles. 'Of course, Frau Lawrence.'

Max is not wearing his uniform today, because it is his day off. He has a white shirt on, open at the neck, with the sleeves rolled up. He steers the bike with one hand and uses his other arm to hold Eve steady. She strokes the beautiful golden hairs curling on Max's arm. His arms are very brown and muscular. They feel warm and firm, like Maggi's fresh-baked bread straight from the oven. Lovely, thick, bluish veins snake along his arms and spread across his hands like secret underground rivers. When Eve touches them gently they squash and wobble to one side, as if they want to escape from her fingers.

Soon they are out of the drive and turning left into Oberrhein

Strasse. Max whistles and sings. Sometimes Eve joins in. Max steers the bike along a track close to the river. He pretends to veer off towards the water, straightening the handlebars at the last minute when Eve screams with delicious fear. The Rhine is grey and dark, sliding noiselessly past them, as huge and silent as a brooding monster. A barge laden with coal chugs and splashes slowly by. Max raises his arm in greeting and the bargeman, steering in his little cabin, waves back.

They pass the big houses, then a few smaller houses. Here and there are bombsites, still un-cleared, which Ben and his friends like to play in – but that's a secret because Della says they're dangerous and she would be angry if she knew. After a few kilometres, there are no more houses, just woods and big fields of pale wheat and barley. Della has shown Eve how wheat has tight little heads of seeds, which you can chew and get a taste of flour. Barley has long straight hair, like a Chinese emperor's beard. Della knows everything about the country. The road changes into a track of dry baked earth now and the bicycle bumps over rough places.

Max holds her tightly and says, 'Not far now.'

The sun beats down on Eve's head and everything is warm and golden. She reminds herself what her mother told her; she must call Max's wife Frau Braun. It's all right to call Max Max, because he is Daddy's driver and that is what *he* calls him, just as they call Della Della and not Frau Rausch. Eve wants to get it right, so Mamma will be pleased.

'There!' says Max.

Eve screws up her eyes and sees a shape dark against the bright sky. They get nearer and nearer. Now she can see a house made of wooden boards, with a sheet of corrugated metal for a roof. Max's house does not look like Eve's house. It is very small and looks old, like an old bent man with a crooked stick, who might fall over at any minute. There are a few other houses nearby which also look old and crooked. A little boy and a little girl come running along the path towards them. The boy looks about six, about Eve's age; the girl looks a bit smaller.

'Papa! Papa!' shouts the boy. Then the little girl copies him and they are both yelling 'Papa! Papa!' at Max. Max tells Eve the boy is called Hansi and the girl is called Klara. He lifts her off the bicycle and the children shake hands with her.

Klara takes her hand and pulls her towards the house saying, '*Komm, komm herein.*'

A tall lady holding a baby comes through the doorway. She is wearing a grey skirt and a white apron. She must be Max's wife. Eve walks up to her and holds out her hand.

'*Guten Tag, Frau Braun,*' she says as politely as possible.

Frau Braun takes her hand. She does not look at Eve; she looks at Max instead. Eve thinks probably she must be shy. She thinks perhaps Frau Braun is not used to visitors, because she gives a little curtsey to Eve, which is strange as she is just a little girl and Frau Braun is a grown-up. Frau Braun is not a smiley person like Max. Eve isn't sure if she's cross or sad; sometimes it's hard to tell with grown-ups. Frau Braun steps aside for Eve to go into the house.

Inside, the house is dark and smells of sawn wood and damp earth, like Herr Eisen's shed. It takes a minute for Eve's eyes to see anything except flashing light from the bright sun outside. At one side of the room there's a little stove and a large basin for washing dishes. In the middle of the room there's a wooden table with five chairs and, beyond it, a curtain shutting off the rest of the house. Eve can't see any stairs. A very old lady comes from behind the curtain and smiles at her. She has a stick to help her walk, and her back is bent over. Max tells Eve this is Grossmutter. She shakes Grossmutter's hand too. Grossmutter grins and mutters lots of words, as if she is singing a song, but with no tune. There are only a few teeth left in her mouth, standing like boulders on a hill with spaces in between.

'Hansi will take you to see everything in a while,' says Max, 'but first, let's have a drink of milk.' He nods towards Frau Braun. She gives the baby a wooden spoon and puts him in a large box with some cloth at the bottom. The baby waves his spoon about, bangs it on the box and sucks it, making long drools of spit. Frau Braun goes to the kitchen area and fetches a metal jug, which she brings to the table.

This reminds Eve about the parcels Mamma has given her. It must be very interesting for the family, because they all gather round to watch as she opens the cloth bag. Each item has been carefully wrapped in paper. Frau Braun and Grossmutter take turns to open each package, as if it were a very special Christmas present. They make little gasps and happy noises about everything they open: a large piece of cheese, a loaf of soft white bread, a lump of butter now almost melting, a date cake, a bag of Maggi's *kipfel*, and a jar of coffee. Grossmutter is stroking the date cake. Eve can tell she would like to eat some cake straightaway, but Frau Braun takes it out of her hands and wraps it up again. Grossmutter looks so disappointed Eve feels a bit sorry for her. The last package has two small bars of chocolate. Hansi and Klara seem very pleased about the chocolate.

Eve watches as Frau Braun carefully puts the food away in a little cupboard dug into the earth of the kitchen floor. She picks up the baby and holds him on her hip with one arm. He reaches to touch his Mutti's hair with his little fat fingers. That makes Frau Braun smile and she twists round to kiss his face lots of times all over. She doesn't seem to mind the snotty mess all around his nose. Then she pours some milk into a metal cup for Eve, and gives some to Hansi and Klara. Maybe there is not enough milk to go round or maybe Frau Braun can't see very well, because she gives Hansi and Klara less milk than Eve. Eve knows this isn't fair and she quickly pours a little of her milk into each of their cups. Frau Braun looks at Max and Max tousles Eve's hair.

Later Hansi shows Eve round the house and the yard outside. There are three chickens scratching about in the dusty earth. Hansi throws them a handful of corn and they peck it up very fast, making soft little crowing noises. He shows Eve a narrow stream behind the house. He says he and Klara make dams and throw stones in the water. They walk on to a field beyond the stream. Hansi leads Eve to a big bank between the field and the stream, and tells her to watch out for the farmer. He jumps down into the field and disappears.

A few minutes later he is back, holding two big orange carrots covered with earth. They pull up a handful of grass and rub the earth off the carrots, and then Hansi washes them in the stream. Then they sit on the grass bank. The carrots taste delicious and sweet. Some bits of earth are still sticking to them and crunch in their teeth when they bite them. Hansi's shorts have a big muddy patch all over the seat, and she wonders if Frau Braun will scold him. Her dress is muddy too, but that doesn't matter – Mamma will know it's not her fault.

When they get back, Frau Braun is cuddling the baby on her lap. She's holding him with one arm and has her other arm around Klara. Frau Braun's dress is unbuttoned, and Eve realises that the baby is sucking at her bosom. Klara is leaning her head on her mother's shoulder, and telling her something about seeing a duckling. Frau Braun is listening to her and nodding and smiling. They look very cuddly and happy, and not a bit sad.

Grossmutter has disappeared and Eve asks where she has gone. Hansi pulls back the big curtain and they peep behind it. Grossmutter is having a rest on a low bed. She is lying with her mouth open, making snoring noises, like Eve's daddy does when he pretends to be sleeping. They tiptoe past her and go through another curtain. There is another bed and a small cupboard. Max's smart grey-green uniform is hanging on the side of the cupboard.

'Mutti and Papa's bed,' whispers Hansi.

'Where do you and Klara sleep?'

'With Grossmutter,' he replies. It is quite a big bed, but not *very* big.

When Frau Braun sees Hansi's muddy shorts, she asks him whether he's been having a mud-bath, and she laughs and hugs Hansi. She's not cross at all. Later, Frau Braun makes soup for supper, with potatoes and cabbage. She gives everyone a slice of the white bread Anna has sent. Eve knows she shouldn't eat it because her mamma wanted them to have it all, but she's not sure how to explain. So she nibbles a little bit of it and then breaks the rest in half for Hansi and Klara.

'Aren't you hungry, child?' asks Frau Braun.

'Not very,' Eve says. She feels quite proud of herself. Mamma would be pleased with her.

It is starting to get dark when Max takes her home. The colours have gone away from the sky and the fields. Everything looks a dull blue-grey. Eve thinks about Max's family. Now Hansi is her best friend. She feels a bit sorry to be leaving. Maybe it would be nicer to live in a little crooked house like his, with everyone so close together, instead of in her big house. The only brightness now is from the beam of Max's cycle lamp, lighting up a circle of road ahead. The dynamo makes a whirring noise, like a tired bee. Eve is very tired and nestles her head against Max's chest. He croons softly to her: '*Es war einmal ein Bebi, es sah genau so aus wie Du ...*' – 'There once was a baby, it looked just like you ...'

Sometimes, if Mamma is in a good mood, she sings that song when Eve is in bed. She likes hearing Max sing it, but it makes her feel a bit sad inside too.

* * *

'But he's not even nine years old yet, Sam – a baby still! A child needs his parents, his home.'

'He's not a baby – he's a very sensible young boy. Of course he needs us and his home and he's not about to lose either, but as I said the last time we talked about it … and the time before that … he needs a good education too.'

Anna glances at Sam. It isn't often his voice betrays impatience or irritation.

'But … what if he's ill? Or unhappy? What if he's terribly homesick? We'll be so far away – we can't do anything to help him. To Ben it will feel as though we've *abandoned* him! Any child would feel that.'

'Now I think you're being a bit melodramatic. It's not as if he's being sent to Outer Mongolia. Humphrey and Constance will be able to visit him at weekends sometimes, and he'll be able to go and stay with them. They're near enough to deal with any problems, should they arise, which I doubt. Mother will go to see him too. You know he can't wait to go. He'll probably love it.'

'He's been reading comics; he just thinks it's all about pillow fights, tuck boxes and midnight feasts. He has no idea what it'll really be like. You can't tell me you were happy at boarding school, can you, Sam?'

'Hmm … well … no, it was a pretty grim time. But that was then, years ago. Things have changed a great deal since I went to school. Much more humane. They actually try to ensure the children are happy and contented these days. Look, darling, we've been through all this so many times. It may take him a little time to settle in, but he *will*. I'm sure of it. You know Mrs Rutter has said she has a special pastoral role with the new and younger boys, especially the ones who live abroad. She's promised to keep us informed. I'm sure she'll look after Ben, take an interest in him. She'll see to it he makes some friends. That's the important thing at his age; once he has one or two pals he'll be fine.'

'I couldn't bear to think of him as lonely and miserable.'

Sam puts his arms around Anna and nuzzles the top of her head.

'I know it's hard for you, and you'll miss him terribly. I'm going to miss him too. But we've got to think of what's best for the boy. His education could determine his whole future life. Surely we can't deny him that, just to keep him with us, however much we want to? And he'll be back home in no time – just a few weeks – and think what a wonderful Christmas we'll all have together.'

'Oh, you're always so very persuasive – all the right answers, as usual,' Anna says, frowning, 'but what about Eve?'

'What about her?'

'You know how close they are. She'll be ... bereaved.'

'He's not dying!'

Anna does not smile.

'Look, of course she'll miss him,' says Sam. 'She may feel lonely for a time. But maybe it'll be a good thing for her too, to be the centre of attention for a while.'

'You don't think Eve gets enough attention?'

'I didn't say that. It seems to me she's been looking a bit peaky lately. Let's just try to look at it positively. An opportunity for us – and especially you – to focus particularly on Eve; to have fun with her, help her develop her interests and her confidence.'

'I don't think Ben's presence at home stops Eve having attention, or stops her developing her interests and confidence.'

Sam sighs and shakes his head.

* * *

A month later, the heat of the summer has given way to a cool, damp September. The whole family drives to Ostende. Anna listens to Eve chattering to Ben in the back of the car. He is quieter than usual, answering only in monosyllables. Anna adjusts her mirror to look at him. Somehow his new school uniform makes him look even younger and more vulnerable. A tousle of reddish hair sticks out from the grey and rust striped cap. Bony knees emerge from long grey flannel shorts. His long woollen socks refuse to stay up, slithering down his skinny calves in bunched folds, despite elastic garters made by Della.

As they left home, Ben stood rigidly, allowing himself to be hugged by Della and Maggi, his face a contortion of self-control. Maggi has filled his tuck box with favourite treats: chocolate biscuit cake, vanilla *kipfel*, cheese straws, all carefully wrapped and packed among the tins and packets.

At the dock, Sam takes Ben for a stroll along the quayside. Anna watches them walk hand in hand together, father and son, deep in some serious conversation.

'No long drawn-out goodbyes,' Sam had said. 'Just prolongs the agony and gives him time to brood.'

Eve is clinging to Anna's arm, looking up at her face.

'We don't want Ben to go, do we, Mamma?' she whispers confidentially.

Anna hesitates, resisting an urge to shake Eve's hand off.

'We want what's best for Ben, sweetie. That's what we want.'

Anna and Ben stand and wave at the ship's rail until Sam and Eve are tiny dots merging into the blur of the crowd. Anna tries to ignore the waves of nausea tightening her stomach, just as she had done years before, as a different ship carried her and Jakob away from Brindisi, away from Europe, and all she had known and loved. Ben is excited by travelling on the ship, appearing to forget his apprehension for a time. He races about exploring and pointing out features of interest to Anna: the lifeboats, the smoke emerging from the funnels, the captain and pilot just visible in the control cabin on the bridge.

They arrive in Dover in a grey dusk and spend one night,

booked by Sam, at a modest guesthouse near the dock. There appear to be only two other guests, an elderly couple. The middle-aged landlady becomes especially friendly when she hears Anna's husband is in the forces. She tells Anna she lost her own husband in North Africa during the war. She searches a drawer and gives Ben an envelope full of golly labels steamed off empty jam jars, promising to save more for his next visit. Ben is delighted. He will be able to send them off for a golly badge, he tells Anna.

Anna studies Sam's directions over breakfast. Later the train takes them to London, through mile upon mile of dreary suburbs. It rains steadily. Ben's special treat is to spend two hours on the underground, puzzling over the map and working out routes that take them to stations with strange names, places they never actually see – Goodge Street, Angel, Monument, Elephant and Castle, Piccadilly – and back eventually to Charing Cross, where they have lunch in a nearby Lyons' Corner House.

Anna is content to let Ben guide her, to take the lead and do as he wants – anything to keep him happy and distracted from their forthcoming parting. Behind her cheery laughter is the knowledge of what is to come, her dread of the moment she will have to leave him, a heavy feeling sitting ominously, like a weight lurking beneath her ribcage, dragging her down. They go into a news-theatre, hazy with cigarette smoke and fusty with the smell of shabby old men in damp raincoats, enjoying an interlude of warmth and shelter. A newsreel is showing.

'When will the cartoons come on?' Ben whispers.

They sit through two cycles of news and cartoons, before catching the train at Waterloo station. Constance and Humphrey are waiting at the station, looking a little older, but otherwise unchanged. They are very welcoming. The two older girls are away: one still at school, the other now at a finishing school in Switzerland. Camilla is still home from her school for the holidays, about to return for the new term. She appears to have grown nearly a metre taller since Anna last saw her. Only just still a child, she has sprouted long legs, and developed the glowering looks of imminent adolescence, but she hugs Anna shyly. Anna recalls the insecurity and anxiety she felt during her previous stay with Humphrey and Constance. This time she feels unintimidated and finds herself surprisingly moved at seeing Constance again, as though reacquainting herself with a very old and close friend.

The following morning Humphrey drives them through gentle Surrey countryside to Hadrian Court preparatory school. It is a sombre Jacobean building, prickly with turrets and towers, a facade of crumbling red-brick, interrupted by dark narrow windows. Large cars line the front drive bumper to bumper. Well-dressed parents talk in loud voices and fuss over trunks and boxes. Humphrey slips his car expertly into a vacated space.

'Why don't you take Ben in, Anna? Find his house and dorm. Get him settled and all that, while I sort out the luggage.'

Dear Humphrey, she thinks, sensitive enough in his way, giving her a chance to say her farewells to Ben in private. She reaches for Ben's hand, but he withdraws it hurriedly, looking about him with hunted, furtive eyes. An older boy, officiously holding a clipboard, approaches them. Beside Ben he looks almost adult, though he can't be more than twelve or thirteen.

'New boy? Good morning. I'm Langley-Hunt. Here to show you the ropes. What's your name?'

'Benjamin Lawrence,' Ben whispers. Anna has never heard him refer to himself as Benjamin before.

'Right. Lawrence … let's see. Yes, here we are, you're on my list for Oak House. This way, Mrs Lawrence.'

Anna smiles and follows the man-boy meekly. He leads them through dark halls and corridors, and into the lighter, more modern extended back of the school. The smell of varnished wooden floors and stale food brings a surge of memories; standing next to Kaethe in a queue of children, clutching her bowl. Anna pauses, overcome with queasiness. Ben looks up at her anxiously. She takes a deep breath and smiles at him. Ahead of them, Langley-Hunt leaps up some steep stairs and strides along another corridor. They break into a trot to keep up, emerging at last into a long room lined with beds, like a hospital ward. Beside each bed is a small cupboard, bookshelf and bedside locker. Langley-Hunt strides towards the third bed on the right.

'This is your bed, Lawrence.' He indicates with a sweep of his arm, looking from Anna to Ben, as if waiting for some comment of appreciation. 'Now, I'll go and see how your pa is getting on with the luggage.'

'Uncle,' says Ben.

'What?'

'He's my uncle. Uncle Humphrey.'

'Oh, right-ho. Better get it right, eh? You might want to say goodbye here, Mrs Lawrence. If you want a word with the Head's wife, her room is on the left on the way out. Mrs Rutter, she's called.'

Anna and Ben sit side by side on the bed and look around.

'Ben, my sweetheart, are you all right?'

'I'm fine, Mamma. I'll be OK. You better go now.'

Anna bites the inside of her lip, willing tears not to betray her. She hugs him. He smiles fixedly. He looks terrified. She suppresses an urge to grab his hand and run with him, and keep running.

'Hello,' says a small voice. A fair-haired boy, even smaller than Ben, is sitting on the next bed. He stands up and approaches Ben.

'My name's Charlie Ballantyre, what's yours?'

'Ben Lawrence ... um ... are you new too?'

Anna takes a deep breath. She gives Ben a last squeeze and tiptoes away.

When Humphrey returns to the car after carrying Ben's trunk upstairs, he pats her knee and offers her his handkerchief.

'Absolutely fine. Talking nineteen to the dozen to young Charlie, and another little fellow. Nothing to worry about, my dear. He'll soon settle in.'

* * *

At this time, just when they are all trying to adjust to Ben's absence, the familiar little world Anna and Sam have built around themselves is starting to crumble and change in other ways too. Della and Herr Eisen are now the only live-in servants. When little Mekki was five, Hannelore had brought her boyfriend Heinz to meet Anna and Sam. A few months later they had been married, and a small celebration party held at the house. Hannelore and Heinz had rented a flat nearby and she had continued to work until a month before her baby daughter Lisa was born. Hannelore was still only twenty-three. Heinz had a steady job driving lorries for a timber merchant. He and Hannelore had decided she would stay at home to care for the children.

Maria, a pleasant woman in her thirties, is engaged to come on a daily basis to help with cleaning and other domestic tasks. Even greater change to the household is wrought by Maggi's departure. Following the death from a heart attack of her former husband Klaus in 1948, Sam helps Maggi to hire a lawyer. After a lengthy legal procedure, a significant proportion of her former wealth is restored to her. She has no wish to wrangle with Klaus's second wife Carla, who inherits the balance.

In addition, the German government is slowly making compensatory payments to those who suffered during the Nazi years. Both Maggi and Della are eligible to benefit from a special pension. Della opts to remain with the Lawrence family, while they still need her. Maggi, at seventy-five, decides she is getting too old to continue regular working. She retires to a small house in an affluent suburb of Düsseldorf.

Anna is deeply unsettled by her departure. Maggi has been a core member of the household for so many years now. Anna's relationship with Maggi has become one of great affection and complete trust, a bond all the stronger because of the early tensions between them. She is not blind to the paradox of her formerly destitute cook returning to a life of leisure and relative luxury, but she does not begrudge her this comfort in her old age. Maggi returns regularly to visit the family, and bring Ben and Eve's favourite baked treats. Sometimes Maggi helps out by supervising the cooking for special social or family occasions, but it is Della who helps Anna take control of the day-to-day cooking.

But why must there be yet another change, another loss – why now? She has to learn to cook from scratch, even down to knowing how many potatoes to cook for four or five people. Eve's behaviour does not help.

'She's so difficult, Della. I sometimes wonder where I've gone wrong.'

'No no, Frau Lawrence, you have not gone wrong at all. Eve is not difficult, not really, just sensitive. She is a child who thinks about things and tries to make sense of the adult world. So hard for a little girl of only six.'

'How did you get to be so wise, Della? You don't even have children, yet you seem to understand them better than I do.'

'No one is more important than the mother, Frau Lawrence, no one.'

'Well, I don't think I'm making a very good job of it. She makes me so angry sometimes. I know I shouldn't let her, I should control it – but I just can't seem to do it.'

'Ah, well, children can be very aggravating at times. She does miss Ben very much. Perhaps she needs to see more friends of her own age? And maybe a pet would help? She's so keen on a having a dog. She has so much love to give.'

Anna looks at Della's open, honest face and feels a brief surge of guilt and regret, overlaid with irritation.

'She has a funny way of showing it sometimes.'

* * *

'D'you know, I think Della's right,' Sam says, as he and Anna get ready for bed. 'A pet would be nice for Eve. All our moving about hasn't helped. She no sooner makes a friend than she's whisked off again to a new house and a new school. Now maybe you see the advantage of boarding school.'

Anna huffs loudly and puts her hands firmly on her hips.

'No, no, no, Sam. Absolutely not!'

'No, of course not. I wasn't being serious, darling. You're right that Eve needs to be at home, but you know the problem with a dog. What if we should be posted back to England? It could happen at any time, and then the poor creature would have to be in quarantine for six months – canine boarding school of the worst sort! Anyway, I've had another idea.'

A few days later Eve is told there is to be a surprise for her.

'Where are we going, Daddy?'

'Wait and see. It's not far.'

Sam and Anna, each holding one of Eve's hands, smile at one another over the top of her head. The first heavy snow of the year has fallen. Their feet crunch on the fresh dry surface. Eve skips along between them, turning round from time to time to examine their trail of footprints, sparkling in the light of the street lamps. Anna registers sadly how happy Eve is to have both her parents all to herself for a while. They come to a cul-de-sac with a semi-circle of neat white houses. Sam leads them to the second house and rings the bell. The door is opened by a small, wiry woman, who introduces herself as Mrs Holland. They remove their boots and coats in the hallway and follow Mrs Holland into the kitchen. Eve looks both puzzled and excited.

'So,' says Mrs Holland to Eve, 'you're the little girl who wants a cat, are you?'

'Really, I want a dog most, but I do like cats too.'

'Right, I see. Well, there are just *cats* here. I've sorted them all out for you. These three in the basket are the boys. The girls are with their mother in that box over there by the stove.' A faint mewling sound comes from both the box and the basket. Mrs Holland crouches down to Eve's level.

'I understand this is a special present for you, dear. You can choose whichever of the boys you like.'

Eve looks round at Anna and Sam questioningly.

'We thought you'd like a kitten for company,' says Sam. 'A sort of early Christmas present. Go ahead. Have a good look at them and choose one.'

'One of the ... *boys*?'

'We didn't think we could manage *lots* of cats,' says Anna, 'and female kittens generally grow up to produce babies themselves. So have a look at the male kittens.' She turns to Mrs Holland. 'Although I don't know how on earth you can tell, when they're so small.'

'It's not always easy.' Mrs Holland laughs. 'Takes years of experience – and believe me, I've had plenty of experience with cats in my time.'

Eve peeps into the cardboard box. The black and white mother cat blinks calmly, as a heaving mound of tiny bodies struggles for her nipples. Eve approaches the basket and studies the three male kittens. She picks them up one by one. First she brings a white kitten with black ears to show to her parents. Next, she brings a very small black kitten with white feet, a white tip to his tail and a white star on his forehead. Lastly, she holds up a striped gold and brown tabby kitten.

'Father was a tabby,' mouths Mrs Holland to Anna and Sam.

'Which do you like best, Mamma?' asks Eve.

'It's your kitten. You must choose.'

'This one is beautiful,' says Eve, putting the tabby kitten on Anna's lap, 'but do you like him too? I want you to like him too.'

Anna stiffens; she is not used to animals. She strokes the little creature awkwardly with one finger, feeling slightly repelled by the frail bones moving inside the furry skin.

'What will you call him?' asks Anna as they walk home, the kitten cuddled warm inside Eve's coat.

'Emil,' says Eve.

Emil is a lively, playful kitten. Eve adores him and spends hours inventing games to entertain him. Emil tolerates being dressed in bonnets and pushed around in a dolls' pram. He seems to enjoy Eve's caresses, and positively seeks them out. Anna notices how much more contented Eve appears when Emil is stretched out on her lap, luxuriating in her passionate cuddles. He follows Eve like a dog, accompanying her to play in the garden or for walks in nearby fields and woods. He grows extremely fast.

After a time he starts to scratch at the kitchen door in the evenings, desperate to be outside. He roams the neighbourhood at night, but no one knows anything of his nocturnal adventures. Three months later he gives birth to four kittens on Ben's bed, three black and one tabby. Anna shudders to see the tiny quivering bodies on Ben's eiderdown, blind and almost hairless, like baby rats.

'Well, either it's a miracle birth, or Mrs Holland isn't quite as skilled as she thought at sexing kittens,' says Sam.

'Perhaps we should call her Emilia ... or Emily?' suggests Anna.

'He ... I mean *she* will always be Emil,' says Eve. 'That's his ... her name.'

They manage to find homes for all four kittens, and Emil is taken to visit the vet.

* * *

Eve, sitting on the sideboard, throws a ping pong ball repeatedly against the opposite wall with a loud clacking sound, and catches it on the rebound.

'But why did he have to go to school in *England*, Mamma? Why couldn't he just stay at school in Germany, like me?'

'Well, because Ben is three years older than you. He needs a different sort of school now.'

The ball bounces in the wrong direction and rolls under the chair. Emil pounces joyfully after it. Sighing, Anna retrieves the ball and hands it to Eve, who resumes her throwing. She had thought Eve would be less needy, less clingy, now that she had Emil for company. Yet she's such a demanding child – nothing seems enough for her.

'So will I have to go to school in England too, when I'm older?'

'Maybe. Maybe not.'

'Why maybe not?

'Because you're a girl. Daddy thinks it's different for a girl.' Eve drops the ball again and Anna brings it back to her. 'Do you want to go and play with Emil in the garden?'

'No, I like it here with you. Why is it different?'

'I'm not really sure. Ask Daddy.'

'Are girls less important?'

'No, of course not.' Eve's ball bounces noisily on the parquet floor and rolls under the dining table. Anna has to stretch to reach it.

'But it doesn't matter if girls go to school in Germany?'

'Well, it's not that it doesn't *matter*.'

'Then why?'

'Oh, for goodness' sake, Eve! Will you stop asking so many questions? Maybe you *should* go to boarding school too!'

Eve frowns. She takes the ball from Anna again and looks silently at the floor. She opens her hand and lets the ball drop from her fingers. Anna gasps in irritation and reaches for it yet again. Eve smiles.

'You know what, Mamma? You're like my *slave*, always getting the ball for me when I drop it!'

Anna flings the ball across the room and yanks Eve roughly from her perch on the sideboard.

'Don't you dare ever to call me that!'

Anna pulls Eve to the kitchen and asks Della to prepare some lunch for her, because she certainly can't be bothered to cook for her when she's in such a silly mood. Della makes Anna a cup of coffee, and then puts a plate of egg noodles and tomato sauce in front of Eve. Eve stares at it, tears welling in her eyes.

'Well come on, Eve. Look what a nice lunch Della's made for you.'

'I'm not hungry.'

'There are plenty of hungry children who would be glad of your good food.'

'Then give it to them.'

Anna stands, her chair crashing to the floor behind her. Tight fists quiver at her sides. She turns to Eve, breathing heavily.

Della calmly steps between them. 'Never mind,' she says softly. 'If you don't want it now, Eve, maybe you'll be hungry later.'

'Della, you'll have to see to her! I can't deal with such a naughty girl!' Anna storms from the room. The sound of her footsteps on the stairs echoes through the house.

* * *

'Would you clean in Eve's room today?' Anna asks Maria. 'We haven't managed it properly since she got chicken pox.'

'Yes, of course, if it won't disturb her, *Gnädige Frau*.'

'Oh no. She's much better. She's not even in bed today. She'll probably be reading or drawing pictures. I'll ask Della to make her some orange juice, and we could all have our coffee in her room to keep her company. She'd like that.'

Della carries a tray of drinks upstairs, with Anna close behind.

They find Eve chattering to Maria. The room looks spotless, Anna notes with satisfaction, Maria is a quick and efficient worker. Eve runs to hug her mother. Anna steps to one side.

'Careful of the drinks, darling!' She waits for Della to put the tray down on the desk and then turns to return Eve's hug, but she has gone to join Emil on the bed again and is sifting through a book of drawings. How pale she looks. She needs some good country air.

'Look, Della, this is you, and Emil is chasing you!' Eve holds up a sheet of paper and giggles.

'Maria, this is you with your broom. It looks like a witch's broom – but you're not a witch, are you?'

'As long as you haven't drawn me riding *on* the broom!'

'And, Mamma, I did you cooking potatoes. Only you've cooked a huge pot of them, and look how hot you are – all red in the face.'

'Little monkey. You're obviously much better – all these funny pictures of everyone. You'll have to do one of Daddy too to show him when he comes home from work. What else have you been doing this morning?'

'I've been reading the new books from the library. This is a good one about a chimpanzee called Zippy. Look, he's got clothes on! And this is Pooh Bear. And look here, this is a new one I haven't read yet. It's got lots of writing – I think maybe it's for older boys and girls. It's about a little girl called Anne Frank. Who is Anne Frank, Mamma?'

Anna holds her coffee cup mid-way to her mouth, as though turned to stone. Della and Maria look startled. The air in the room has grown thick and heavy. Eve looks from one face to another.

'Mamma, I said who is Anne Frank?' she says, more loudly this time.

'Ssshhh!'

'What? Why … Mamma, who is—?'

'Psshht, Eve! Don't ask that! Don't talk about it now. Not now!'

'But I just—'

'Did you hear me? I'll tell you about it *later*. *Not now!*'

Eve flings herself backwards on the bed and buries her face in Emil's body.

* * *

Anna is sitting on the wooden seat encircling the great chestnut tree, concealed by a beech hedge, trying to concentrate on reading. It is one of her favourite secluded spots in the garden, sheltered from the wind and catching early evening sunshine. Lately, she has come to the solitude of this place more and more often. Through the leaves of the hedge she can see Herr Eisen and Eve kneeling side by side in the vegetable garden. Anna holds the book open on her lap, but the lines of writing swim before her eyes. Her attention is not on the book; it is drawn firmly to the gardener and the child, to their quiet conversation and shared activity. A pressure grows behind her eyes as she watches.

They are planting garlic. Eve makes a deep hole in the earth with a wooden dibber, and drops a clove of garlic into it. She carefully spreads her hands wide, side by side, three times to measure the correct distance from the last hole, and presses the tool into the soft earth again. Herr Eisen studies her progress. When Eve looks up at him, he nods and smiles encouragingly. Anna can see Eve's small hands working diligently in the soil. Herr Eisen's hands, by contrast, are large and bony, with lumps swelling the joints. The skin is folded into loose wrinkles and speckled with patches of brown, like a hen's egg. Anna watches as Eve looks back along the line of small mounds marked by a length of green twine pulled taut between two wooden stakes. The sight of Eve chewing her lip and frowning with effort and concentration is enough to trigger the release of the tears that have been welling.

'You are working hard, little one,' Herr Eisen comments softly. Eve does not look up. 'I have to.'

'Oh?'

'So Mamma will be pleased.'

'Ah, yes.'

'I'm going to pick her some flowers. That might make her happy, mightn't it?'

Quietly Anna picks up her book and tiptoes back to the house.

* * *

For two weeks Anna determines to extend to Eve the warmth and affection she knows she so craves, and which she herself knows she *feels*, yet which it sometimes seems to take a supreme effort on her part to show.

'You know, Frau Lawrence, I think it is harder with Eve, because she is so like you. Ben is a boy; it is different. But she reminds you of yourself, perhaps?' As usual, Della's wisdom and perception astounds Anna. Of course she is right. So often, she wants only to punish herself, but it is Eve who is there.

Events take over, which punish them all. Herr Eisen, dear, gentle Herr Eisen, dies suddenly of heart failure. Sam finds him lying outside his garden shed one morning.

Anna holds Eve on her lap, hugging her, stroking her hair, kissing her. She rocks her gently, as she did when she was a baby. It feels so good, so close; how she has missed her. Why did he have to die now, of all times? she wonders. So many losses to deal with, just when they all need some stability. Is nothing ever permanent?

'Can we go and see him, Mamma? I want to see him, before he goes to heaven.'

What harm can it do? It is right for the child to understand death. Anna has discussed it with Della, as she does most issues of importance. When Della was growing up, the bereaved – even children – were expected to kiss dead loved ones goodbye. She told Anna she still recalled the feel of her mother's face, as she lay in her coffin on the scrubbed kitchen table, the flesh hard, cold, and unyielding. Of course, Della had been older than Eve, and familiar with the relentless cycle of life and death, like any farmer's daughter. Anna almost envies her this intimate contact with the dead. She had been so far away in Palestine when her own mother died in Vienna, and far away again when her father died in Esther's home in America. Far away too when Jakob died alone in Auschwitz.

She pushes these thoughts away with a violent shudder and stands up, sliding the child off her lap and taking her hand briskly.

'Come then. But remember, Eve, Herr Eisen cannot wake up or speak to you.'

''Course I know that. Why did he die, Mamma?'

'He was very old. His body was tired. His heart was tired of sorrow. He will be happy to join his wife and children, with the angels. How he must have missed them over the years.'

'Won't he miss *me*? Won't he miss living here with us?'

'I think he will miss you, I'm sure of it, and Ben too. But Herr Eisen was a good man, so I expect he hopes that in heaven he'll be reunited with all those he has loved and lost before. And one day we may join him there too.'

Eve thinks about this silently. Anna leads her to the salon where the simple, dark coffin stands on two tables in the centre of the room. On the sideboards at either side, two silver candelabra cast a gentle, intimate light. She lifts Eve, settling her into the hollow above her hip. They gaze down at Herr Eisen in silence for a few minutes. His white hair has been brushed up from his forehead and back behind his ears. His beard is white and clean, with a trace of golden streaks near the jawline. He is no longer wearing his worn brown jacket, his striped blue and white shirt frayed at the cuffs, nor are his old leather braces supporting thick, green loden trousers. Herr Eisen is smart and spotless in clothes neither

Anna nor Eve have ever seen before: a black suit of a fine, slightly shiny cloth, double-breasted and buttoned right through, a shirt of pure white cotton with starched cuffs showing at his wrists, and a high collar at his throat. Around his neck is a red and white spotted kerchief, tied with a flourish.

Yet despite all this finery, or perhaps because of it, Herr Eisen looks quite unlike himself. His face is of a pale almond colour. Gone is the ruddy, outdoor vigour. His expression is strange too, fixed in a smooth and rigid smile, so uncharacteristic of a man whose face was usually serious and contemplative, only rarely breaking into a network of creases and ridges as he allowed pleasure to soften his features.

'Herr Eisen?' Eve says doubtfully. Anna cuddles her closer reassuringly.

'Is it really him?'

'Yes, *Schätzel*, he is dressed for his Maker.'

'He looks … beautiful.'

* * *

Not long after Herr Eisen's funeral, Anna again seeks Della out to discuss her concerns about Eve.

'I just told her we were having a reception for the mayor this evening, and I wanted her to help by handing round trays of hors d'oeuvres for the guests – and do you know what she said?'

'What?' Della smiles indulgently.

'She said "I don't think I can. I'm much too shy to do that."'

'Oh, did she? Too shy?' says Della.

'Yes, and then she said, "Maybe I'll go and ask Herr Eisen what he thinks"! Imagine! What on earth is going on in that child's head? We all thought she understood that Herr Eisen is dead and not coming back. Yet she goes down to the garden shed to "talk to him" every day. It's not healthy. Maybe I should forbid it?'

'Hmm. I wouldn't do that, *Gnädige Frau*. He was a very special

160

friend to her, almost like a grandfather. She misses him, and now with Ben away too, it gives her comfort to feel Herr Eisen's presence, in her own way.'

'We all miss Ben, and Herr Eisen too of course.'

Children should be with their mothers, Anna thinks. No one knows just how much she misses Ben, how his absence has become a constant presence, blocking her feelings for Eve. At times she worries for Eve's sanity. She does not mention to Della, or to Sam, that she herself regularly converses with Ben, when the agony of her longing for him becomes unbearable. That is different: she *knows* Ben can't hear her – it is just a way of feeling close to him, of keeping the black shadows at bay.

Sam seems quite relaxed about Eve's conversations with the dead gardener. As he and Anna dress for the reception that evening, Eve suddenly appears in her parents' bedroom wearing her favourite lemon yellow party dress. She smiles at them both and sidles up to her mother, turning her back.

'Can you fasten my dress please, Mamma?'

'Yes of course, my sweetheart. How lovely you look. Have you decided to come to the party after all then?'

'Yes.'

'So did you ask old Eisen's opinion?' asks Sam, winking at Anna.

'Yes I did,' Eve says solemnly. 'I told him I didn't want to go because I was too shy.'

'Oh, and what did he say?'

'He said, "Just pretend you're not shy."' She looks from Sam to Anna. 'So that's what I'm going to do.'

'Excellent advice.'

Chapter 10

Sam stares at Dr Ehrlich. He presses his hands against his trouser legs, feeling their heat and dampness. He takes a deep breath and closes his eyes, as if hoping he might be transported away from this place, far away. When he opens them again, Dr Ehrlich is still there, sitting behind his large polished wooden desk, nodding in his understanding, sympathetic way. Bloody, bloody maddening, sitting there nodding like a puppet, like a mechanical doll. The best in his field, so they say. A specialist in healing the damaged and displaced of Europe, those who have suffered unimaginable cruelty and loss, those who have survived and don't know why. If anyone can help Anna, he can. Someone must help Anna.

Eve is playing at a little table in the corner of the room, murmuring softly to herself. An imaginative child, her teacher had pronounced, dreamy. She lives in her own head a little too much. Just as well, Sam thinks. Right now, inside her head is probably a safer place, a good deal more comfortable than the real world.

Every so often Eve stops what she's doing and gazes across the room at Sam with her large dark eyes. Anna's eyes. Confused thoughts swirl around his brain, painfully abrasive, like grains of sand whisked onto an eyeball by an eddy of wind. He stands up. He remains motionless for a moment, as though surprised at his own action and unsure what he might do next. The sound of his chair scraping back fills the room. Dr Ehrlich stands too and smiles up into Sam's face. A full foot taller, Sam suddenly feels more in control.

'Thank you, Doctor.' He extends his hand. Dr Ehrlich takes Sam's hand in both of his and holds on to it.

'Time, Brigadier,' he says softly. 'It will take time. There is only so much suffering the human psyche can stand before breaking. We are none of us made of iron, you know. Not even you.'

Sam glances at Dr Ehrlich's face, searches it, and sees the remark is meant kindly.

'No, of course not.'

'She needs to feel secure and safe,' continues the doctor. 'At the moment she feels frightened and ashamed.'

'Ashamed?'

'We are all ashamed of what we perceive as weakness, Brigadier Lawrence. I believe you understand this. She does not want to let you down, to admit she can't go on, to admit she needs help. It is important that she knows you love her – unconditionally.'

Sam shifts his weight from one leg to the other, tries to stand still and upright. Sweat is trickling down his back under his uniform, tickling, like a caress. He closes his eyes and pictures Anna's fingers tracing a gentle journey along his backbone.

'I'd like to see my wife now.' His voice is gruff and shaky.

Dr Ehrlich smiles. 'Yes of course,' he says. He moves swiftly to press a buzzer on his desk. After a moment, a neat young woman knocks and enters the room.

'Ah, Monika, please take Brigadier Lawrence to see Anna.'

The child stands motionless now, watching. She holds a small toy figure mid-air in each hand.

'Come, darling, we're going to see Mamma,' Sam says. Apparently so absorbed in her play just a moment ago, Eve instantly drops the toys on the table as if they are nothing to her, and walks towards her father, her eyes never leaving his face. He takes her hand. It feels soft and warm, like a small animal. Suddenly Sam feels like weeping. He follows the young woman to the door.

'Say goodbye to Doctor Ehrlich, Eve.'

'Goodbye, Doctor Ehrlich,' Eve responds solemnly. Doctor Ehrlich bends towards her as if bowing slightly.

'Goodbye, my dear. Your mamma will be very happy to see you.'

* * *

Sam concentrates on following Monika's clicking heels and neat stocking seams down the long grey corridors – a welcome distraction from the monotonous and dispiriting surroundings. He wonders how she manages to arrange the seams in such a straight line. A faintly medicinal smell penetrates his thoughts, carrying him back to his father's surgery years ago in Cumberland.

He tries to focus his mind on what Doctor Ehrlich said. Certainly, the man meant well and was highly regarded. But if you stripped away the psychological drivel, what was left? That Anna was mad? No, not that surely. But unhinged, perhaps. 'A breakdown'. What did that really mean? He had tried to care for her – God knows he wanted to. Of course he loves Anna 'unconditionally', as the doctor put it. Perhaps he doesn't go in for fancy words and romantic gestures, not as often as he should, but surely Anna knows how he feels?

'Daddy!' Eve hisses at Sam in a loud whisper. She pauses in her step and frowns up at him. With her eyes, Eve indicates his hand. He realises suddenly that he is crushing her small hand in his firm, rigid grip. He releases her and smiles down reassuringly.

Most of the doors they pass are shut, but one or two are open, revealing simple bedrooms inside. In one, a young woman sits motionless with her head clasped in her hands; in another, Sam glimpses an older woman, very thin, her face drawn and beaky, pacing back and forth.

Monika halts outside a closed door. She knocks on the door and enters immediately, without waiting for a response.

'Visitors for you, Anna.'

She is standing by the window. A faded, greyish cotton shift clings to her shoulders and hangs limply to her knees. Sam knows all of Anna's dresses; he doesn't recognise this one. How pale she is as she turns towards them. Her look of bewilderment changes slowly into a wan smile. Sam and Anna stand and stare at one another, frozen into inactivity. Eve has no such inhibitions. She pushes past Sam and runs to her mother, her arms outstretched.

'Mamma, Mamma!' she shouts. Anna crouches down, hugging Eve, kissing her, stroking her hair. She buries her face in the child's neck and breathes in deeply, as though trying to absorb her into her own body.

Monika has withdrawn. Sam leans against the doorframe, watching. He hears a strangulated sob, and realises to his alarm that it has come from him. Anna stands up and looks at him, her hands still clasping either side of Eve's head.

'Sam,' she says, 'Sam.'

In a moment he crosses the room and wraps his arms around her frail body, and holds her, holds her.

* * *

Later that evening, Eve is sleeping in the large bed in their hotel room, as dull and dreary as the hospital had been. Sam watches her unconscious, vulnerable form. A small, pathetic version of Anna, her curls dark against the white bed linen.

Eve had cried desperately when it was time to leave Anna. She had clung to Anna, her arms fixed around her mother's waist, hanging on like a limpet when he tried gently to draw her away.

At her bedtime he tries to cheer her up. He reads some of her favourite stories and tries to amuse her with her beloved 'Creepy Crawly' tickling games. She smiles, as if to please him, but remains largely silent and unresponsive.

'I want Mamma to be with us.'

'Soon, darling, she'll be home soon.'

Eve frowns at him. 'Why does she have to stay in the hospital?'

'Mamma's sick.'

'Then they should give her medicine to make her better,' Eve retorts without hesitation. 'Why don't they do that, those doctors?'

'Well, she's sick in a special way – not with anything like flu or measles, but she's been sad in her heart. And that's a kind of sickness too.'

Eve's face shows her struggle with this concept. A sudden look of panic enters her eyes. 'Mamma said Herr Eisen was sad in his heart – before he died.'

'Mamma's not going to die, sweetheart. But she has had some sadness.'

'Who's made her sad?' she asks accusingly. Her face clouds with anxiety. 'Is it me? Have I made Mamma sad?'

Sam shakes his head and holds her closer. 'No, Eve. It's not you, not at all.'

'Can't you make her happy, Daddy?'

'I am trying very hard. But the sad things happened to Mamma many years ago.'

'Before you got married?'

'Yes, before we even met.'

Eve's eyes wander around the room, as though searching for a solution. 'Maybe you could buy her something nice, Daddy? Or we could take her out for a picnic. Would that make her happy again?'

'It's a good idea – it certainly might help.'

The questions and answers follow round and round, exhausting them both. Sam suggests Eve draws a picture for Anna, to take to her the next day. She settles at the desk with her coloured pencils. Sam leans back in the chair and tries to relax. He can think of nothing but Anna.

Once, early in their relationship, before Ben was born, Sam had told her that sometimes he feared he was turning into his father, grim and sombre. Anna had surprised him by claiming that the very opposite was true.

'No, Sam. You are not like your father, from all you have told me about him. Not one bit. You take much more after Mother.'

'I see. You mean long skinny legs, and losing my marbles?'

'That's not fair, Sam – Mother still has many marbles. She remembers everything very well. Anyway, you know I didn't mean those things. I mean that you are an emotional man – you have so much love and affection to give, just like Mother. Only she hasn't had the chance to give it, and I think it's been the same with you.'

How could Anna have perceived this, when he himself had not? Her entry into his life is a continuing wonder to him. Her willingness to express her feelings, and her absolute expectation that he do the same, has changed his life, and sometimes takes his breath away. Yet, though she is so open and communicative in some ways, Sam always has a sense that there is something at the very centre of her being which she does not – which perhaps she *cannot* – share with him, even now. Perhaps it is always so. Perhaps no two people can ever expect to know everything about one another. We all select what thoughts, feelings and experiences to reveal, even to those closest to us.

Sam knows much about Anna and her former life; he knows about her great distress at having to separate from her family, about her marriage to Jakob and their flight to Palestine; he knows of the tragedy of Jakob's return to Austria. Anna has never uttered a word of criticism against Jakob, but Sam is aware that she felt loyalty rather than true love for him. Somehow Sam feels no jealousy of the poor devil. It is almost as though Jakob's role had been to bring Anna to Palestine for *him*, for the two of them to be together, although of course Jakob wouldn't have seen it that way. Before Anna's arrival in his life, Sam had given up all thought of children. Now there is the miracle not just of Anna, but of Ben and Eve too.

Eve finishes her picture and brings it to show him.

'That's beautiful, Eve darling. Mamma will love it. Tell me what's going on here.'

'That's you and Mamma, and that's me and Ben doing somersaults on the grass. And that's Emil chasing a butterfly. We're all having a picnic in the country. It's lovely and sunny. I did Mamma wearing her turquoise dress, 'cause it's your favourite and she looks so pretty in it, even though she wouldn't really wear a long dress for a picnic.'

Sam pulls her onto his lap.

'Shall I read you a bedtime story now?'

'Will you *tell* me a story, Daddy? Tell me a story about when you and Mamma met. I want the story about Mamma and the mice. Do a Mamma voice.'

It's an old favourite; she's heard it many times before. So Sam leans back in the armchair, cuddles her and begins.

'Long ago, when Mamma and I first met in the far-off land of Palestine, I thought she was the most beautiful lady I'd ever seen.'

'Was she like a princess?' Eve interrupts.

'Well, not the sort of princess with long golden hair and a crown, but she was a princess to me. We fell in love and after a while I asked her to marry me. I was so happy when she said yes. We came from different countries and had different ways. Mamma had grown up in Vienna and I had grown up in England. We didn't speak each other's language perfectly. We had to learn about one another.

'One evening we had been to the cinema to see a film, and when we came out and walked in the streets, Mamma said she was hungry. I asked her what she would like to eat and quick as a flash she replied "Mice!"

'At first I thought she was joking, but when I looked at her I saw she was deadly serious. I asked her where she could get mice to eat – I suppose I was playing for time. Mamma was getting a little impatient – she was hungry after all. She frowned and replied that we could buy them at any street stall.

'"And how are they cooked, these mice?" I asked. I was feeling a little worried about what my future wife was going to serve me up for dinner, I can tell you. I knew these foreigners had funny ways, but eating mice was going a bit far!'

Eve chuckles and snuggles in to Sam's chest.

'"Oh," Mamma replied, "they can be boiled, but I like them best roasted over a fire, with lots of butter on."

'Then Mamma led me to a stall in one of the little cobbled alleys, where a man was roasting great heaps of corn on the cob over a fire in a brazier.

'"There you are," Mamma said triumphantly, "*Mais!*"

'What an idiot I felt! Of course, then I realised the German word for maize sounded exactly like "mice". It was a great relief, believe me, to know we weren't going to have to eat roast mouse and gravy for dinner every Sunday.'

'Silly Daddy,' says Eve sleepily, and allows him to lift her into the bed.

Later that night she wakes sobbing, as if from a nightmare, her thin chest convulsing. Sam lifts her out, and holding her to him he realises she is wet. He rings the desk staff, and they bring fresh sheets willingly, but he insists on dealing with the bed himself. He washes and changes Eve, and eventually she settles back to sleep.

He can't remember the last time she wet the bed. Not for years, not since she was a toddler. Enough, enough – this can't go on. Anna must get better. He must make sure Anna gets better. Why on earth was she wearing that drab, colourless garment? It totally swamped her sweet body. He thinks of her body with great longing. Anna was so particular about her appearance. He decides to go shopping with Eve and return to the hospital the next day with some new outfits for Anna. That will make her feel better, and Eve would like it too. And surely there must be a hairdresser in that dreadful place too? He would see to it the following day. He kisses Eve's forehead gently, determined to sort everything out – and to take Anna home.

* * *

Anna presses her knees together, the way Esther had always instructed her when they were girls, her feet in the new navy blue high-heels tucked neatly to the left. The skirt rides up a little as she sits. She tugs absently at it to smooth the hem. It's a good colour for her. How clever of Sam to know her taste so well. How many other husbands could choose perfect clothes for their wives in just the right size? Her hand caresses the silky fabric of the sleeve of her new blouse. The trilling notes of a blackbird outside in the garden drift in through the open window.

Dr Ehrlich looks at Anna with his patient, gentle smile, and waits. Do they teach patience as part of psychiatry training, she wonders. Would he simply sit and wait quietly for the entire morning if she does not speak? Some patients fall in love with their doctors – she knows that. Anna is not in love with Dr Ehrlich, but she does trust him. It is time. Today she has to speak – she knows it. This is not a game they are playing. Without honesty there can be no progress, no recovery. Sam needs her to get better; he is close to breaking down himself. The children need their mother – and not a sick mother absorbed in herself.

Take the worries, the painful memories, one by one from your heart, Dr Ehrlich says, and put them on a shelf. Do not hold them inside, to fester and torture you. High on the shelf, where you can see them, take them down and examine them when you wish – but then put them back where they belong, on the outside, at a distance.

Anna has already told him much: about their flight to Palestine, their lives there, hers and Jakob's, of Jakob's return to Austria, his death, and her remorse and guilt. He knows too of her meeting with Sam, how he restored her with his persistent and insistent love, how she came to love him as no other man in her life. She has talked of the difficult time in England following their marriage, and the even more difficult move to Germany, with its consequent adjustments and trials. She has told him more of herself than she has told anyone else, other than Sam.

Yet a secret remains, a malevolent voice at the very core of her, proclaiming her badness, a secret she has not revealed. She knows it is there, and Dr Ehrlich knows it too. Is there nothing she can keep from him? Perhaps there is not; he wields his benign power over her again and again.

Anna closes her eyes, and pictures, as so often before, that day of incongruous sunshine and beauty in the Vienna Woods, when she told Jakob of her pregnancy. And as one image follows another in her mind, she opens her mouth and begins to speak. Once she begins, she cannot stop. She tells Dr Ehrlich everything, almost everything. He listens silently, only nodding his head faintly in encouragement. At last she pauses. There, it is done; she has told him. He gathers himself straighter in the chair. His eyes burn into hers.

'And the child?' says Dr Ehrlich. 'Tell me about the child. What happened to your child? Please do not be afraid. Tell me, and then, more importantly, you must tell Sam.'

He is without mercy. Nothing can be withheld.

Chapter 11

20th April 1957, München-Gladbach
My Dear Esther,

I hope you and Reuben and all the family are well and flourishing.

It may surprise you to receive this letter from me, but the time has come when I must communicate with you, if only for Anna's sake. I could not do otherwise. Forgive me that my first direct communication with you has to be one of such length and emotional intensity. When you read this letter I hope you will understand.

From the earliest time of our marriage, I have been puzzled by Anna's relationship with you. When she talked of your childhood and early adulthood together, it was clear to me that you were the most beloved, the most special of sisters – that she had always regarded you as her guide, her mentor and her supporter, as well as her very dear companion. Of course, I know that she also feels great fondness for Margaret, but it seemed to me that there was a particular bond between the two of you, which went beyond sisterly affection.

Why then, I have wondered all these years, was she so

reluctant to maintain meaningful contact with you? By contrast, Margaret and her family have visited us here in Germany, and Anna and Ben have been to stay with her in England, especially during the time Artur was living there. There is a regular exchange of letters between Anna and Margaret, and occasional telephone calls. All as you would expect between sisters, particularly those who have been separated for many years by cruel circumstances.

Yet, despite all my urging and encouragement, she has not wanted to invite you here, nor to visit you in Boston. Letters in both directions have been relatively few, and she has told me little of their contents. I couldn't help noticing that each of your letters to Anna left her deeply agitated for some time afterwards. The only time I remember her telephoning you was when Artur was dying. I have always known that there are aspects of her life that Anna has felt unable to share with me – with anyone, except perhaps her dear friend Yael in Haifa – and I have sensed that to pressure her too much could have greatly distressed her, and perhaps driven her further from me.

In the last year or two, Anna's vulnerability and emotional frailty has gradually overcome her. Things came to a head a few months ago when she had a complete breakdown and spent some time as an in-patient in a German clinic some distance from here. As you can imagine, this was greatly upsetting, not just for me, but for Eve too. At least Ben is at school in England, and so has escaped much of the trauma.

Part of the therapeutic process recommended by her excellent psychiatrist was that Anna should try to share the distressing events in her life, which she has kept hidden all these years, and which have been eating away at her. So, Esther, I am glad to say that in the past few weeks I have learned the full truth: of the birth of Anna's baby in Switzerland, and of how you and Reuben so willingly took

174

the child with you to America, adopted him and raised him as your own.

Please understand that I am not judging Anna and will never judge her – though, God knows, she judges herself harshly. Anna is the woman I love beyond words, and I will always do so, no matter what emerges from her past. My only concern now is to restore her health and sense of equilibrium, and to do that I believe she must acknowledge the events of the past openly – and get to know Shimon. This may be a disturbing prospect for you and Reuben, having brought Shimon up as your own child from his earliest babyhood. In that sense you will always be his mother and father, and Anna knows that.

Really, it should be Anna who writes to you and not me, but although she is so much better than a few months ago, she is still very fragile. She is full of fear, guilt and shame, though no one has given her cause to feel these emotions – they are all her own. With encouragement from myself, and from Yael, who is due to visit us shortly, and from yourself, Esther – if you can bring yourself to communicate it – I hope that she will not only write to you herself, but that she will agree to visit you and Shimon in time. So I beg you to write to Anna, in the knowledge that I know all about Shimon and that she has nothing to hide and nothing to fear. Please try to reassure her and to tell her about the child she has missed so desperately and yearned for these nearly twenty years, as she has missed and yearned for you, her sister.

> *With most sincere regards to you and your family,*
>
> *Sam*

May 29th 1957, Boston

My dear Sam,

I cannot tell you how much joy your letter brought me. As soon as I saw the envelope, I knew somehow that it was from you. My hands trembled so much it took me some time before I could open it. I have waited for that moment for over twenty years. Over the last year, when I heard nothing from Anna, I have been almost mad with worry. In the past, when Anna did write one of her rare letters, she told me very little of herself, but she did tell me what a warm, affectionate and sensitive man you are – and through reading your letter, I have seen that for myself.

At that terrible time so many years ago, Anna was desperate. It is her nature to be secretive – a legacy perhaps of having to suppress so much of ourselves as children, due to our mother's illness. Her feelings of shame and guilt pushed her even deeper within herself. Perhaps we were wrong, but it seemed that the only solution at that time, was for us to take the child. No one else was allowed to know, not even our parents or Margaret. Of course, I have never regretted it – Reuben and I love Shimon like a son, and Marta and Leila regard him as their brother.

But the cost for Anna has been unimaginable. She felt she had betrayed Jakob, and had to agree to his terms. He believed Anna would forget her pain when they had children of their own. Of course, that did not happen, and in any case, no mother can forget her first-born child, regardless of her love for children who come after. Anna insisted that no one speak (or write) of the past. She could not bear to know anything of Shimon except that he was well – and we had to respect her wishes.

Reuben and I have always told Shimon the truth about his

birth. We told him that we love him and that nothing will ever change that, but that Anna – his mother – loves him too. We always hoped that Shimon would come to know his mother one day. It is what Shimon wants too.

I will write to Anna to tell her all this. How lucky she is to have you, Sam.

With loving greetings from all of us,
Esther

June 12th 1957, Boston

Liebste Anna,

How are you, meine Liebste, my dearest? Your lovely Sam has written to me and told me about your illness. I hope that you are growing stronger and happier day by day. I am so sorry to know how you have suffered, and so sad not to have been with you and put my arms around you. But, Anna, I am glad – yes glad – if it means that you can at last share your secrets and your pain with those who love you. All these years you have kept it inside you. Why, Anna? You think others will condemn you, but it is not so. Now Sam knows what happened to you – and does he love you any less? Not one bit.

Now at last, I feel free to tell you of your beautiful son, your Shimon, who has been nothing more than a shadow at your shoulder for so long. He is determined to emerge from the shadows, let me tell you, he will not be kept hidden any longer! First of all, he was a darling baby and a sweet little boy, full of fun and curiosity, full of love and affection. As soon as he was old enough to understand the words, I told him about you, Anna. I told him he was extra lucky, that he had two Mammas – one was his Auntie Esther Mamma, who cared for him and loved him from day to day. The other was his Anna Mamma, who gave birth to him and loved him with

177

all her heart, even though she had to give him up and flee to Palestine.

Shimon asked many questions. He wanted me to tell him all about you. When he asked why you had not come to visit him, I explained that you were afraid that he would blame you; that you were afraid he might hate you. He always answered that he would never hate you, but he came to call you his 'Frightened Mamma'.

Do not worry that Shimon's life has been one of sadness – it has not. He has had a happy and full childhood, surrounded by family who love and admire him. Marta and Leila worship their big brother, but of course he has another brother and sister who have never met him. Shimon has grown into a fine, intelligent, perceptive and secure young man. You may wonder what he has inherited from you, and what from his father. There is no doubt he has inherited Otto's good looks. That is where any likeness to his father ends. Girls hover round Shimon, but he is not vain and never takes advantage of his attractiveness. He is kind and caring, with a strong sense of right and wrong. This comes from you, I think. He has a riotous sense of humour. This too comes from the Anna I remember. He also has a quick temper and expresses his outrage without hesitation or inhibition. Where does this come from, Anna …?

Liebste, we all long to see you. Shimon is desperate to meet you. Please come to visit us. We have a nice home here in Boston, and plenty of room. Please come soon. There is nothing to stop you now, no reason to hold back.

Reuben, Marta, Leila, and above all, Shimon, send you much love –

as I do, my dearest sister. I long to embrace you,

Your Esther

Chapter 12

Düsseldorf 1957

Anna sits at her dressing table, fiddling aimlessly with jars and bottles. All day she has been unable to sit still. Now, as the time draws near, she can barely contain her excitement – and her apprehension. It is nearly fifteen years since she has seen Yael. Will they be able to re-create the closeness, the friendship they once had? Certainly, their regular long letters over the years have kept alive a depth of warmth and intimacy she has never again found with anyone new. Clutching Yael's most recent letter, she re-reads it for the hundredth time. Just thinking about Yael, and Rachel, and the times they shared in Haifa, brings a heaviness, an aching to her throat.

She knows Sam has written to Yael, as he wrote to Esther. She does not blame him for that – it was an act of concern, not one of intrusion. In fact, it brings her great peace to reflect that three of the most precious people in her life now know everything important there is to know. The relief of the confessional; she has often envied Catholics that comfort. Why did she deny the truth to Sam for so long? It seems an impenetrable question. Sam has never reproached her, but he did ask if she could not have trusted him. She always trusts him absolutely, Anna tells him, and without reservation. It is *herself* she did not trust. But only now, slowly, she is learning to trust herself too, and even to like herself, just a little.

And Rachel, what of her? What will she be like now, *who* will she be? Anna pictures herself back in the warm courtyard with the beloved little girl, whose innocent charm and physical presence comforted her so much all those years ago. Rachel had been a small child at that time, younger than Eve is now. Now Rachel is a young woman of nineteen. Will she even remember Anna?

Sam opens the door quietly, and puts his head round tentatively.

'Anna, we should be going. Are you ready?'

She turns to him and smiles. Immediately his face relaxes. These days he often looks tense, she notices, and tired. His face is drawn; he seems to have lost weight. He is always dismissive of his own health. A lengthy bout of flu has sapped his strength recently.

'Fit as a flea,' he assured her, as she urged him to rest in bed a little longer. Yet the doctor is concerned for his chest, and reminds her sternly that Sam is no longer a young man. They should plan a holiday together, perhaps without the children.

Sam bends down and puts his arms around her. She twists round to look at him.

'I'm coming. Do I look all right? Look at the shadows under my eyes. Will she think I look much older?'

'Of course not. You look lovely as always. She'll just be glad to see you. Time hasn't stood still for any of us.'

'You think it's the right decision to leave the children with Della?'

'I do. The entire family party could be a bit overwhelming. Gives you two a chance to talk together a bit on the journey back too.'

* * *

Normally Anna hates airports and train stations, the scene of so many sad partings and departures, but this is different – a welcome arrival. The information board indicates Yael's plane is on time. Anna's stomach squirms and contracts. The gates open and passengers begin walking through with their luggage, some alone, others in couples or groups, their eyes anxiously scanning the waiting faces. For a moment Anna can scarcely breathe. Sam strokes her shoulder. Suddenly there she is: a short, stocky figure with dark, olive complexion, her broad face enlivened by a huge smile. The blackness of her hair is streaked with grey, and the cut more sophisticated than formerly, but otherwise she is hardly altered. It is her, Yael.

They stop just inches apart, as if separated by an invisible screen. They embrace for a long time, both crying, and the long years turn around them, swooping like swallows about to leave. Anna takes a step back to allow Sam to move forward. He bends his height to hug Yael. Only then does Anna's attention transfer to a striking young woman, standing like a shadow, deliberately in the background. Alert eyes, so like Yael's, study Anna with great interest. A subtle look of Yael, yet quite a different version, like variations of fruit from the same tree. She is slender, and taller than both her mother and Anna. Long dark hair frames her face. High cheekbones sweep down towards a heart-shaped mouth and small pointed chin. Her mouth tilts slightly higher on the right side when she smiles, just like Yael's.

'Rachel …?'

'Anna! I am so happy to see you.'

They embrace, with more tears.

'Do you really remember me, Rachel?'

'Of course I do. You are just as I remember you. I have pictured you so often. You were one of the most special people of my childhood. How could I forget you? But I'm afraid *I* must have changed a lot.'

'You have become quite beautiful.'

On the drive back from Düsseldorf airport, Rachel sits in the front seat next to Sam. He takes pleasure in pointing out the sights to her, explaining points of history: the Oberkasseler bridge over the Rhine, Carlsplatz, Kaiserswerth, Königsallee, the Altstadt and Rathaus. Rachel exclaims with genuine interest at each. She asks lots of questions, delighting Sam with her curiosity. Anna and Yael, meanwhile, sit in the back of the car together, hands clutched, knees pointing inwards, scarcely taking their eyes off each other, just talking, talking, and during the hour of the drive, fifteen years shrivel up and drift away, leaving their friendship to return.

At home Ben and Eve run out into the drive to meet their visitors.

'Oh my goodness!' exclaims Yael, hugging Ben first. 'Just look at you two! Such a fine, handsome young man. But I thought you went to school in England?'

'I do, but it's the holidays at the moment. I'm home for eight weeks.'

'Eight weeks! But that's wonderful, Ben. What good times we will all have. And now, who is this lovely young lady? She looks just like her mamma.'

Eve smiles shyly and looks from Yael to Anna. She allows Yael to hug her, but her eyes are fixed firmly, admiringly, on Rachel.

'Oh, I think you like my Rachel, don't you, Eve?' asks Yael.

'Yes I do. Would you like to see my cat?' she asks, turning her face to Rachel. 'She's called Emil.'

'Emil? What a good name. I would like to see her very much.'

Eve stretches out her hand to Rachel and leads her into the house.

'Ben,' Anna calls softly, 'keep an eye on them and see that Eve isn't bothering Rachel.'

He raises his eyebrows slightly, gives a knowing nod, and strides after his sister, pleased with the adult responsibility he has been given.

Yael links her arm firmly with Anna's. She looks penetratingly into her friend's face.

'Lovely children,' she says. 'Both of them, lovely. But, Anna, *you* have become so thin, and your face ...'

'Don't say it, I know. My face looks like an old woman's.'

'No, not at all. You don't look old, dear Anna, you look ... *lost*. Like a lost child. We must help you find yourself again.'

'Yes, that search is a project Sam has taken on too.'

Yael extends her other arm to hold Sam too, and walks into the house with them both.

'Then let us begin immediately!'

* * *

'I can't believe you would leave Israel. It's impossible to imagine you living anywhere else.' Anna shakes her head, frowning. Della places a large tureen of soup in front of her.

'Rachel and I have been considering emigrating for a long time. Re-emigrating, in my case. You know how things were when I left Russia. We *had* to leave. What choice did we have? But it was always David who was the true Zionist – I was a pragmatist, just trying to save my skin, and my parents. So much has happened since then, to me and my life, but to Israel too. The dream of Zion has gone sour for me. All that idealism. A Shangri-La for the Jews – that was the idea. But at what price? Haven't we Jews seen enough of cruelty and victimisation, of one group of people pitted against another?'

'Israel is the only home I have ever known,' puts in Rachel. 'I am a Sabra. I *do* find it hard to imagine living anywhere else. If we remain, I would soon have to join the military and fight for my country. Of course, if there were truly a threat to Israel, an outside enemy—'

183

'Like Nasser perhaps?' interrupts Sam, circling the table with a bottle of wine. 'Now the Egyptians have taken full control of the Suez Canal, God knows what their next move might be.'

'Perhaps. I'm not sure how much of a threat the Arab world really is. If it were, I guess it would justify joining forces with my comrades to defend Israel. But we can ask ourselves, who *are* most of the people defined as enemies? Our own neighbours. Those who have lived in Palestine for generations and whom we, Israelis, have forced from their homes and villages, and into new ghettos. And as if it isn't enough to discriminate against Arabs, increasingly there are divisions among Jews themselves: lighter skins against darker skins, Ashkenazim against Sephardim, pre-war Sabras against Holocaust survivors. You know what Ben-Gurion called them? "Human dust".'

'Pah! Shameful!' says Anna.

'Look, we don't want to talk politics with you all evening – we do enough of that at home,' says Yael. 'The fact is Rachel has been offered a place at MIT, and I've decided to live in America too – at least while she is studying there.'

'MIT? But that's wonderful, Rachel!'

'Brains as well as beauty,' says Sam.

'That's right,' says Yael, looking at Rachel with pride. 'I'm not sure where the brains come from – must be from her father. Not from me, that's for sure.'

Anna watches them: their closeness and ease, laughing together, the strong bond between Yael and her daughter.

'Total nonsense, Yael. You always were sharp as a needle.'

Conversation pauses for a moment. Yael and Rachel exchange meaningful looks.

'Another reason for us both to go to America,' says Yael, 'is for me to join … a … friend, who lives there.'

'A *friend*?' Anna laughs delightedly. She passes a bowl of salad round the table. 'Who is he? I assume it is a "he"? Come on, out with it!'

'Leave the poor woman alone,' says Sam. 'Can't she have any secrets?'

'Absolutely none! And certainly not from me. We are none of us allowed secrets any more. Revealing all is so liberating!'

'How much wine have you had, darling?' asks Sam.

'Of course I don't mind telling you,' says Yael. 'He's called Hal Stonehouse and I've known him about a year, since he first came to Haifa. He was on a "fact-finding mission", looking at legal systems in different countries. He's a lawyer, and he's been divorced for about five years. That's about it. He needed somewhere to stay, and one of his colleagues recommended my house. You wouldn't believe how smart it is now: a high-class guesthouse! Well of course, over time we talked ... and talked ... and talked. I showed him round a bit and introduced him to one or two people. To cut a long story short, we became good friends—'

'Just good friends?'

'Anna!'

Yael smiles.

'Hal's a really nice man, Anna,' Rachel adds. 'I can quite understand what Mum sees in him.'

'Oh, thank you for that vote of confidence from my daughter! We have to have the approval of our children for our relationships, don't we? Anyway, we are *very* good friends. Since that first trip, he's made three more visits to Israel, and he has invited me – *us*—' Yael looks at Rachel '—to stay with him in Boston.'

'Boston! But that's where my sister Esther lives!'

'I know, Anna. There's more than one reason for you to visit Boston now – no excuse not to.'

Anna's hands clutch her face. She looks down at her lap, then turns towards Sam. He reaches his hand across the table to her.

* * *

185

Rachel is exploring the city centre. She says she needs some new clothes for America. To Eve's great joy, Rachel has offered to take her along too, promising a girls' shopping expedition, perhaps with a visit to a coffee house for a drink and a cake. Anna is delighted to see the blossoming relationship between them. It reminds her of her own special attachment to the young child Rachel was years ago. Yet the memory is overlaid with a sense of some sadness and regret. If only her times with Eve could be as uncomplicated. She resolves to do more with her herself, to devise some special times for the two of them together.

It is a fine early summer's day. Anna and Yael walk to the Rhine and stroll arm in arm along the riverside promenade. Across the great, heaving expanse, small waves glitter silvery in the warm sunshine. They find a bench facing the water and sit down side by side, the growing heat of the sun penetrating their heads.

'Mmm, we could almost be back in Haifa.'

'You know, Anna, when Sam first used to call at the house for you, I thought he was charming, so handsome and so courteous – and there was no doubt about your feelings for each other – but sometimes I used to wonder how compatible you two were. There was Sam, an English army officer, and you, brought up in Jewish intellectual and socialist circles in Vienna. It was as if you occupied opposite poles of the social and political spectrum.'

'Oh? Did you think Sam was a reactionary old stick-in-the-mud?'

'Well, maybe not reactionary exactly, but he did present himself as … conventional.'

'I think that was part of the attraction. It was almost like marrying a kindly uncle – but a sexy one! I felt so safe with him.'

'What an idea! A sexy, kindly uncle! Anyway, I was quite wrong to think there was such a gulf between your beliefs. Sam's attitudes are actually much more radical and liberal than I realised. It's just that he disguises them with that traditional English gentleman persona.'

'No, you're right. Actually, Sam is much more socially sympathetic than me. I'm the reactionary, hard-bitten one.'

'You're not hard-bitten – just a realist, like me.'

'Sam always believes in the basic good of human beings. It's a wonderful quality: what makes him so special. It colours his whole view of the world. I'm not sure I share his faith in human-kind or human kindness.'

'Perhaps you've had more evidence to the contrary. That's bound to change you, though I know Sam hadn't lived a life protected by cotton wool either. You were still young and innocent those first days in Palestine. You had suffered, but you had no idea how that pain would fester in you over the years to come. But, Anna, maybe you should try to take a lesson from him, and believe in the positive, at least until proven wrong.'

They sit quietly holding hands and contemplating the river. Barges slide past, water churning in their wake. On the near side of the river, the barges sit deep in the water, laden with coal, heading north and east towards Rotterdam.

Yael draws Anna's hand up to her chest.

'So, Anna, when are you going to America? When are you going to see your Shimon?'

The peace of the moment is broken. Anna's breath comes in short gasps. She withdraws her hand and picks absently at the skin around her nails.

'I'm so afraid, Yael. What if he hates me – and who could blame him after what I did to him? Will he ever understand? And what of the children – how can I leave Ben and Eve to go so far away? And … what will I tell them?'

'What if, what if! Yes, there are some aspects you will have to think about. What to tell the children, sure, you need to consider that carefully. But leaving them for a few weeks is no problem. You have Della, and they are not babies any more. They will have school, all the usual routines – they'll be fine. Shimon – your son – your child? You're so hard on yourself, Anna. Of course he won't hate you; Esther has told you he's longing to meet you. Be honest with yourself – you are just making excuses.'

Anna is silent. She stares at the dark water of the river striving constantly for the sea.

'You're right. I must go. Will you come too, Yael? Will you come with me?'

Chapter 13

Boston 1958

Anna's entire body trembles out of control, as though attempting to drill her into the floor. The immigration officer frowns at her passport and visa. Without moving his head, he switches his gaze to her, pale eyes peering over the top of his wire-rimmed glasses.

'Is this a vacation visit, Ma'am?' His voice drifts faintly through thickened air.

She concentrates all her energy on not passing out, on staying upright, on continuing to breathe. Perspiration glazes her forehead and prickles her neck, yet she feels cold as a North Sea mist.

'Ma'am? Are you OK? I said, are you visiting the US for vacation purposes?'

Anna tries to focus on the question. She raises her head and blinks up at the man. He is large, heavy, with a pitted red face. Thick flesh bulges over the collar of his uniform. He regards her with a mixture of puzzlement and suspicion.

'I am visiting my son. My son and my sister.'

'OK!' His tone is ironic, as if to say 'now we're getting somewhere!' 'So he is working over here, right? Your son?'

'He lives here. He is an American citizen. And my sister is too. I haven't seen him for twenty-three years.'

'Twenty-three years?' The man whistles through his teeth and regards her with disbelief, as though no one but the most hardened criminal could fail to visit a son for such a lengthy period.

'How long do you plan to visit?'

'Four weeks.'

Another long hard stare, and he waves her through.

'I will meet you on my own,' Esther had written. *'Reuben thought he and the girls should stay home so that you and I can get over all our tears and "histrionics", as he calls them, beforehand. Shimon too will wait at home to see you. We'll make sure you have some special private time together. He is so excited he hardly knows what to do with himself.'*

Anna moves forward slowly along a long corridor, staggering under the weight of her suitcase, other more rapid passengers passing her.

'Do you really need to take so much?' Sam had queried.

'Yes, I do!' Anna had retorted. 'Esther said it could be very warm or very cool in Boston at this time of year. Anyway, half of it is presents: for the whole family, and for Yael and Rachel too. I could hardly go empty-handed.'

At the end of the passage, wide double doors swing open automatically, as if to embrace her, as she approaches. She squints into the sudden light of a spacious waiting hall beyond. Small groups of people are hugging or talking animatedly; others stand or stroll, waiting to be reunited with travellers who have yet to emerge. Anna puts her suitcase on the floor and rubs her palm, red and indented from the weight. Her head is throbbing; she stands swaying. The whole scene is moving in and out of focus. She cannot make out individuals, cannot see faces. A shape looms, dark against the fluorescent brightness.

'Anna.'

She turns. 'Esther.'

So here she is, her sister. They embrace, shutting out their surroundings, shutting out more than twenty years, oblivious to all around them. Two middle-aged women of similar height and build, one auburn-haired, the other dark, clutching each other like statues in an intricate pose of intertwined limbs. They stand back and look at one another's tear-streaked faces. They laugh, they cry, they hug again. For a long time, they cannot speak. At last, the sobs, the laughter, the gulps for air subside.

'Oh my God, Anna. What have you done to my face?'

'What do you care? You can't even see it.'

'I see yours. Mine must be worse: red nose, rivers of mascara, smudged lipstick. What a sight, huh?' Esther strokes Anna's cheek tenderly. 'So many years, so long we haven't seen you, my little sister.'

'Here I am.'

'Here you are. Let's go get some coffee before we go home.'

* * *

She stands momentarily on the terrace. The sun has warmed the pinkish flagstones. They radiate a gentle heat upwards; she feels it enveloping her trembling legs. A gravel pathway snakes from the terrace, weaving among neatly pruned shrubs and trees, around a small pond, and disappears into the hidden rear of the garden. Someone cares for this garden, Anna thinks. Is it Reuben? How sad that she doesn't really know him. Sam would be so interested in the garden. She must try to remember what she sees, memorise the names of the plants and trees to tell him all about it.

She breathes deeply, steps onto the path and walks, slowly. She pauses at the pond and gazes at it for a moment, wondering if there are frogs, or fish. How Eve would love to see frogs. Concentrating simply on walking steadily, Anna pursues the winding track of the path. The trees are just beginning to take on the yellows, reds and browns of autumn. Boston is famous for its autumn colours, Sam had told her, especially the maples. He had shown her a picture of a maple tree, with a drawing of its leaf, so that she would recognise it. A light haze of dew still clings to the grass in the shaded patches between the bushes.

She emerges into an open area, lit by a dazzle of slanting sunlight, and for a moment she is blinded. Using her hand to shield her eyes, Anna walks forward. The path runs out and she steps onto the damp lawn and looks around. A figure is seated on a wooden bench almost hidden in a semi-circle of small overhanging maple trees, as if in a fairy arbour. As she approaches he watches her and stands, very still and straight, his arms by his sides, only his fingers moving. He takes a step towards her. Anna pauses. Her legs turn to liquid and begin to give way. He surges forward and wraps his arms around her, supporting her slight weight.

'Shimon,' she whispers, 'my boy.'

'Mamma.'

He leads her to the bench, one arm around her, almost lifting her. They embrace, and cry, embrace again, laugh and cry. She pushes him back and holds him at arm's length.

'Let me look at you.'

He is tall, not as tall as Sam, but nearly six feet perhaps. Broad-shouldered, slim-waisted, slender-limbed. His skin has the smooth colour and texture of melted caramel, flawless. Otto's skin, she realises with shock. She has rarely thought of Otto over all these years. He is an irrelevance, except in leaving his seed behind, and so dictating the path of her life. Now something of his physicality returns to her, his beauty.

But this is not Otto; she feels nothing for *that man*. This is Shimon – her son – and he is beautiful. His hair falls in soft, black curls around his ears; small ears, like Eve's. His eyes are soft hazel brown, with flecks of green and gold. They have a slight downward slant, giving him an air of sadness, counteracted by laughter lines in each corner. For a moment she thinks she sees something of Sam in the shape of his eyes. But no, how foolish. She has to remind herself that there is no blood connection between them; Sam is not his father, of course. Both Sam and Ben have blue eyes: clear, pale, piercing blue. Shimon's eyes have a dark ring around the irises, as do her own, emphasising the colour. A strong jawline, speckled with black stubble. She strokes his chin.

'Sorry, I'm rough. I did shave, honest.' He laughs.

She laughs too. 'You are perfect.'

They continue their exploration of one another, eager as children, exclaiming over the similarity of their noses, the difference in the shape of their hands.

'See how your fingers taper,' he says. 'Mine are blunt, like Gramps's. He always said he had the solid hands of a peasant.'

She realises with sadness that he is talking about Artur, her own father. Artur, whose life ended here in America, and who never knew that his eldest grandson was not Esther's child but hers, Anna's.

'Shimon, beloved Shimon,' she whispers as she strokes him. 'It is as though I have been given my baby back … no, not just that, it is as though I have been given my *soul* back. I feel complete at last.'

'Me too, kind of.' He looks at her a little shyly.

'You too?' she says. 'But you have had Esther for your mother, Esther and Reuben – your lovely family always here for you. I never imagined you would even think of me.'

'I *do* have Mom and Dad, and a wonderful family. 'Course I'll always love them. But … sometimes I felt there was a … nothingness inside, a … a vacuum or a hollow that could never be filled. From the time I was old enough to understand, I was told … I knew I had another mother. I guess this sounds crazy, doesn't it? Meeting you, it's as if a big weight has been lifted off me. I needed to know … I needed to know *you*, for my own identity, what makes me *me*.'

* * *

The weeks pass with frightening speed. Over twenty years of family interactions are compressed into a month. Anna reacquaints herself with Reuben, a mild, quiet, intellectual man – Esther was always the noisy one. She begins to get to know her nieces, Marta and Leila. So many echoes of former times. As Anna watches the girls, it is sometimes almost as though she is observing a film of herself and Esther when younger. Above all, she spends time with Shimon, answering questions she had never allowed herself to consider before, exploring with him half a lifetime of painful emotions.

For Esther and Anna, it is not so difficult. The foundation of their relationship is so strong, and established so early, that it endures the strains and traumas of the past. Somehow they pick up where they left off, the intervening years quickly fading. Theirs is the relationship of close siblings, with all the ups and downs of such a bond. Just like when they were teenagers, Esther sometimes sees it as her role, as older sister, to advise, protect, and even control Anna. Like when they were teenagers too, Anna sometimes resents what she regards as her sister's bossiness. On one occasion they go walking together in the Arnold Arboretum. When Shimon arrives in his car later on to pick them up from an agreed spot just outside the park, he finds them standing on opposite street corners, pointedly ignoring each other. As soon as they get into the back, one each side of the car, they start bickering furiously about the misdeeds of the other.

'She thinks just because she's the eldest, she can tell me what to do! Does she think I'm still a child …?' rages Anna.

'She always did think she knew best – she won't listen to my suggestions. Haven't I lived in this city twenty years? Don't you think I know where a good eating joint is?' retorts Esther.

'Hey, girls, girls!' says Shimon, laughing at them. 'What is this? Are you two returning to your childhood, or what?'

They look at one another and collapse giggling into each other's arms.

* * *

Yael and Rachel have already visited Esther and her family on several occasions before Anna's arrival. Yael and Esther, both strong women and neither reticent about speaking their mind, instinctively like each other; they are drawn into an instant friendship. They also have a shared common interest that holds them together: Anna.

A further complication adds to the complex melting pot of family relationships; no one can fail to notice an immediate magnetism between Rachel and Shimon. Shimon, studying for his doctorate at Harvard, is ideally placed to act as Rachel's guide to Boston and its universities. He does not resist this opportunity. They enjoy one another's company intellectually and in time romantically too, the two of them soon becoming inseparable.

Towards the end of Anna's stay, Esther and Reuben arrange a special dinner for her. Marta and Leila are having a sleepover with friends, but Yael and Rachel are invited for the evening. Anna is aware that Shimon's attraction to Rachel deflects some of the intensity of their own burgeoning mother–son relationship. She feels no jealousy; it seems natural, strengthening her maternal feelings towards Shimon, towards both of them. She notices Esther and Yael watching Shimon and Rachel too. Anna, Esther and Yael: a convoluted triumvirate of mothers.

Tension starts to build during the meal. Anna senses that Esther is leading up to some sort of climax.

'So, Anna,' says Esther, as they relax over coffee, 'only three more days in Boston and you're back to Germany.'

'You don't need to remind me. I don't know what to feel about it – torn between joy at seeing Sam and the children again, and despair at leaving all of you.'

'All the more reason to plan another visit, maybe with all the family next time?' suggests Reuben.

Esther's fingers drum the table. 'But I guess the next step is for Shimon to travel out to see you all, right? Maybe in the Christmas vacation?'

'Come on, Esther, no need to put the pressure on,' says Reuben. 'Anna may need time to talk it over with Sam first.'

'What's to talk over? Sam's such a warm and friendly guy, he'll be happy with anything that makes Anna happy.'

'Sam would be very welcoming to Shimon, I'm quite sure, from all I know of him,' adds Yael, looking carefully at Anna.

'It's not as simple as that. I don't see Sam as the problem,' Anna says slowly.

'Problem? Is there a problem? Am I a problem, Anna?' Shimon asks.

'Of course you are not a problem, darling Shimon …'

'But …?'

'I would like nothing more than to introduce you to all of my family, for you to become a part of *us*, as well as of Esther and Reuben's family …'

'I feel another "but" coming on.' Shimon looks at her with sombre eyes, a muscle in his temple and another in his jaw twitching alternately.

Yael stands up. She steps behind Anna's chair and hugs her shoulders, nestling her cheek against her friend's.

'I think we should leave you to talk this through in peace, Anna. Come on, Rachel, we'd better go home.'

'No, you stay, Yael, and Rachel too. I need you all to understand.'

Anna looks at the five faces around the table, all sympathetic and tender, but despite that she feels besieged.

'I've been thinking about this for some time. Of course Sam would welcome Shimon with open arms. As you say, Esther, he wants nothing more or less than for me to be happy – and stable. He knows all about you, Shimon, and how important you are to me. But Ben and Eve are a different matter. They are still very young; they know nothing about Shimon. How could they understand that their mother had a baby, a baby they know nothing about, and that she *gave him away*? How could I explain it to them, when I have not admitted it, even to myself, for all these years?' Anna covers her face with her hands.

'Anna, you should not have to struggle with this in front of all of us. It is too painful,' says Reuben quietly.

'What, should she keep the pain hidden again? Have another breakdown?' Esther retorts. 'Of course she should speak about it. What are you saying, *Liebling*? You don't want Shimon to come over and meet the children?'

Anna looks at Shimon, his young face drawn and agonised. She longs to run to him, hug him, rock him, take away the sadness.

'No of course I'm not saying that. I'm saying I don't think Ben and Eve are ready for all the information – not yet. In some years, maybe. But just now they are too young to understand. It could unsettle them, frighten them even.'

'I wonder if you underestimate the understanding of your intelligent and sensitive Ben and Eve,' says Yael gently. 'Children are so much more resilient than we give them credit for.'

'Maybe, but I don't think I can take the risk. Anyway, you haven't let me finish. Of course I want you to come and stay with us, Shimon, for you to get to know Sam, and Ben and Eve, but … I would have to introduce you as Esther and Reuben's son, rather than my son. That's not a lie, is it? You *are* their son; you will always be their son, as well as my son.'

'You would deny me?' asks Shimon, so quietly he is barely audible. Rachel reaches for him, tears running down her cheeks.

'Never, never, never. I will never deny you, Shimon. But these are young children. Try to understand how it might distress them.'

'Of course. I do understand the distress of children,' he says slowly.

'Let them first get to know you as their cousin – their much beloved cousin – and then later they can learn that you are their brother.'

'Haven't there been enough concealments and half-truths, Anna?' asks Esther.

'Please think about it, Shimon. Let us welcome you to our home in Germany.'

'But only on your conditions?'

'I'm sorry.' Anna stands abruptly and rushes from the room, her hand clasped to her mouth.

* * *

Anna watches as Shimon, Ben and Eve bend over a complex new jigsaw puzzle, a Christmas present from Shimon to Ben, their three heads intent on studying the picture on the box lid and searching the wooden pieces spread over the floor. Sam is sitting in an armchair reading, legs stretched towards the fire, puffing at a cigar.

'Here are two more bits of the engine,' says Ben. 'I'm going to see if I can find all the black and gold parts. Why don't you just look for straight-edge pieces, Eve?'

'Because that's boring. I want to look for windows on the carriages. Look, I'm going to find that lady's head.'

Eve's arm is draped loosely around Shimon's shoulders, her fingers playing at his neck. Periodically she rests her head against his arm. Gently, he lifts her arm and separates himself to lean forward.

'Look. Here's the feather in the woman's hat. See if you can find the rest of it.' Shimon jerks his leg forward suddenly.

'Aagh! My leg's gone to sleep – I need to stand up a minute.'

He hops towards the Christmas tree and then circles it doing an imitation of a war dance. Eve giggles.

'Has your leg woken up now, Shimon?'

He notices Anna in the doorway watching them, and smiles. She moves forward and hugs him hurriedly, always aware of not allowing herself to demonstrate her feelings too openly. Has Ben sensed something special between them? He sometimes appears watchful to her.

As if responding to her thoughts, Ben glances up, looking from Anna and Shimon to his father. Sam raises his cigar to Anna in greeting.

'There you are, darling. That's the new dress is it? Do a twirl. Yes, very charming – really suits you. What do you think, Shimon?'

'Very beautiful.'

'Sam,' says Anna, 'the doctor was quite clear that you shouldn't smoke so much.'

'Nor am I. He said cut down on the cigarettes and that's exactly what I'm doing.'

'He didn't say take up cigars instead!'

'No cigarettes *or* cigars? What a martinet, eh Ben? A man's got to have some pleasures in life.'

'Mamma's quite right, Daddy. You shouldn't smoke so much. It's supposed to be bad for your health.' Ben sighs loudly and looks sternly at Sam. He walks from the sitting room and slams the door.

'Oh dear, beginning of the terrible teens, I suppose,' says Sam, looking at Shimon.

'I remember being thirteen. It's not an easy age.'

'Ah, that's more than I can,' replies Sam.

'Hmm. So much changing inside and outside – and always trying to put a brave face on things.' Shimon says.

'True,' says Anna. 'He's found the new school a big adjustment.

After being top dog at Hadrian Court for the last year, now suddenly he's one of the new boys again.'

'And of course,' says Shimon, 'he's had to get used to having a brand-new … *cousin* suddenly appear on the scene.' He looks at Anna. She frowns.

'But that's all right, Shimon,' says Eve from the floor. 'We *like* having a new cousin, don't we, Mamma?'

'Of course we do.'

'Except that he's *not* your cousin, is he, Mamma?'

The colour drains suddenly from Anna's face. She holds on to the back of an armchair.

'No …?' she says faintly, her eyes opening wide.

'No, course not! He's your nephew!'

* * *

Why is it that recently, life seems to have been spent at airport arrival and departure lounges? Reunions and partings; intense pleasure followed by deep sorrow. Sam has gone with Shimon to find him a drink for the flight. She sees them approaching, deep in conversation, Sam's hand on Shimon's shoulder. *What did I do to deserve him,* she wonders, *so generous with his affection?* She's not even sure whether she's thinking of Sam or Shimon, or perhaps both of them.

'I hope you don't regret coming, Shimon? I know it hasn't been exactly as you wanted …'

'Of course I don't regret it. How could I? You have all been very good to me. Ben and Eve are lovely kids. I do want to know them as my brother and sister though, and for them to know me as their brother.'

'Yes, and you will, in time,' says Anna.

'Sooner rather than later, I hope,' adds Sam.

* * *

They watch until the plane disappears from view. Anna fights a black cloud of melancholy and despair, which threatens to descend.

'Well, we'd better go,' she says brightly. 'At least we've still got two children at home.'

Sam holds her to him, stroking her hair.

'However far away he is, you have Shimon too. He'll always be a part of us now.'

Chapter 14

Chislehurst 1962

A day of humid summer heat has turned into a sultry evening. The sun has just set, leaving a salmon glow behind the trees. The air still hangs warm and close as a heavy curtain. A late blackbird claims his territory, his insistent tones piercing the stillness. Anna and Sam sit on uncomfortable deckchairs sipping glasses of chilled Moselle wine, and survey their unruly garden.

'I know I said we need to see it through a whole year before making major changes, but I'm just itching to get started. It's starting to take shape in my head …'

'In your head? In your *dreams* too! You're so completely preoccupied with it, Sam – even when you're asleep. You were muttering something about "dig it, dig it in here" last night.'

'A likely story. Probably one of Eve's ghastly pop songs drilled into my brain. Anyway, I've been thinking about it, and I think we should make this whole area into a terrace. It's sheltered from the wind and gets the last of the evening sun, so it would be perfect. Over there, summer borders with traditional perennials. And over there on the left, a small rose garden. At the bottom, there's room for some fruit trees and bushes, and a small vegetable plot. You'll have to tell me what you'd most like in it.'

'Will you take any notice? You've got it all worked out already.'

Anna smiles and strokes the bleached hairs on Sam's arm. He exudes joy and contentment. If she'd had any worries about him missing the camaraderie of military life, or his role as a senior officer, those concerns have long been dispelled. She can't remember when she last saw him so relaxed. It is over forty years since Sam last lived in his homeland. At first, he is like an alien, an awestruck visitor from another world, which in a sense is exactly what he is. The volume of traffic on the streets amazes him, as does the variety of foods, restaurants and shops on offer. He is astounded by the colourful, bizarre clothes and hairstyles displayed by young people, and by the general lack of formality with which people of all backgrounds appear to treat one another. Yet he adapts quickly to his new environment and the changes in lifestyle.

Four days a week, dressed in a dark city suit, Sam cycles to the station for his commute into central London and his retirement job at the War Office. He entertains Anna with stories of the office girls: their complaints about the old-fashioned attitudes of their parents, the attractions or shortcomings of their current boyfriends. His secretary Linda suggests that calling him 'Brigadier Lawrence' is a bit stuffy, and she is happy to address him as Sam, if he doesn't mind. Sam doesn't mind.

For Anna too, life in England is major adjustment. The four years before their move had begun the process of preparation for a great change in circumstances. In 1958, at the age of sixty-five and still robustly fit and energetic, Della had retired to a cheerful flat in Berlin. While still living in Germany, Anna and Eve were able to visit her from time to time. They would sit on her sunny balcony drinking coffee and eating hazelnut wafers. Della's diary was crammed with activities: meeting friends, painting, swimming, country walks and much more. She had entered into her new life with characteristic determination and enthusiasm. She claimed to miss living in the bosom of the family, but Anna doubted she had much time to reflect on it.

Since Sam's retirement and their move from Germany, Della has been planning a trip to stay with the family in Chislehurst. It will be her first experience of England. She prepares herself culturally by reading every conceivable reference to members of the British Royal Family in 'Bild-Zeitung'. Over the years, her letters, with their detailed pronouncements on the marriage-ability or otherwise of 'Charles' and 'Anne', cause Anna amusement and exasperation in equal measure. Nevertheless, she misses Della's down-to-earth wisdom, and the warmth of her company.

In civilian life in England, she learns, live-in servants are regarded as the preserve of the seriously rich. Instead, a stout, good-natured Londoner, Mrs Potts, is engaged to clean for four hours twice a week. The two women grow friendly and comfortable together, and gradually develop their own routines. Each morning at eleven, Mrs Potts is called from her work, to sit in the kitchen, where a slice of bread and butter and a cup of milky coffee await her. When Anna asks if she might ever like to vary her mid-morning snack, perhaps with a biscuit, a slice of cake or some fruit, she purses her lips and looks into the distance to consider the matter.

'I don't mind 'avin' a scrapin' of Marmite on it, once in a while,' she concedes.

Occasionally, if Anna goes out, Mrs Potts lets herself into the house with her key, but generally Anna remains at home and joins her cleaner at the kitchen table with a cup of coffee of her own, and sometimes even a cigarette.

'I like the smell of it, but I never fancied smokin' myself. 'Course Mr Potts 'as to 'ave 'is smoke.'

Anna becomes familiar with the characters of Mr Potts, of the steady, loyal older son and of the acquisitive, ne'er-do-well younger son, who holds a special place in Mrs Potts's heart, despite his undeserving behaviour. She learns of the lives of the daughter, and her lazy husband, who does little but get her pregnant again and 'take avantige' of Mr and Mrs Potts's generosity.

Apart from Mrs Potts, Anna manages the household alone. Her cooking has become confident, and she is known in particular for her Viennese specialities. Esther had encouraged her to take up sewing again; after all, she had asserted, dressmaking is in their genes. Anna, like her mother long ago, has a flair for designing and making stylish outfits. She sews for herself and also for Eve, although Eve is becoming increasingly choosy over what she wears, and is learning to sew for herself.

For so many years Anna had longed to put down roots. Now at last, she feels able to do so. In the first proper home of their own she and Sam have had together, she is determined to make a success of it. After years of living in temporary army accommodation with borrowed furniture, they nest-build excitedly, like young newly-weds. For the first time, they choose their own furniture, carpets and curtains and equipment for their home. Sam is particularly interested in gadgets and labour-saving machines: mixers, washers, driers, electric mowers – and central heating.

'Britain has a mild, maritime climate,' he had assured the family before their departure from Germany, though Ben had looked doubtful. One winter spent huddled in thick pullovers and blankets is enough to convince Sam – all of them – otherwise, and central heating is installed throughout the house.

Neighbours have been welcoming and friendly, inviting Anna and Sam to dinners, drinks parties and coffee mornings. They introduce Anna to friends of their own, and gradually her social circle expands. Many of her new acquaintances and friends are also European; Chislehurst increasingly regards itself as cosmopolitan. While some snobbery exists, there is not the same pressure of rank in suburbia. For the first time since she left Austria, Anna feels settled, accepted, and at peace with her surroundings.

At home, things have become easier with Eve. Perhaps because the transition to school in England has been difficult for her, Eve regards her mother as an ally and confidante as never before. She detests the rigidity of school and finds herself in constant conflict with authority over one issue after another: her liberal interpretation of uniform rules, her refusal to eat many of the unfamiliar and unappetising meals, and her surly rebellion with all but a small number of favourite teachers.

At first the other girls too regard Eve as odd and foreign. Observing her daughter's fury, Anna recognises the familiar pain of the outsider, watching the world from the periphery, and pretending not to care. How best to help her? As Esther is fond of saying, too much sympathy just results in self-pity. Don't all adolescents believe they are 'different'? Eve needs to find her own way. Time will bring some relief, although of course she won't see that yet. Anna listens to Eve's complaints as they sit together after school, but tries to encourage her to seek her own solutions.

* * *

In the spring after their move, to Anna's great joy, Shimon and Rachel announce their intention to marry. The whole family is invited to a traditional Jewish wedding in Boston but, problematically, the date falls within school term time for both Ben and Eve. Ben is taking two of his A level exams a year early and can't possibly be taken out of school. Sam and Anna agree it is fairer for neither child to attend.

'Which really means you'll have to go on your own, doesn't it? We can't possibly leave Eve at home on her own – not at fourteen – and it's too long a time to expect friends to put her up.'

'She'll be terribly disappointed. Don't you think she could stay with Emma and Dori?'

'No, darling, I really don't. No, I'll have to stay here with her. I know Esther will be sorry we can't all go …' says Sam.

'And so will Shimon and Rachel!'

'Yes of course they will, but you're the most important one in this. There's no way *you* can miss the wedding.'

Anna spends just over three weeks in Boston, the wedding occupying the middle weekend. When she returns, Ben has just arrived home following his exams. Anna is bubbling over with excitement. She brings photographs and special gifts for Ben and Eve. Marta and Leila have written cards to their cousins and there are personal letters from Shimon and Rachel, Esther and Reuben, and from Yael. At first Eve tries to feign indifference, wanting to demonstrate to all her feelings of resentment at having been left out of the great event, but she's unable to keep the facade up for long.

'Look at Rachel's dress in this one,' she exclaims, passing a photograph to Anna. 'See how it fits her waist perfectly.'

'I know. It's just right for her. Doesn't she look gorgeous! Esther has such good taste.'

'She let Esther choose it for her?'

'Not just choose it, *make* it. Her friends did all the catering, but following Esther's instructions.'

'The cake looks quite a work of art,' Sam says.

Ben looks up from reading his letter. 'Shimon says they're going on honeymoon to *Alaska*. They're going to see grizzlies, black bears – and whales! Fantastic.'

'Brrr! I wouldn't want to go to Alaska for my honeymoon – too cold,' says Eve.

'Well, that's all right then – there's no chance of that anyway,' says Ben. 'Who'd want to marry you?'

'Now, now,' says Sam, 'I guess they'll have love to keep them warm.'

'Aaaaghh!' says Eve, clutching her throat and making a grimace. 'Yuck!'

* * *

Later that evening Sam raises, once again, the issue of when Ben and Eve should be told the full truth about Shimon.

'I did speak to Shimon about it in America. Of course, he wanted me to tell Ben and Eve the whole story long before now. I understand that. But in the end, he seemed pleased that I'd agreed to what he regards as the first step at least.'

'And that is?'

'Well, telling them that long ago I made a mistake, I did something wrong; that I had a baby. I'll try to explain something of the circumstances, and that I couldn't keep the baby – that I had to give it away.'

'That is quite a step forward. So what *aren't* you telling them? What else did Shimon want you to reveal?' asks Sam.

'You know he wants me to tell them everything. But I'm just telling them as much as I think they can handle, at this stage … I'm not going to say that the baby was … *is* Shimon.'

Sam draws deeply on his cigar and looks into the fire.

'Sam? Don't you think that's right?'

'Hmm. I'm just wondering if you won't leave them with rather a lot of questions. What if one of them asks about what happened to the baby? Surely they'll want to know that. What are you going to say?'

'Then I'd just say he was adopted by a lovely family. A family who loved him very much, who cared for him well. That's the truth at least, isn't it?'

'Ye-es. It's just not the *whole* truth, is it? It's hard to know how satisfied they'll be with that information.'

'Well, they'll just have to be! That's all I'm going to tell them right now. I don't believe they're ready to know all about Shimon, and that's that!'

Sam puts his arms around her.

'You must do what feels right for you, darling. No more, no less.'

* * *

Eve runs into the hall to answer the telephone. She always appears to be waiting for an important call and is usually disappointed. Anna and Sam hear her impatient tone, and exchange glances.

'What? *Who* d'you want to speak to? Uh-huh. What's it about? What did you say your name is? Yes, OK. OK! Just a minute.'

'Perfect telephone manner,' murmurs Sam, raising his eyebrows.

'It's for you, Mamma. Some foreign guy. Sounded German.'

'What's his name?' says Anna.

'Maxim something. Couldn't make out what he said his surname is.'

'Well, what else did he say?'

'He just said he wanted to speak to you.' Eve shrugs and gives an exasperated sigh. Anna raises both hands to her mouth for a moment.

'What if it's …? Oh, I hope everything's all right with Della.'

Eve looks suddenly fearful. Anna turns anxious eyes towards Sam. He flings his paper to one side and scrambles to his feet. 'I'll go.'

Sam's deep voice carries clearly from the hall. He conducts what appears to be a long and predominantly one-sided conversation, his contributions being mainly brief responses.

'Ah yes? I see. Maybe so. When was that?'

Anna is uneasy. Eve sits on the arm of the sofa and rests her head on her mother's shoulder. At last Sam returns to the sitting room and looks at their questioning faces. He sits down next to Anna and picks up her hand, cradling it in his own, as if it were a fragile bird that might attempt to fly away at any moment.

'Sam? What? Who was it?'

'Don't worry – nothing to do with Della. She's fine.'

'Well? Who was it then?'

'His name is Maxim Henkelmann. He's the son of Fritz Henkelmann.'

'Fritz Henk …? Oh God. Oh God, what did he want?'

Sam looks cautiously from Anna to Eve and back again. Anna realises he is unsure whether to speak of her first marriage in front of Eve. She frowns and nods her head impatiently, as if to say 'it's OK, you can talk in front of her'.

'All right. Well, it's quite a long story. It seems Fritz Henkelmann died not long ago. His son, Maxim—'

'Who was Fritz Henkelmann, Mamma?' interrupts Eve. Anna looks at her. She takes a deep breath.

'He was a friend of my first husband, Jakob, when they were growing up in Vienna. They were very close as boys. But Fritz was a Roman Catholic and Jakob was a Jew, like me. When the Nazis grew in power, Fritz became interested in their policies and beliefs. After a while he became an ardent Nazi himself. You know how the Nazis despised Jews. Fritz told Jakob they could no longer be friends. But he did do two good things for Jakob, and for me. First, he warned Jakob that he was in danger and had to leave Vienna, and he also got us some papers to enable us to leave the country. Then, years later just before the war, when Jakob returned to Austria from Palestine, it was Fritz who told me he had died in Auschwitz. Otherwise I might not have known for years.' She strokes Eve's arm gently.

'So really that's three good things he did,' says Eve.

'Yes, I suppose it is. What were you going to say, Sam?'

'Yes, the phone call. I was saying, Fritz died, of cancer I think.

Maxim told me that after the war, Fritz had deeply regretted ever becoming involved with the Nazis, that he had been beguiled by their propaganda; it became a young man's obsession. Eventually he realised he didn't really believe in any of their policies, and—'

'Oh that's very easy! It's what they all say!'

'Yes, maybe. But I suppose he did try to help you and Jakob, even if only in a limited way. Anyway, I'm telling you what Maxim, the son, said to me.'

'Go on then.'

'Apparently Fritz had spent years trying to trace you after the war, but was unsuccessful. It seems he did discover your address in Haifa and turned up there, but Yael didn't trust him and wouldn't give him any information about you. It didn't occur to him that you might have married an Englishman, at least not until recently. When he began researching that avenue, of course eventually he found you, or rather us. That is, he learned your new name, and where you were living. But by then it was too late – he was dying.'

'Well, I hope I'm not expected to feel sympathy for him.'

'Maxim said his father desperately wanted to meet you and atone for his actions. Of course, that's impossible now, but he said *he* would very much like to talk to you, on his father's behalf.'

'Absolutely not! I don't want to meet him.'

'Of course, it's your decision, darling. But maybe it would be cathartic in a way. Maxim actually sounded rather nice. Gentle and … very upset.'

'I think it's so sad, Mamma,' says Eve. 'After all, you can't blame the son for what his father did. Not all Germans and Austrians were bad, were they? Look at Della, and Maggi.'

Anna gets up and paces from one side of the room to the other. She sighs deeply.

'No, we can't blame them all. Not all were Nazis. Certainly after the war, hardly anyone admitted to being a Nazi, but in reality it was a tiny minority who had actively stood against them.'

'Probably they were scared,' says Eve.

'Yes,' says Anna, regarding her daughter with a new respect, 'I think you're right. They were.'

* * *

'I'll be with you all the time, unless you want me to go out,' says Sam. 'Eve will bring in a tray of coffee, but I've told her to leave us after that.'

'Yes, thank you, Sam. I want you to stay with me. Don't go out of the room, will you? Not at all. There's nothing you can't hear.' Anna twists a handkerchief in her hands. She pushes it up her sleeve and picks absently at her fingers. 'I hope we did the right thing, letting him come here. I feel a bit sick.'

'It will be all right, believe me. Do you want to get some air for a short time?'

'I want a cigarette. I'll go and smoke it in the garden. Have I got time?'

'Yes, of course. He's not due for a few more minutes.'

Eve joins Anna on the bench on the terrace.

'You're brave to see him, Mamma. Don't feel worried.'

'I know, darling. There's nothing to worry about really.'

The front doorbell rings. Anna crushes the remains of her cigarette underfoot and goes inside.

'Herr Henkelmann.' Anna gestures towards a chair. 'Please sit down.' She is conscious of standing stiffly, not extending her hand, not offering to shake his. She is aware too of the formality and brusqueness in her voice, her unsmiling face.

'Please, Mrs Lawrence, call me Maxim,' he says diffidently, almost fearfully.

She does not reply. He is young, twenty-one or twenty-two perhaps. He resembles his father. Fritz's face looms suddenly in her memory. The last time she saw him, he would have been about Maxim's age. White skin with ruddy cheeks, like those of a little boy who has rushed into the house, breathless and hot after playing outside. Apple cheeks, Kaethe would have called them. Large eyes of a blue so pale as to be almost white, like water reflecting light. Pale hair too, the blond of Scandinavian flaxen. Fritz's face and Maxim's merge into one; one that gazes anxiously at her. Everything about him communicates innocence. Looks can be deceiving though. What about his father?

'Here you are, Maxim,' says Sam, touching him lightly on the arm and putting a cup of coffee on the table beside him. 'Milk? Sugar?'

'Just a little milk, thank you, Mr Lawrence.'

'Brigadier,' Anna says.

'I'm sorry?'

'My husband. Brigadier.'

'Oh, I'm sorry. *Brigadier* Lawrence ...'

'Not at all. I'm retired now. Plain old Mr will do very well. Or Sam for that matter.'

Anna sits opposite Maxim, their chairs at a slight angle. Sam sits a little further back in his favourite armchair.

'I am grateful that you were willing to see me, Mrs Lawrence. I do understand it is not easy for you. My father—'

'Your father betrayed his friendship with my first husband.'

Maxim wrings his hands and licks his lips. 'He knew that. He would agree with you. But ... in the years that followed, he suffered terrible remorse for what he did.'

'He *suffered*? People uprooted from their homes and countries, fleeing halfway across the world with nothing but a bundle of clothes, they suffered. The "lucky" ones who managed to send their children to safety far away, in a foreign country, knowing they would probably never see them again, they suffered. Those sent to concentration camps, old people, men, women and children, even tiny babies, they suffered. Fritz was a part of that suffering. Can you even imagine what those people endured?

Seeing their loved ones starving, sick, wrenched from their arms and slaughtered – and being unable to protect them.'

'I cannot pretend to imagine what they must have gone through … What the Nazis did was an abomination.'

'Your father knew what went on in the extermination camps. Not only did he not try to prevent it, he *believed* in it.'

'Forgive me, Mrs Lawrence, but I must contradict you there. My father has talked a lot to me of that time. He told me that when the true brutality of those places was revealed to him, he was horrified. At first, yes, he *had* supported the expulsion of the Jews from Austria, the so-called purification of the Aryan race, but he had never believed the Jews would be *exterminated*. Once he learned what was really going on, he did his best to make conditions more tolerable, and to advocate for the Jews. He tried desperately to get Jakob released. He even tried to get him reclassified as a Catholic – against Jakob's will – pretending he was a distant relative. When he failed to save him, he was completely distraught, a broken man. His reputation in the Nazi Party was in ruins, of course. He was expelled from the party and conscripted to fight. He was wounded at Stalingrad and taken prisoner. It was 1949 before my mother and I saw him again. I had last seen him at the age of about four. I barely remembered him. His health never fully recovered.'

'He died this year?'

'Last September.'

'I suppose he would have been about fifty-two?'

'Yes.' Maxim takes a handkerchief from his pocket and wipes his eyes.

Sam stands up and walks towards them. He rests his hand on Maxim's shoulder for a moment. Then he sits on the arm of Anna's chair and puts his arm around her.

'I'm sorry for the loss of your father,' she says, regarding Maxim. 'If Fritz had found me, what would he have wanted? I don't feel it is for me to forgive what he did as a young man.'

'I don't think he expected forgiveness from you, although he spent the rest of his life trying to atone for what he did. After the war, he became part of a movement to educate German children and young people about what happened, to make sure it never happened again. He spent every spare moment visiting schools to talk to the pupils, and he was completely honest about his own role.'

Maxim looks plaintively at Anna, and then at Sam. 'What he really wanted was to reassure himself that you had survived the tragedy reasonably intact. He wanted to know if you had found some happiness.'

Anna twists her head to look up at Sam.

'Well, it's a pity that he didn't live long enough for you to tell him that yes, I have found happiness. I have survived "reasonably intact."'

* * *

Anna decides to talk to Ben and Eve alone. Sam agrees that this is best. Knowing how teenage volatility expresses itself, she's concerned that neither of them should walk out of the discussion before she's finished saying what she wants to say. She arranges to take them both, as a surprise, for supper to a little French bistro that has opened nearby. This fits in with her idea of telling them now – now that she considers they are adult enough to understand. She has requested a quiet table at the restaurant, and is relieved when they are shown to a secluded alcove in the far corner of the room.

Ben is curious about his mother's motives.

'Are we celebrating something?'

'In a way. You could say that we're celebrating the two of you becoming mature young people. So mature in fact, that I feel able to talk to you about something, something that previously I didn't think you would understand.'

'What?'

'I'd like us to have our meal, and then we'll talk about it afterwards. You might even like a little taste of wine tonight.'

'Sounds like bribery to me.'

Eve is excited by the novelty of eating in a restaurant, and being offered free choice from the unfamiliar menu.

'*Escargots*. Aren't they *snails*? I'm certainly not having those!'

'There're plenty of other things to choose from.'

Anna herself can scarcely eat at all. She nibbles a little bread and picks at her plate of food, while her stomach churns. She drinks rather more wine than she is used to. When the plates are eventually cleared away, she begins. Ben and Eve watch her expectantly.

'A while ago I talked to you about the time before I met Daddy.'

'You mean about Jakob in Palestine? About how he was killed by the Nazis?' asks Eve.

'Yes … and even before that time, when I lived in Vienna …'

'We know how there wasn't much to eat when you were little, and how the British soldiers fed the Austrian children – and how you weren't in the least bit grateful!' Eve chuckles.

'Yes, that was when I was a small child. I'm talking about later, when I was a young girl, a young woman. There are things I need to tell you about that time.'

'Is this to do with that Maxim Henkelmann coming to see you?' asks Ben. 'Did he upset you?'

'His visit was quite upsetting. It brought back many sad memories, but that wasn't his fault. And it's not really to do with Maxim, or his father, except indirectly. I need to tell you, and it's not very easy, so I want you just to listen.' Anna looks at the two expectant faces and takes a deep breath.

* * *

'But why? *Why* did you have an affair with Otto, when you were engaged to Jakob? How could you do that?' Ben's outraged question echoes Jakob's words from decades before.

'It's hard to explain so you can understand. I made a terrible mistake. It was very wrong of me. First of all, I was fond of Jakob, but I didn't love him *enough*, not as much as he loved me. That too was wrong of me. I don't want to make excuses, but I hope you'll understand some of the reasons why things happened as they did. I should have been more honest with Jakob, but I liked the idea of being engaged and of getting married. I hoped – I *thought* – my love for him would grow. I think I really believed that. Then, Otto came into my life unexpectedly. He was extremely charming and handsome. You've heard the expression "he swept me off my feet"? Well, he really did sweep me off my feet. I was terribly attracted to him. In fact, for a time I was convinced I was in love with him. I suppose I persuaded myself that he loved me too, although it was ridiculous. I was immature and naive.'

'So you were pregnant,' says Eve. 'What happened then?'

'I told Jakob I was expecting a baby. I had to, of course. It was so difficult. It was awful. He was terribly upset and angry at first, and very disappointed in me.'

'Not surprising,' says Ben.

'He told me he still wanted to marry me, but that he would not keep or bring up another man's child. He asked me to agree to give the baby up for adoption.'

'Did you do it?'

'At the time I felt I had no choice. Even now, having an illegitimate child is a terrible disgrace – but in those days a young woman's reputation would have been completely destroyed. The idea of having to tell my parents I was pregnant – of all our friends and acquaintances knowing – was quite inconceivable. I would have been ruined.' Anna pauses, her heart pounding, suddenly thrust back into the turmoil of that terrible dilemma so long ago.

'I was young, remember, and in the early stage of the pregnancy I hadn't yet developed love for the baby inside me; it just didn't feel real to me. I didn't yet feel ... connected to it. I was still in shock. I had no idea how I would feel about it later.'

'So what happened?' Eve repeats.

'We went to live in Switzerland, Jakob and I, for the whole period of the pregnancy. We kept it secret from the whole family ... except Esther. She was my only support. As time went on and my stomach grew bigger, I started to feel closer to the baby. I hadn't expected to develop such strong feelings for the child, such intense love. I began to dread having to give it up, but there was nothing I could do. When the time came for the baby to be born, I went into a small Swiss clinic. The adoption had already been arranged. After the baby was born, he was immediately removed and taken to the adoptive parents. He has lived with them ever since.'

'He?' queried Ben.

'The baby was a boy.'

'Did you know the people who adopted him?'

Anna pauses a moment, her mind frozen in panic. 'I ... I knew they were good and loving people, who would always care for him.'

'How could you do it?' screams Eve, starting to sob. 'How could you give away your own baby?'

'It was a very difficult time – it was agony for me. But I had no alternative.'

'If there had been other difficult times, would you have given away me, or Eve?' asks Ben, his voice gruff with bitterness.

'Of course not!' Anna says, reaching out to hold his hand on the table. He pulls his away and thrusts both his hands between his knees.

'Didn't you miss him?' he asks. 'Did you ever think about him?'

'I missed him more than I can say. I have thought about him every day.'

'Does Daddy know?' asks Eve. 'Does he know you had a baby before you married him?'

'Yes, he does know.'

'Wasn't he angry?'

'Your father is a wonderful, understanding man. He knows we can all make mistakes in our relationships sometimes. So no, he wasn't angry.'

'So why didn't you tell *us*? Why didn't you tell the truth? Didn't you trust us?' Eve's face is contorted with anger.

'It's not that I didn't trust you. I wanted to wait until you could understand better. I didn't even tell Daddy until I was so unwell at Ellwangen. I think I was too ashamed.'

'You're always telling us how important it is to be honest.'

'I still believe that – even though in this situation I haven't been totally honest with you.'

'Not *at all* honest,' says Ben.

Ben never mentions the discussion again. He asks no further questions of Anna. From this time onwards, she senses that he withdraws from her, and she is deeply saddened. Eve, on the other hand, frequently throws the revelation back in her mother's face, uses it as a weapon, particularly at times of confrontation, of which there are many.

'I suppose you're sorry you didn't give me away, aren't you?'

Of course not, Anna assures her, she would never, never have considered giving her away. What a terrible thing to say. Yet … yet Yael is the only person on earth to whom she could ever admit that in years gone by, in those darkest moments, she would sometimes torture herself by playing a terrible game. Against her will, despite herself, she would sometimes imagine … if you were put in the position of *having* to select one child to give away, never to see again, which would you choose: Shimon, Ben or Eve? There is no answer.

She tries to convince herself that the children's negative reaction to hearing her story, part of her story, proves that she was right not to tell them sooner, and that she is right not to tell them everything now. Yet sometimes in the night, she wakes with a lingering doubt gnawing at her. If she had simply told them everything when they were younger, might they just have accepted it, and accepted Shimon?

Chapter 15

1970

The old plane rumbles and shakes westwards, heading towards Tehran airport. Over the mountains, clouds thud wetly against the portholes and batter the aircraft with violent turbulence. Breaks in the clouds show brief glimpses of mountain ranges far below, ridges sharp as knives, bright with sun on one side, dark and shadowy on the other. Eve cannot settle to read. She looks around her. Across the aisle, the elderly tribesman sits rocking in his seat, incanting his prayers ever more fervently. His face has turned grey-green.

His son nods and smiles at Eve. He has told her this is his father's first experience of air travel, his first departure from Afghanistan. They are going to a conference of leading Muslim elders in Tehran. The old man takes a small rug from his pack and lays it in the central aisle. He glances nervously out of the windows. At the sight of the vibrating wings, he raises his eyes beseechingly, fingers working their beads furiously. He looks out again, glancing from one side of the plane to the other, trying to work out which direction it is facing, which way is Mecca. Then he kneels down and starts to pray in earnest.

The air hostess peeps out from her little compartment near the front of the plane. The safety belt warning light is on due to the turbulence. She appears to be considering whether to tell the old man to return to his seat and fasten his belt, but decides against it and shuts herself away behind the curtain again.

Eve's weariness and grief wraps her in a blanket of numb unreality. She pulls the shawl around her shoulders and takes out Ben's letter, crumpled from many readings. Was it coincidence or fate that his letter had arrived at the central post office in Kabul just the day before she did? All those months living in a distant valley in the Pamir Mountains, Eve had been completely out of touch with her family, many days' travel from the nearest town, let alone the capital. Yet there, on top of the pile of correspondence waiting at the *Poste Restante*, was Ben's airmail letter. Their father had died of a massive heart attack only three days previously. Why always a 'massive' heart attack, she wonders; it's not as though anyone would die of a minor heart attack. How could Sam be dead? A world without her father. It wasn't possible. It was just too final to conceive.

Travelling alone in wild and remote mountain regions, Eve had rarely felt fear, never considered herself in potential danger, despite all of Sam's dire warnings before she left. 'The Afghan is a fierce and warlike chap, not given to following rules,' he had informed her in his old-fashioned manner. He had always referred to those of other nations in this way – 'the Sikh', 'the Serb', 'the Arab' – an expression belying the great respect and courtesy he showed to other peoples.

Often, on family holidays, Eve's mother had expressed exasperation about Sam's insistence that to lock the car in a foreign city was an insult to the local people, implying a suspicion that they might have dishonest intent. Amazingly, it was a trust that was never betrayed; nothing was ever stolen. One time Sam's wallet, packed with holiday money, had gone missing from his back pocket in a down-at-heel town in Yugoslavia. Eve recalls

Anna's response: the lift of her eyebrows, the knowing smile, how she had come close to trumpeting 'What did I tell you?' But Sam had strode calmly to the local police station and made enquiries, to find that the wallet had been found in the street and handed in intact.

Perhaps her father's belief in the goodwill of others had contributed to Eve's lack of fear while travelling; like Sam, she assumed everyone she met would be well disposed towards her, that none would harm her. Nothing in her growing up had prepared her for the wilds of the Hindu Kush, but she was young enough, flexible enough, to learn new ways of dealing with a totally unfamiliar world. Yet now, suddenly, about to re-enter urban civilisation, she feels at a loss to know how to behave.

The official at the British Consulate had been kind and helpful, perhaps glad to handle any case not simply another hippy run out of money or in difficulties over a drugs deal. He had arranged Eve's immediate repatriation, involving first flying on this small local plane, followed by an overnight stop in Tehran, and then a scheduled flight to London the following day. Eve anticipates her return home to suburban Chislehurst with complete terror. By the time she arrives home it will be nearly two weeks since Sam's death.

* * *

A taxi speeds her, together with a middle-aged British couple, from the airport through the noisy streets of Tehran to a large modern hotel, overnight stay care of the British Consulate. The woman appears intrigued by Eve's bizarre appearance; after nearly a year away she wears a colourful mixture of local tribal garments and the ragged remains of her own clothes. She questions Eve persistently.

'Have you been in Afghanistan a long time, dear?'

'Yes, nearly a year.'

'Oh my, that's a long holiday! Or perhaps you were working?'

'No … just travelling.'

'Ah, travelling. You don't look very well, dear. You're terribly thin.'

'Mmm.'

'Have you had any treatment?'

'No.'

'Oh, you should. You never know what you might have picked up over there.'

Eve stares at the woman and nods. She turns to look out of the window. She does know what she has picked up; a pleasant doctor at the American Hospital in Kabul has explained that she almost certainly has severe amoebic dysentery, and will need to visit the Hospital for Tropical Diseases in London as soon as possible.

The hotel is half empty. The few guests in evidence are mostly American businessmen or engineers, recognisable by their conspicuously large-sized and garish clothes. Like all men far from home, they are lonely, bored and open to opportunities. As Eve stands in the bar and asks for an orange juice, she is immediately propositioned by an American, despite her strange clothes and wild hair. He looms over her with a blue and white checked shirt, crew-cut hair and a large, reddish face. He tells her his name is Warren and he is thirty-six, which Eve regards as impossibly old, but apart from the man at the British Consulate in Kabul and the woman in the taxi, she hasn't spoken English with anyone for a year, and is strangely drawn to this bulky and diffident man.

Warren offers to buy her a drink, which she accepts, and dinner, which she declines. She explains she is not well and can eat very little. Warren tells her he is an engineer with a multinational company building an oil pipeline in western Persia. The project area is remote and hot, and Warren longs to return home to the hills and forests of Vermont. He's been away for three months and misses his wife and children.

Eve likes his honesty. He asks – in a half-hearted sort of way – if she would sleep with him, and doesn't seem surprised when she says she'd prefer a hot shower and a long sleep. They wish each other good luck and Eve retreats to her room.

* * *

The first morning back in England, Eve wakes in her old schoolgirl's bedroom with its yellow curtains and posters of the Stones, Jimi Hendrix and Fleetwood Mac. She wonders if it is real or a dream, or if perhaps she has dreamt her entire time away. She pads across the polished floorboards of the landing and opens the door to her parents' room. Her mother, always an early riser, is already downstairs. The two single beds stand side by side, like children's beds. They are neatly made, with white sheets, cream woollen blankets and shiny green eiderdowns.

On Sam's bed his blue and white flannel pyjamas are just visible between the two pillows, neatly folded. A small Indian woven rug on the floor separates the beds. On the bedside table is a thick copy of *Seven Pillars of Wisdom*. He must have been in the middle of reading it; a bookmark peeps out two-thirds of the way through. Gently, tenderly, Eve removes it. She recognises it as one she had embroidered for him at the age of eight or nine. How she had sighed and sweated over those uneven red cross-stitches to write the words, 'For Daddy – with love from Eve'.

She pulls out his pyjamas and presses her face into them, breathing in the smell of him. His shaving brush and razor, his toothbrush and toothpaste in a plastic mug, stand on the glass shelf above the basin. The chintz curtains are half closed. Eve opens Sam's side of the wardrobe. On the left, white Aertex vests and pants fill one shelf, socks and handkerchiefs another. Below them is a little heap of folded sweaters – 'jerseys', he would have called them. His shirts, trousers, jackets and suits hang from a rail on the other side. Everything ordered with the precision that dominated his life.

At the extreme right end is his uniform, unworn for the last ten years. It is all there, just as always before. It seems inconceivable, impossible, that her father is not. She is overwhelmed by a sense that it is not true, that this is a conspiracy. Of course he isn't really dead; how could he be? Why have they hidden him away? What have they done with him? Where is he? If this is supposed to be a joke, it isn't funny, not at all. Surely it's about time to reveal the truth.

* * *

She gazes around the crematorium garden, searching everywhere for some trace, but there is none. He's not there, no part of him in evidence. Below them the red-brick buildings of the crematorium and chapel stand solid and ugly as factories. A narrow roadway separates the crematorium from a cluster of low office buildings. Two metal dustbins stand outside a door. Eve notices, with a dull shock, that the lid of one is slightly skewed. Her heart thumping, she is overcome with a feeling that *that* is where he must be: her father's remains dumped in that dustbin; that is surely what must have happened. His precious ashes discarded like clinker from a cleared-out grate. She sways precariously, nauseous, empty. *Get a grip, Eve,* she tells herself, *you're starting to lose it.* Her breath comes in jagged, uneven gulps. Ben looks at her face and grasps her arm.

'There's a plaque,' he says quietly. 'No grave, of course. He wanted a tree planted and his ashes scattered around it.'

He stands patiently, looking at Eve, waiting for her to regain control and move forward.

'I guess it's hard to take it in. That he's … gone. You do understand we couldn't wait for you? I mean, we had to go ahead with the funeral. I wasn't sure when you'd get my letter, or *whether* you'd get it at all.'

'Yes, I know.'

'This way,' he says, steering her towards a smooth green hillock beyond the buildings; a grassy mound, a grassy knoll, Eve thinks, sparking the memory in her mind of the grassy knoll in Dallas, Texas, a few years before, where Kennedy was shot. Ben and she had lain on their stomachs watching events on TV, crying, not believing it was really happening. Ben had gone upstairs and written a poem about it, full of sixteen-year-old anger and passion.

Eve clenches her fists. She almost stamps her foot, but controls the impulse, aware that Ben would interpret it as childish.

'Why do they have to give everything such stupid, bloody names? "Book of Remembrance", "Chapel of Rest". Nobody's resting in it. Such idiotic euphemisms.'

'Yeah, I know,' says Ben, shrugging. 'Look, here it is.'

A tiny tree, no taller than Eve's shoulder, stands in the mown grass, upright and straight, like a determined toddler reaching upwards as if trying to touch the sky. It is a silver birch, its bark pale and peeling. Silver birch, her favourite tree. Sam knew that, just as he knew her favourite flower was a pure, pale yellow rose. Every summer he would come in from the garden to present her with the first yellow rose in bloom. Had he chosen the tree himself? Had he planned this in advance? Did he know he was going to die? Low down, near the base of the tree, a rectangle of shiny coppery metal is fixed to the trunk at a slight angle. On it is written:

In loving memory of
Brigadier Samuel Richard Lawrence.
Born 24th March 1902. Died 26th August 1970.

Eve strokes the smooth, cool surface, allowing her fingers to feel the indentations of the script, as if reading Braille.

'That's it? This is all that's left of his life?'

'No, of course it's not all! There's everything he was and did and achieved. There's our memories of him and who he was. That doesn't stop. There's our love for him. That doesn't stop either. And ... well ... I'm proud he was our father.'

This is more, of a personal nature, than Eve's brother has ever said to her before. It makes her cry for the first time since her return.

* * *

At home, Anna is in the kitchen. The pastry for apple strudel is rolled out on a cloth on the table and Anna is stretching it rhythmically with her hands. She stops when she hears her children come in and wipes her floury hands on her apron. She gives Eve a questioning, anxious look.

'Darling ...?'

Ben kisses her, then turns and runs upstairs. They hear his clomping feet leaping two or three steps at a time. His bedroom door bangs shut. Eve and Anna hug for a long time, each feeling the convulsive gulps of the other. Eve washes her hands and together they complete the stretching of the strudel pastry. They add the filling of sliced apple, sultanas, brown sugar and baked breadcrumbs, which Anna has prepared. Then they roll it up, careful not to tear its surface, seal the edges and put it away in the cool of the larder.

Anna makes a pot of coffee and they smoke a cigarette together at the kitchen table, like they used to sometimes when Eve came home from school. Anna's hands tremble whenever she lifts her cup.

'Are you OK, Mum?'

Anna sighs. 'It's hard, very hard ... for all of us. Sam – Daddy – was everything to me – my core, my centre. I loved him so much. I don't know how ... I always thought he was so strong.'

'But he wasn't strong. He was sick, wasn't he? Why couldn't they help him?' Eve frowns and roughly brushes tears from her cheeks.

'You know Daddy. He never complained about anything. Never made a fuss. If only he'd said something about the pain sooner ...' Anna's voice tails off.

'You didn't know? Are you saying you didn't know he was ill? How could he hide it from you? Surely you must have known about it?'

Eve makes an involuntary tutting noise and Anna glances at her. She sighs deeply. She repeats, '*T'ja, ja, t'ja, ja* ...' She twists a pathetic scrap of tissue in her hands.

'*Ja*, I should. I should have realised ... but Sam hated anyone to make a fuss about him. He always wanted to be the strong one, to be in control ... and I suppose I *wanted* him to be strong too. He always said it was nothing, and I wanted to believe he was right.'

'It's not your fault, Mum. Of course it's not your fault. I just wish I could have seen him again. Before I left all we ever seemed to do was argue. And now, it's like he's just disappeared off the face of the earth. There's no time to tell him ... well, anything.'

'Daddy would have been so happy to know you are home safely, so happy. He worried about you very much.'

'Did he? He worried? I wish we could have *talked* more, now that I'm more of an adult – but now there's no chance to say anything.'

'I know, darling. I'm so sorry.'

'It's not your fault,' Eve repeats. Yet *was* anyone at fault? Shouldn't Anna have realised that the pains, the warning signs, which Sam had just dismissed as 'a touch of flu' or 'running out of puff', were really serious angina, foretelling his fatal heart attack? All those years her father had cared for Anna, guided her and protected her, almost as though she were a needy child. If only Eve had been there when he was at his most vulnerable, instead of on the other side of the world, might she have been able to help him? If only she had had the chance to care for him. If only she had said some of the things that would never now be said.

Anna seems to be following the same line of thought. She plays with her trembling fingers, as though rolling prayer beads.

'There is so much that wasn't said. I tried to be honest with Sam, even though it was hard. I *was* open in the end, but it took a long time. Maybe I should have been more honest with you and Ben too ... Sam wanted me to ... but I thought I should wait ...'

'Wait? What are you talking about, Mum? Wait for what? What do you mean?'

'Wait for you to grow up, to be more mature. To understand ... how things were. There were such difficult times, such cruel and confused times. How could you possibly understand what really happened – the choices I had to make?'

'What are you talking about?' Eve repeats, her voice rising shrilly. 'What choices?'

Chapter 16

Anna has taken to wandering the house, not exactly aimlessly, but as if puzzled and in confusion. Everything appears familiar yet unfamiliar, as though she has been deposited in a house devised by someone who has attempted to copy her home, but has done so badly, omitting the most vital elements. She feels as if she is always searching, but exactly what for is unclear. Sam, perhaps; to hear his voice, to see some sign that he has not gone from her for ever, that he is still there. Perhaps just the need to recognise something that has meaning. Peace perhaps. Peace was so long coming to her life, and it was Sam who helped her to find it. Whatever that peace was, now it has gone, and Sam too.

She cannot settle; she is compelled to drift from room to room, yearning for something nameless, something vague and nebulous. She is not even sure she would recognise it if she were to find it. She has forgotten why she set off on this search in the first place, if ever she knew. She treads softly, on tiptoes, as though afraid of disturbing another occupant of the house. Yet she knows she is alone.

She opens the door to Ben's room. The air is warm and stuffy. His travel bags are stuffed behind a chair, clothes scattered like autumn leaves across the room. She picks up a pair of jeans and smoothes them over the back of the chair. She takes a T-shirt from a heap on the floor, caresses it for a moment and folds it on the rumpled bed. In a few more days he will be gone, back to his flat and post-graduate studies in Cambridge.

She moves to the window and pushes back the curtains, still half-closed. Light pours into the room. She gazes out onto the garden. The grass needs cutting. Guilt surges through her. Sam wouldn't have let it get so long. Maybe Ben will have time to cut it before he goes, or Shimon, or Eve. Anna retraces her steps to the door and out onto the landing.

She moves to Eve's room. The walls and curtains are as Eve chose them six or seven years before, when they first came to the house, her love of sunshine and warmth expressed in the shades of yellow colour scheme. Anna strokes the wallpaper and smiles. Eve's room is considerably tidier than Ben's. The curtains are open; the bed is neat. Clothes are draped over the back of the chair. Despite the wild-child image Eve likes to cultivate, Anna knows she needs the security of order. Like her father.

Anna breathes in deeply. Eve too will soon be gone. Back to a temporary shared flat in Notting Hill. Shared with a motley group of people about whom Anna knows little and has not enquired too closely, but whom she knows Sam would have called 'dubious'. She has learned not to question her daughter about her friends, or her life. Eve says she *might* take up her offer of a university place in the autumn; she can't commit herself at this stage. She is impatient when Anna reminds her she has only two or three weeks in which to make up her mind.

Anna steps out across the landing again. The polished wooden floorboards near the stairwell creak, just as they always have. She runs her hand along the top banister, feeling its smoothness, and opens the door to the guest room, now neatly prepared for Shimon's imminent arrival. It is the smallest

232

bedroom, homely and comfortable. Every need has been thought of: a spare blanket folded at the foot of the bed, a selection of books and magazines on the bedside cabinet, fresh towels and flannels by the basin, flowers on the table. Yet it exudes the drab anonymity of a hotel room. Shimon will occupy this room, be part of their lives for a week, and then move on to meet with academic colleagues in Cambridge. He too is a temporary visitor. All her children, now transient guests in her house. She is the only permanent occupant. They will go; she will remain, alone.

From downstairs, Anna hears the sounds of arrival – footsteps on the front path, keys jangling, a door opening and shutting, voices and laughter. Then, Shimon's call: 'Anna!'

She stands and clutches a handful of the fabric of her blouse to her chest, her heart beating through the flimsy material. As always, she is terrified Shimon will inadvertently let slip their true relationship, before she is ready. Recently, when they have been alone together, he has been calling her 'Mamma' more readily, more spontaneously. She shakes her head faintly at the irony. Just at a time when Shimon is starting to feel at ease using 'Mamma' – privately of course – her two younger children are beginning to feel *less* comfortable with it. Both Ben and Eve sometimes test out calling her 'Anna', but are hesitant and self-conscious about it. Ben in particular sometimes mumbles an incomprehensible mixture of 'Anna', 'Mum' and 'Mamma', and often avoids calling her anything at all.

'I'm here!' She clears her throat. 'I'm coming!'

The three young faces watch her as she slowly descends the stairs. Even before she reaches the bottom, Shimon steps forward and envelops her in his embrace. He holds her tight, rocking gently, absorbing her sorrow.

'Anna. I'm so, so sorry about dear Sam, and I'm sorry we couldn't be here with you for the funeral.' He murmurs into the hollow of her neck.

'Don't apologise, Shimon. Sam wouldn't want you to reproach yourself. He wouldn't have wanted Rachel to be at risk. We all know she couldn't possibly travel right now. It's just a pity Boston is so far away. Is she quite all right again?' She steps back to look at him.

'Really, she's fine. It was just a bit scary at the time. Apparently slight bleeding at this stage isn't unusual, but it really freaked us out. She had a few days resting, the bleeding stopped and she felt great again. She sends her love to all of you. And Mom does too of course, everybody does.'

'What a relief. Now come, you must be exhausted after the journey. Let's all sit down and have a cup of coffee. I want to hear about all the family. You can unpack later and we'll have some lunch.'

'I'll bring the coffee in,' says Eve.

'Thank you, darling. It's all ready on the trolley.'

Anna resists the urge to sit next to Shimon on the sofa, where she can touch him, and instead sits on the chair opposite. She studies her son. He looks tired, but fit and content. Fatherhood is suiting him.

'Tell me about little Eva. Is she talking much?'

'Oh yes, she never stops! She deals mainly in commands and questions. "Why doggie bark?" "Mommy sit here!" "Daddy play!" She's a miniature tyrant. Rules the house.'

'Well, quite clearly, you thrive on it.'

'I've some photos to show you in my case.'

Eve wheels the trolley in and parks it next to her mother. Anna pours coffee into the cups and hands one to Eve. Eve passes it to Shimon.

'Did you call her Eva after me? I've always wondered.'

'I guess, in a way. We liked the name, but we also wanted something that would … link our families, keep up the continuity.'

'So I'll expect Benjamin for the new baby, right?' says Ben with a grin. Shimon laughs.

'Might not be so appropriate if it's another girl. We've got a few ideas, but we'll have to see what he or she looks like. We did think maybe Samuel for a boy.' He looks questioningly at Anna. She glances at Ben, who is stirring his coffee with concentration.

'What a lovely idea.' Anna takes out her handkerchief and blows her nose.

'Daddy would have been very pleased, don't you think, Ben?' she says.

'Well, maybe he would. We can't really know that.'

* * *

In the park Anna links arms with Shimon and adjusts her step to his. Eve has gone to see a former school friend, and Ben says he has a paper to read at home. Anna is glad of the time alone with Shimon.

'You must miss Sam very much, Mamma.'

'I can't tell you how much I miss him. I can hardly comprehend the reality. Sam gone? How can it be – my Sam not here? Sometimes I think of all the possible years ahead, and I wonder if I can really bear to live them without him. But what can I do? I *have* to live without him, unless I throw myself under a bus. I have no choice.'

'I didn't know him for very many years, but he was one of the most lovable human beings I have ever encountered, a very special man.'

'Yes he was. Oh God, Shimon – "*was*". How I hate talking about him in the past tense!'

'What will you do?'

'Do? I really don't know. Sam gave meaning to everything I did. Without him ... nothing really seems to matter to me. I'm still giving conversation lessons at the high school of course – that's been an important routine. I like the children, though they're terrors, some of them. Also, right now, with Ben and Eve at home, there's always something to do, something to think about. Just practical things: wash clothes, shop for food, cook meals, make some favourite cake to please one of them. But soon, what *will* I do?'

They pause, watching a squirrel nibbling a remnant of sandwich next to the pathway. It notices them and hurriedly stuffs the last corner into its mouth before scampering up a tree.

'For some people, their faith gives them great comfort and strength, but I'm not a religious woman. In time, I may develop some new interests, but at the moment it's hard to feel motivated to do anything. I can't seem to concentrate on anything.'

'You know you have an open invitation to come and stay with Mom, and with Rachel and me, whenever you want, and for as long as you want.'

'That's very sweet and I'll certainly come, after a while. I'd love to meet Eva, and the new little one when he or she comes. I am so blessed with loved ones over there: Esther and Reuben and the girls, you and Rachel, Yael and Hal. Yes, it would be wonderful to spend some time in Boston again. But right now, I think I need to be here. I want to be available for Ben and Eve. They're both going through a difficult time themselves, of course. I do so want to see Eve settled, to have a direction. Study, work, marriage, whatever. I feel she's a bit of a lost soul at the moment. She doesn't know what she wants, except that she doesn't want to live here at home, with me.'

'I can't bear to think of you being on your own and lonely in the house.'

'The house is fine. Sam and I loved it, but we thought we'd have longer in it together, much longer. Without him I'll be lonely anywhere. It's not as though I haven't got company; Ben and Eve won't be far away, and I have some good friends. People here have been very kind – and you know dear old Della is coming to stay for a fortnight soon.'

They sit side by side on a bench and stare at the ducks and swans drifting on the pond. 'Also, you wouldn't believe how much there is to do, all the business to complete when someone dies. I absolutely detest it, but I suppose it keeps me occupied.'

'If there's any way I can help you with the business, or anything else, just let me know.'

'Thank you, my darling. I've got a good solicitor. Sam's brother Humphrey recommended him. He's very kind and supportive.' She pauses and turns to him. 'There *is* something you can help me with though, something I've been thinking about for some time.'

'Oh?'

'Shimon, the time has come to tell Ben and Eve the truth, the *whole* truth. Of course it has. I know you felt I should have told them years ago, and perhaps you were right. I'm not sure I managed the partial revelations very well the last time. They were both very angry with me. This time I want us to speak to them together. You and me.'

'Really? Are you sure this is the right time? You said yourself this is a difficult time for them. They're both still pretty raw about losing Sam.'

'I'm not sure there'll ever be a perfect time. I already indicated to Eve that I have important things to tell her. I didn't really mean to, but it just slipped out. I can't go on putting it off for ever.' She grasps his arm and pulls him round to face her. 'Surely this is exactly the time when they would both benefit from having an older brother?'

'However you want to handle it, I'll do my best to help.'

* * *

After supper, they remain sitting around the dining table, talking and drinking wine. Shimon's presence has changed the dynamics in the family; the atmosphere is more relaxed. Ben, Eve and

Shimon are discussing music, laughing as they tease one another, each denigrating the musical tastes of the others. Anna watches them silently for a time, gathering courage to introduce a very different topic of conversation, not wanting the light spirit of the evening to be totally destroyed.

'I need to tell you something,' she suddenly blurts out, her voice raised above theirs. All three faces turn towards her. 'It is something I hinted at to Eve the other day.'

No one speaks; they watch her. She feels a knot gather and churn in her stomach and her hands begin to tremble, but there is no going back now.

'About six years ago, I took you two out for a meal. You will remember how I told you something of what had happened to me, many years ago as a young woman.' She pauses, a heavy silence descending. Then, as if they might need clarification, she adds: 'I told you how I had a baby and gave him up for adoption. At the time, you found it difficult to hear that news. I think you were angry with me for revealing faults, and angry that I had not told you about them sooner. Children do not always want to hear about their parents' frailties and imperfections. Perhaps I shattered some of your illusions.'

'Mum,' Ben interrupts her, 'what an idiot I was at the time ...' Anna raises her hand to stop him.

'You were still very young,' she continues. 'I hope that over the years, you have both come to terms with what I told you, and feel that it was at least right that I *told* you. Now that you are older and more experienced yourselves, you may have learned greater insights into the complexities of human relationships, and into what happened to me ... and some of the reasons why.'

Ben looks around at all those seated at the table, his face betraying a struggle with puzzlement and uncertainty. 'So did you tell Shimon all about it too?'

'Shimon has known about the baby ... for a long time. In fact,

I want to tell you more about that time and that baby, and I have specially asked Shimon to be here with us today.'

Both Ben and Eve look from Anna to Shimon, their faces clouded with anxiety, and perhaps the beginnings of suspicion.

'As you know, my first son was born in 1935, and for reasons I have already described to you, he was immediately removed from me and taken to his adoptive parents. What I did not tell you before is that those adoptive parents were your Aunt Esther and Uncle Reuben.'

Ben and Eve stare at Anna. Ben looks white. Eve gasps and covers her mouth with her hand. Tears flood her eyes and roll down her cheeks, leaving trails of mascara. Ben clasps his hands together in his lap and looks down at them, frowning.

'You see, the baby I gave birth to, was ... is ... Shimon.'

There is the sound of another gasp, an intake of breath, a soft sob, followed by a long silence. Shimon reaches out to hold Anna's hand. After a few moments, Ben, his eyes glistening, says quietly, 'So Shimon is ... our brother?'

'Yes, he is your brother. Or strictly, he is your half-brother.'

'So why the pretence? Why the secrets? Why did you pretend he was our *cousin*?' Eve is barely in control of her voice.

Anna shakes her head, and looks at Eve beseechingly. 'You may well ask. The timing seemed so important to me ... now I wonder if the pretence and concealment was pointless. Perhaps I was terribly wrong.'

Shimon reaches out his hand and opens his mouth to speak. Anna raises her hand to stop him and nods slowly.

'It was very difficult to know when to tell you, how to tell you. I had only outwardly acknowledged Shimon as my child in 1957, remember, after my stay in hospital at Ellwangen. You have to realise, Sam knew nothing about him until then. Once I told him, it was Sam who helped give me the strength and confidence to make contact with Esther again, and with Shimon.' Anna presses a handkerchief to her eyes.

'You were both still very young. Ben was getting used to boarding school … being apart from the family. I did not feel you could deal with the knowledge then. Later, when I told you part of the story, you were teenagers. We had not long moved to a completely new environment in England. Eve, you hadn't really settled at school – you didn't know quite who you were and where you belonged. I was afraid the sudden entry of a *brother* into your lives was more than you could cope with at that time, either of you. The last thing I wanted was for you to feel … displaced.'

Ben looks steadily at Shimon.

'Had we been displaced?'

'Not at all. If anything, finding Shimon again, after burying him inside me for all those years, *intensified* my love for you. It was as though a part of my heart that had almost been frozen was freed, was thawed. Of course, I have always loved both of you more than I can say. From the moment you were each born, you brought me – and Sam – indescribable joy. Yet, at the back of my mind was always the knowledge of another child. I can't pretend otherwise. I longed for that child; I yearned for him. Perhaps that longing sometimes inhibited my relationship with you, but I never, never loved you any the less, not when you were children and not now.'

Ben stands up and walks unsteadily around the table. He opens the curtain and presses his forehead against the cool glass of the window.

'I think … I think there is a part of me that has known this for some time,' he says slowly, his back to the room, 'or at least, has sensed it. Not the details, and maybe not consciously … but it just feels like … a kind of confirmation.' He turns and looks at the gathering. Shimon stands and pushes his chair back. He strides towards Ben, his hand outstretched. They clasp hands and then pull each other close, into an embrace. Eve gets up too and touching her mother's arm with her fingertips, she draws her hand gently around her shoulder and then approaches her brothers. They open their arms to include her in the embrace. Anna watches them, crying softly.

In turn, each of her children return to the table, hug and kiss Anna and sit down again. Ben picks up the bottle of wine, still half full, and offers it to the room.

'Shit, Ben, I could do with something stronger than that. How about the rest of you?' Shimon mops his face with his napkin.

'Not for me,' says Anna, 'but there's a bottle of Sam's whisky in the sideboard.'

They talk for hours, pausing only to move to the armchairs after a while. By two in the morning all are exhausted and variously drunk. For once, the debris from the dinner table is left unwashed and ignored.

'My darlings, I must go to bed. We can talk more in the morning. Goodnight to you all, my dear, dear children.' Anna gets up and kisses each of them.

As she approaches the door they respond, almost in unison, 'Goodnight, Mamma,' and subside into tipsy chuckles.

'We should all go to bed,' says Ben, 'but just before Mamma goes, can I ask you one thing, Shimon? Have you ever tried to contact your father ... Otto, I mean?'

'I have thought about it occasionally, and Rachel and I have talked about it. But no, I never have, and I never will. Otto would be over seventy by now, and his children with Karin – assuming he is still with Karin – must be middle-aged. Anna never told him she was pregnant, so he knows nothing of my existence. What would be the point? He's an irrelevance to me. All my life I have had Reuben, who's been the best father anyone could wish for. A few years ago I acquired a stepfather, in Sam, whom I also grew to love. Two good fathers are surely enough for any man?'

Anna smiles and blows a kiss into the room, before shutting the door behind her. Intense sorrow and joy flood through her simultaneously, like two rivers interlaced, each struggling to dominate the other. Her body is racked with uncontrollable sobs as she staggers up the stairs. She feels cleansed, scoured of all the secrets and lies. At last, at last, she has done the right thing. Her fear of alienating her children was unfounded; she has united her family. If only Sam were there too.

Chapter 17

Sam is not there, yet time passes, the years go by, and Anna grows old, very old, without him. How is it possible to be so old? Today they, she and Eve, are going to the house Sam, Anna and the children lived in when they first moved to England. Anna can hardly believe that was fifty years ago. *Fifty years ago!* How they loved that house, the first proper home of their own. Before that she'd never been able to put down roots anywhere. All those houses in Germany, none of them truly homes. It meant so much to her, and to Sam.

Of course, he loved the garden. It was extra special for him, knowing they wouldn't have to move on before his beloved plants matured, as so often before. In the event, he didn't have as long to enjoy their home as they all expected. Strange to think how significant the time in that house was for them both, yet they had only six or seven years in it together. Anna lived on there alone for another twenty-five years, but it's the time they spent together she remembers most. How odd the notion of time is, especially when you're old. Some periods seem to go on and on, others condense into a moment.

It's nearly twenty years since she moved into Ben and Nadia's house in Islington, into a 'granny flat', as they called it. She knows how good they were to her, how welcoming, yet those years are a bit of a blur. Trying to settle in a strange part of London, where she didn't know anyone, was very hard. She didn't even know the butcher or the postman at first. She hadn't realised how important those little contacts were; she even missed dear old Mrs Potts.

But she had tried to make a life there: joined a bridge group though she hated cards, took up Spanish, attended a local history class, and a music and movement class, and helped out with the family in whatever way she could. At first, she had made cakes or puddings for special occasions. Ben and Nadia expressed appreciation, even though they were excellent cooks themselves. Charlie, Guy and Alma were sweet and affectionate to her, but they'd been outraged when she suggested 'babysitting' for them one evening, while Ben and Nadia went to the theatre. It's easy to forget that even grandchildren grow up.

In the end Anna had become unwell and spent two weeks in hospital. It had turned out to be pneumonia. No one thought she would survive. She had to remind them she was the skinny girl from the soup kitchen in Vienna! Not swept away so easily by a little cough on the chest. Her illness did age her though. She wasn't very steady on her feet after that. The doctors thought she might have had a small stroke too. After much discussion, everyone had decided she needed more care than Ben and Nadia could provide, so she moved to Morden House.

She had hated the idea at first, but she didn't want to be a burden for the family. Now, after four years there, she's used to it and reasonably contented. It's comfortable and she feels safe and well looked after. The staff are kind, but there aren't many residents she can talk to. She can't hear them, even the ones who make any sense. The family visit a lot – at least one person comes every day. Even so, there are long periods of time when she is on her own; time to think, maybe too much time.

* * *

Eve is due in a few minutes. She must have thought about this outing for some time. Thought about what would give her mother pleasure, have special meaning for her. Anna smiles to herself. She knows she annoys Eve. She can't help it. Sometimes it's as though she's *compelled* to annoy her, even hurt her. She doesn't mean to really. Or perhaps she does, she's not sure. They're very different in some ways, she and Eve, and very similar in others. She's not certain whether it's the similarities or the differences that are more provocative. Eve is oversensitive, always was, even as a child, though Anna knows Eve hates it when she tells her that. Says it's a 'cop-out', an excuse for being cruel. Perhaps she hasn't always been as kind to Eve as she should have.

There's a pounding on the door. Eve always makes sure Anna hears her come in.

'Hello, Mamma,' she says loudly, bending over the chair to kiss her mother. 'You look nice. When did the hairdresser come?'

'This morning. I asked her to do my hair first thing today, so I'd be ready for you. Stand there by the window. Let me look at you. Do I know this blouse? I like that green on you – it suits you.'

'Well, there's praise! No, I don't think you have seen it before – it's quite new. The trousers are old though.'

'I can see that. I recognise them. Never mind, I suppose the Masseys will be casually dressed. People usually are. You haven't put any weight on have you?'

'Do you have to look me up and down like that? No, I don't believe I've put on weight.'

'You're slim; that's why you can even get away with wearing old trousers. Have you dyed your hair?'

Eve gives a long sigh. 'No, Mamma, I haven't dyed my hair. Can we change the subject?'

'What? What subject?'

'Change the subject. Can we talk about something other than what I look like?'

'You look nice.'

'Thank you.'

Eve often tells Anna she's obsessed with people's looks. Perhaps that's true. Well, outward appearances are important. Looks have always been important to her, her own and other people's. Maybe it's a foolish attitude at her age. Why bother now? She can hardly claim to be an example of physical perfection herself, not any more. Everything sagging and bulging and wobbling and fading – bah, how horrible! Eve switches Anna's hearing aids on and gently inserts them.

'Are you ready? It'll take a good hour to get there, so you may want to go to the loo first. I noticed there's a nice café opened in that little shopping centre by the post office. D'you remember where I mean? Just round the corner from the house? Everything's on the ground floor. I thought we'd go there first for a light lunch, and then on to the house. The Masseys expect us about two-thirty. Does that sound OK?'

'It sounds fine, darling. How clever of you to arrange it all.'

* * *

It makes a pleasant change going out in the car with Eve. It's a fine, bright day. Late spring – one of Anna's favourite times of year. As so often, she wonders briefly whether it might be her last. Not that it matters, she doesn't mind, but she tries to notice all the details, just in case. The leaves are still pale green and fresh, everything looking new and young. It's good to see the outside world again; it feels like such an exciting expedition, she might as well be on safari in Africa.

In places the traffic is so thick the car has to crawl along. Eve tuts impatiently and drums her fingers on the wheel, but Anna doesn't mind the delays at all. It gives her a chance to watch the people in the streets. Amazing how they dress these days. Just look at those girls! Showing great bare folds of tummy flesh, even the plump ones. You'd think they'd want to hide it, not show it off. Some of the boys are just as bad, trousers hanging halfway down their behinds.

'Do we really need to see their underpants?'

'What?'

'Those young men – showing everyone their bottoms.'

'Oh … yes. Just a bit of a fad at the moment I suppose. You didn't think much of me wearing mini-skirts years ago, did you? But I seem to remember you weren't much happier about the long flowery skirts a year or two later.'

'Mmm. Your hippy phase. It wasn't so much the flowery skirts I didn't like, it was everything and everyone that went *with* them.'

'Well, I'm thoroughly respectable now.'

Eve finds the café and manages to manoeuvre the car into a small space very near. She starts to lift the wheelchair out of the back of the car.

'Leave it – it's not far. I can walk if I hold your arm.'

As they approach, a waitress holds the door open for them, and customers pull chairs out of their way. They're shown to a table by the window. One of the few benefits of being very old, and looking it, is that at least most people go out of their way to help you.

* * *

As the little car turns the corner into the cul-de-sac, Anna feels her stomach tensing. Twenty years disappear in a moment. She glances at the Ryecrofts' house next door, almost expecting to see dear old Sandie lying sprawled by the front gate as always, lifting his head half-heartedly and thumping his tail on the pavement in greeting. But of course he's not there, poor old mutt. No doubt the Ryecrofts themselves will have moved on too. The Beaumonts' house has been repainted – rather an odd shade of peach to choose.

'Fancy painting the house that orangey colour – Melissa Beaumont always did have strange taste.'

'Mmm?'

How tall the cherry trees in front of Number Four have grown. After an overnight shower, the browning petals lie in soggy clumps on the path and on the pavement. Must be slippery, quite a hazard for people walking past. A great mistake planting cherry trees so close to the house, Sam always said. Fifty weeks of shade for two weeks of strawberry pink.

A woman – it must be Helen Massey – comes scurrying to the front gate, a broad smile on her face.

'Oh here we are! Hello, Mrs Lawrence, how lovely to meet you. May I help you?'

'I can manage, thank you,' Anna says, heaving her legs sideways, where they dangle helplessly over the pavement. Mrs Massey hovers uncertainly. Eve walks around the car, walking frame in one hand, and hauls Anna efficiently into a standing position, holding her steady while she gets her balance. Then she places the frame in front of her.

'We may need the wheelchair if Mum gets tired,' Eve tells Mrs Massey, 'but she likes to walk when she can.'

'That's marvellous! You're doing very well, Mrs Lawrence.'

'Fortunately, I learned to walk as a baby, as most of us do.'

Mrs Massey glances at Eve, who raises her eyebrows.

'Well, do come inside. Take your time.'

Anna pauses and looks up. The windows have changed. Mrs Massey follows her gaze.

'We had double glazing put in after we moved here. It does make it much warmer.'

'When did you move here, Mrs Massey?'

'Ooh, let me see. It must be about eight years ago – 2005 or 2006 I'd say. We bought the house from the MacCarthys. I think they bought it from you, didn't they? They were here a good few years. And please, do call me Helen.'

248

'Our front door was natural wood, solid oak. My husband varnished it each autumn.'

'Was it? I think the MacCarthys painted it blue. This white one was new when the windows were fitted.'

New windows on either side of the front door have lightened the hallway. The polished wooden floorboards have been replaced by a pale cream carpet. Not very practical, Anna thinks.

'You don't have children?' she asks loudly.

'We have two actually, a girl and a boy. They're both away at uni at the moment.'

'Where?'

'At university.'

'Ah.'

Anna's automatic navigation takes over and propels her towards the kitchen.

'*Sorry. Is it OK?*' Eve mouths at Helen Massey as her mother shuffles ahead. She nods and smiles back. They follow Anna's retreating figure.

'It's quite different. Very modern,' says Anna. She looks around with interest. 'We had the cooker here. And what is this?'

'It's a fridge-freezer.'

'So big?'

'It is rather big. It's useful having the space though, especially when the children come home. You know how much young people can eat! Now, I'm just going to put the kettle on for coffee. Why don't you go on into the sitting room and make yourselves comfortable? I'm sure you know where it is! Just look at anything that interests you.'

Everything so familiar, yet so different. Like landing in a parallel universe, Eve says. More like a dream, Anna feels, where nothing is quite as it should be. On the way home they discuss their impressions.

'Dad wouldn't think much of the garden now, would he?'

'No, they've designed it to be labour-saving. He'd hate all those fir trees. And that wooden veranda – what did she call it?'

'Decking.'

'Yes, decking. More suitable for a ship.'

'Anyway, it was kind of her to let us visit – and give us a tour.'

'I'm glad I couldn't go upstairs.'

'Why's that?'

'I don't think I wanted to see our bedroom, with all their things in it. It was *our* place, mine and Sam's. I wouldn't want to see signs of another man in our room.'

Chapter 18

2014

Just as the party is starting to break up, he arrives. Just look at him and Ben, walking towards her together, each with an arm around the other's shoulder. Her two sons. How handsome they both are, yet so different: Shimon with his smooth brown skin and dark eyes; Ben with his pale complexion and reddish hair, just peppered with grey at the temples. And behind them, Eve and Rachel. Rachel, elegant and striking, even in her seventies, Anna observes approvingly.

'Shimon! You've come! I'm so glad.'

He crouches by her wheelchair and hugs her.

'Of course I've come. I'm hardly going to miss my mother's hundredth birthday, am I?'

Anna's eyes fill with tears as she strokes Shimon's hand.

'She's very tired, aren't you, Mamma?' says Eve. 'Why don't we all take you up?'

'No, no! Not yet. Shimon's only just arrived …'

'I'll be here all week – we all will,' he says, looking at Rachel. 'We'll come back tomorrow – spend all day with you, and Eva and Samuel want to visit with you too. There'll be plenty of time for a proper talk.'

Shimon and Ben run up the stairs to meet Anna and Eve as the lift doors open. Anna smiles to see the childlike pleasure on their faces. With Shimon's help, Eve settles her in the armchair next to her bed.

'Thank you, my darlings, for all you have done, for all you are, and for your lovely families. What an extraordinary day!' She kisses each of her children, but lingers, as always, over Shimon. She clutches his hand and reaches up to stroke his face and the short white hair at his neck. He takes her hand and gently presses it to his lips. Anna shakes her head, as if not quite believing he is really there.

After more hugs and goodnights, the two men retreat downstairs.

'Shall I stay and help you to bed, Mamma?'

'No, you go back home, darling. It's late and you've a long journey. You and Richard must be tired too. Besides, I feel like sitting here a bit longer. I'm not ready to sleep yet.'

'Don't be too late. It's been a long day.'

'Yes it has. Thank you for a very *special* day today. You know …'

'What?'

'You know I do appreciate you, and all you do.'

'I know.'

Anna leans back in her chair and luxuriates in the pleasure of being alone. She looks at the clock. Soon the evening carers will arrive and help her to bed; it's always such a relief to switch off, close her eyes, and wait for sleep to carry her away. But tonight she has her thoughts to occupy her. The day has filled her mind with thoughts and impressions and memories. She reflects on her life – if only there wasn't so much of it! – and tries to order her thoughts.

Her eye is drawn to the bookshelf in the corner of the room.

Anna struggles to rise out of her chair and stands for a moment, clutching the bar of her walking frame tightly to get her balance. She shuffles towards the bookshelf. Straight ahead of her, at eye level, is the large maroon-bound photograph album. Ben and Eve had bought it two years previously for her ninety-eighth birthday, and helped her to compile it. Margaret, her younger sister, had just died at the age of ninety-four. Now there was only Anna. The photos were to be a comfort for her, a gallery of the most important people throughout her life. She holds herself steady with her left hand and carefully extracts the album from the shelf, staggering for a moment from the shock of its weight as it slides off the edge.

Breathing heavily with the effort, Anna lifts the album onto the top bar of her frame, and holds it in place with her thumb, using the rest of her fingers to grasp the bar. Slowly, she makes her way back to the armchair. She swings the photograph album onto her low table. It lands with a thud. She's feeling a little dizzy now. Beads of perspiration punctuate her forehead. *Keep steady, don't fall,* she tells herself. She takes a deep breath and edges herself round, turning her back to the armchair. When she can feel the front of the seat against the backs of her knees, she reaches behind to find the arm of the chair and starts to lower herself. The last part of her descent comes in an unexpected rush and she lands panting in the chair. She sits for a few minutes getting her breath back and waiting for her heart to slow.

There's a loud knock at the door. Sofija, the young care assistant from Latvia – or was it Poland? – comes in, smiling. A pretty girl, always neat.

'Hello, Anna, how are you? Happy birthday! Would you like cup of tea, or some cocoa?'

'Tea, thank you.' She pushes the album towards the back of the table to make room for the cup. Sofija disappears into the corridor and comes back with a cup of tea, a bit too milky.

'Have you had a nice day, Anna? I'm sorry I wasn't here for your party. A big day for you today.'

'Yes, thank you, Sofija.'

'Oh, you have photographs, Anna?'

'Yes, I'll show you some of them one day, if you like.'

'Yes please. I love to see photos. You want biscuit?'

'No, thank you. Are you working tomorrow, Sofija?'

'I'll be here. Day off Saturday – I go see film with Jacek .'

'Good. You should enjoy yourself.'

'See you tomorrow, Anna.'

* * *

Where to start? So many people to choose from, to think about. The pictures are organised in chronological order. She opens the first page and looks first at her mother and father, Artur and Matilde. Her mother sits rigid in her chair, her back ramrod straight – this is before her illness – voluminous skirts spread over the seat, her waist drawn tightly into a tiny, narrow isthmus. Artur, stiff in a dark suit, stands behind, one hand resting on her shoulder, the other on the back of the chair. They stare at the camera with sombre concentration, unsmiling, in the style typical of photographs of the period.

Anna strokes their faces gently with the back of one finger. Images caught in a moment in time. Accurate enough as facial likenesses, yet telling little of their personalities. Her father, a simple, down-to-earth man. Such an apt phrase for him, quite literally a man of the soil. A man of wisdom and honesty, without guile or graces, a robust, brave and passionate man. Matilde, more refined than her husband, was the artistic and creative force in the business and the marriage. Forced by circumstances to spend the years of his prime caring for a sick wife, Artur had applied himself to the task with affection, devotion and without complaint.

Only much later, after reconnecting with her sister Esther, does

254

Anna learn that for many years some of his regular expeditions to 'clients' were in fact visits to his mistress in a country village, with whom he had two sons.

'Don't look so shocked,' Esther had said, laughing at Anna's astounded face. 'He adored Mamma, but she was an invalid. What do you expect a healthy young man to do?'

Anna nods in silent agreement, as she recalls the conversation and pictures Esther, her red hair swirling as she stands with her hands on her hips and flicks her head to one side. How can it be that Esther, always so alive, so vibrant, is gone, like Artur and Matilde? Yet gone she is, dead these last twelve years, and even little Margaret, the baby of the family, dead for two years. She turns on a few pages and studies photos of Esther and Reuben, and their children, Marta and Leila, and of course, Shimon.

Next Jakob, who has always come to be referred to as 'poor Jakob' in the family. It was started by Sam in his mischievous way; 'poor old Jakob,' he would say, 'poor old chap.' But Jakob never was old. How young he looks in the few photographs she has of him. Young and handsome and full of misplaced hope. He deserved better. She thinks of their journey together, which took them so far from the lives and the people that had been a part of their growing up. So many periods of loss, sadness and trauma.

Yet compared to the lives of many others, she has been lucky. At least the bad times have been balanced with times of joy and love. At least she was old enough to have some choices when she and Jakob left Vienna. Not like the poor children sent abroad by desperate parents in order to save their lives, knowing they might never see them again. Yet, like for those children perhaps, her life has been a constant search, a yearning for home, security and love. Almost half her life has been an unspoken, unacknowledged search for her son, her Shimon.

The loss of homeland and loved ones is so crucially painful to human beings, Anna feels, but those who have not experienced

255

it cannot fully understand the depth of longing and need. It is a longing so fundamental to the Jews, Yael would say, bred into them by their long suffering, a longing that is not diluted by time. No, on the contrary, it grows in strength, even passing from one generation to another.

Here is Yael in the early days in Haifa, sturdy in the *kibbutznik* uniform of khaki trousers and shirt, squinting into the bright sun, her limbs brown and strong. Next, one of their days at the beach together, Anna and Yael, sunburned arms intertwined with little Rachel. More pictures, more time. Yael the proud mother, arm in arm with Rachel at her graduation in America – and again, locked in embrace with Hal, both grinning broadly, following their marriage in Boston. Yael was always so generous with her love, always ready with affection.

Her dear, dear friend. How she misses her. How she misses her all-enveloping hugs, her deep, unrestrained laugh. Such a cruel irony. Yael was so happy with Hal those last few years. The only thing she truly missed after moving to North America was the heat and sunshine of a Middle Eastern summer. Yet in the cool of New England, it was the sun that killed her; an aggressive melanoma sending its outriders all around her body, finally to multiply in her liver.

A few pages on and Della, another precious friend and help-mate, is cradling toddler Ben in one arm and infant Eve in the other, sitting in the dappled shade of a mature cherry tree, around which Herr Eisen had constructed a rustic wooden seat. Della, who tolerated all Anna's early suspicions and reserve, and patiently, gently, won her trust. Della, who accepted her initial role as servant and performed it with warmth, loyalty and sensitivity, until all in the family knew she was much, much more than that. Three times she visited England, the first time in 1963, the year after Anna and Sam moved there.

There is a picture of Della and Anna taken by Sam in the garden. They are sitting on the low wall together, a climbing yellow rose – Eve's favourite – cascading all around them. Further on, another picture shows Della a few years later, formally dressed in her best coat, after Sam's funeral. She is leaning on Ben's arm, Sam's memorial tree in the background, holding a handkerchief to her eyes. She must be about seventy-five there, Anna thinks. That same year she returned to England again to spend time with Anna and support her through her loss. Two years later she died peacefully in her sleep, in bed in her little flat in Berlin. Her life had not been easy, Anna knows, but she appreciated every simple pleasure; she had the gift of a joyful heart.

The next pages show herself and several pictures of Ben and Eve at various ages and sizes. One photograph is taken around the time of her stay at Ellwangen; how anguished she looks – and Eve, so small and pinched and sorrowful. If only she had been able to protect her from suffering. Whoever said suffering is good for the soul? Anna cannot recall where or when she has read or heard those words. Has her suffering made her a better person, more sympathetic, insightful, caring, tolerant? Probably not. She has battled with insecurities all her life, and passed them on to her children, even her grandchildren. All in their way have felt 'different', outsiders. That has created obstacles and hardships for them, but perhaps at the same time given them strengths – self-possession, stamina, resourcefulness, imagination.

Once, long ago, Anna recalls, when Eve was perhaps fifteen or sixteen, she had accused her mother of prejudice.

'You of all people! How can you stereotype people like that, after all your experiences?'

Eve had had a boyfriend, Lester, a sweet, handsome, lonely and affectionate boy. They had met at a party and been instantly attracted to one another. It was impossible to dislike him; he was polite and appreciative of any slight kindness. He had worshipped Eve, and she had been drawn to his innocence and vulnerability. But Lester came from a children's home, with an uncertain past and complicated parentage. Anna had not been able to ignore his broad Cockney accent. She had found it threatening somehow.

Gradually she had begun to chip away at Eve's pleasure in the relationship. He was not articulate enough for her, not educated enough. What was his future? Yes, he was kind, but she would soon be bored with him. How much more hurtful to string him along, allow him to become more deeply involved. Better to end it before things got too serious. What had been a friendship full of simple joy and affection – working on homework together, walks in the park, visits to the cinema – had become fraught with new stresses and dark predictions, awakened from elsewhere. To Eve's later shame and remorse, she had not been able to handle the situation. It had ended in sadness and pain, for her but especially for Lester. For years she had wept at the memory of his wounded face, the hunch of his shoulders as he walked away for the last time.

Anna too felt many regrets. She had to acknowledge that many of the boys who came to Eve's door after that – all from richer, classier homes, all with crisper accents – had far less attractive personalities and less admirable morals than Lester.

Anna sighs, and reflects that the distinction between good and bad people is never straightforward. Even defining good and bad has so many pitfalls. In the end, most of the people she encountered were basically good, or tried to be. Even Fritz Henkelmann, whom she had condemned and vilified for so many years, had had principles, however misguided, and had tried to demonstrate his loyalty and friendship. He had spent his life tortured by guilt, and bequeathed the suffering of his soul on to his unfortunate and innocent son Maxim. So many people have passed through her life, each leaving behind their particular influences.

With a leap of excitement and pleasure, Anna turns to the pages of Sam pictures, as though she had been waiting for this moment all along. First, one of him leaning nonchalantly against a palm tree in Palestine not long after they first met, looking very tall and handsome in his army uniform. Then, a smaller album version of the studio photograph of Sam she arranged after he had requested one of her.

Anna glances over to her chest of drawers. Both framed pictures stand at an angle, she looking young and glamorous and, beside her, Sam with his characteristic twinkle, his slightly lopsided smile and Clark Gable moustache. Beautiful Sam. She bends slowly towards the album on her lap and kisses the photograph of him. Here too, the two of them in the garden of the lovely house in Chislehurst. Anna could never find her yearned-for peace and security in a place alone. It was what her mother had once called 'running towards the rainbow', that search for what feels right, for what you need and desperately want, a place you can put down roots. Only with Sam could she find it, only through his generous and unquestioning love.

Now Sam has gone. He has been gone for so many years, more years even than they had together. Has the peace gone with him? Is the rainbow unattainable once more? His legacy must be here with her, in what they built together. Their three wonderful children – for Shimon is as much his son as hers – and their many grandchildren and great-grandchildren, whom Sam never met.

Anna is exhausted. Why is she still here when all have gone, all these loved ones? Of all her generation, why is only she left alive, the last survivor? She feels so alone – the loneliness of survival. How easy it would be to give up, to sink into desperation. She knows what Yael would tell her, and Esther, and Della, and Sam too. She closes her eyes and for a moment hears a cacophony of voices. Stop feeling sorry for yourself. Have you learned nothing? Think positive – you are the *lucky* one.

Yes, she decides; she is *not* alone. She has her children, her grandchildren and her great-grandchildren. She has her memories. She is greatly blessed.

Acknowledgements

Without my father Jim Darley and my mother Trude Darley, this book would never have been conceived. I give thanks for the richness of experiences to which they exposed me, and for their many anecdotes and stories which enriched my childhood, and which somehow remained in the depths of my memory, to be reproduced in various forms in my writing. For every story told, there were enigmas and secrets hinted at or left untold. Some of these were researched; others had to be composed from my imagination, to fit what *might* have happened. Sadly, neither my father nor my mother lived to see the completed book.

My thanks too to my brothers Peter Darley and James Darley – both writers too – who gave positive support at every stage of the book.

Thanks to Ann Coburn, my mentor during the first writing of this book, for her wisdom and insight. While this story is a work of fiction, it is based on real experiences, and recounts and alludes to many real events. It has been important therefore, to ensure it tallies with historical truth. My appreciation to Brigadier John Sharland, who helped keep me right on military matters.

Special loving thanks to my family – Luke, Jo, Thomas and Rose – for their interest, and pertinent comments, and especially to my husband Terence, for his unfailing encouragement and support.

ONE PLACE. MANY STORIES

If you enjoyed *Beyond The Storm*, why not try another sweeping historical novel from HQ Digital

Dear Reader,

Thank you so much for taking the time to read this book – we hope you enjoyed it! If you did, we'd be so appreciative if you left a review.

Here at HQ Digital we are dedicated to publishing fiction that will keep you turning the pages into the early hours. We publish a variety of genres, from heartwarming romance, to thrilling crime and sweeping historical fiction.

To be the first to hear about new releases, competitions, 99p eBooks and promotions, sign up to our monthly email newsletter: po.st/HQSignUp

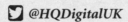 *@HQDigitalUK*

f *facebook.com/HQDigitalUK*

Are you a budding writer?
We're also looking for authors to join the HQ Digital family!
Please submit your manuscript to:

HQDigital@harpercollins.co.uk.

Hope to hear from you soon!

ONE PLACE. MANY STORIES